A Necessary Killing

PAUL WALKER

First published in 2019 by Sharpe Books.

CONTENTS

A NECESSARY KILLING

One

Devonshire, England – June 1579

The three men circle warily. Rough and soldierly in appearance, two have daggers and the other a short sword. A fourth stands up the wooded bank holding our horses with my killed companion at his feet. I edge carefully back into the stream. The water is chill and fast-flowing. I must take care not to stumble. Will it be quick, or will I endure agonies from terrible wounds while they have sport with their victim and prolong their moment of victory? I have height on all of them, but they are thickset, dark and grim-faced in their determination.

This cannot be my end. Yet, it seems my time on earth is finished – and in this small place. I should be pricked with fear, wild and alert for a means of escape. Instead, I am curiously resigned with an overwhelming sense of loss and injustice that my passing from this world will be slight and unremarked. There is no sanctuary in this quiet, wooded valley; no sign of any help. We are too remote. And what of Helen? Gone is the promise of our sweet closeness in the marriage bed and cozied comfort in our fading years.

I cup my hands and shout, 'Edward, Henry, to me.'

They stop and the two with daggers look at the man with sword. He is their leader.

Again, but louder, 'Edward, Henry. Murder. Thieves. Here.'

Their leader bares his teeth and replies, 'Ha, there is no one. Those words are worthless shit - your threat holds naught.' He is right. There is no Edward or Henry; names I plucked from the ether.

'You will soon learn of your error. They are near.' I must stay resolute and firm. To show fear will hasten my end.

'Come,' he says, 'this need not lead to more harm. Your horse, coin and value about your person is all we seek. Throw your boots, cloak and trinkets at our feet and we will leave you to your dabbling and splashing in the water. We would keep our hose dry.'

They are no more than twenty paces from me. If I show doubt, or move in a way that accedes to his words, then I am done, and quickly. I try again, 'Edward, to me. Now.'

He chuckles deep in his throat and takes a pace forward. The others follow. I grip the handle of my dagger. A low noise escapes my clamped mouth as I prepare for what is to come. I stamp and splash a foot to stop a trembling in my leg. Helen, I am sorry. Fear is in me now, but also indignation. Surely…

The tautness in the air is broken by a cawing of crows and clattering in the trees. Another sound follows – is it a voice, distant and high?

They have stopped.

Someone answers my call. I try to shout but can only croak. I clear my throat, fill my lungs and roar, 'Here. Foul murder. The stream.'

They are uncertain. The man with sword is closing. He growls. The others are still. Do my senses play tricks? Again, there is a distant hailing. Unmistakeable this time, and a little closer. A man's voice shouts, 'Ho there,' and other words I do not recognise. There is no alarm in his calling. He will think we are making merry at our gathering. Once more, with as much urgency as I can muster, I bellow, 'Foul murder!'

The leader curses and swipes his sword in a wide arc. He hesitates, jerks his head at the others. They turn and make their way back up the hill towards the horses. He continues to close with me, but I sense that his resolve is weakened.

I point my dagger behind him. 'You are too late, they are here.' There is no sign, but I must convince, so take a step forward.

He raises his sword; glances over his shoulder; returns to face me. A cry from one of his men. There is movement on the hill; a flash of colour in the trees; a glint of steel. He stretches his sword to me and raises the other hand behind him; makes a half-turn. More cries from the hill. A yell. The image of a horse flickers at the edge of sight - perhaps two mounted horses. The sword man takes a step back; then another. Our eyes meet. He stares, opens his mouth, but naught comes. Turning slowly, he leaves his sword pointing at my chest. There is action up there; a blur of movement. He lurches away, lowers his sword arm and starts up the slope. I am fixed for a long moment, then follow him. I forget I am encumbered by water and too slow. On the bank, I am near him, but trip on a rock and stagger. He sees me falling and readies to strike. I make a despairing lunge. My dagger punches through flesh and strikes something hard. There is a crack. He yells. My dagger is broken. I meet the ground with a thump; taste the earth; smell foul breath as he rolls over me. I am on him, stabbing at his throat with my broken dagger. It will not do; will not cut easily. An eye. I jab the dagger as hard as I can into the eye. Four times; ten; more. I am frantic; must take his life force quickly or I am lost. Suddenly, he is still. I see the blood; hear a gurgling in his throat... and more. It is me. I am grunting, sobbing, panting... pounding my useless weapon into his head... I must... stop.

Have I done this? The head beneath me is a grotesque misshape of cut flesh, white bone and blood; my hands slick with gore. I drop the dagger and move my eyes slowly to the scene amongst the trees on the hill. Two new men stand with swords in hand gazing at me. Where are the other attackers? I push myself up on the shape under me and try to stand. My legs give way and I am back on my knees straddling the body. One of the new men sheaths his sword and walks towards me. I watch as he approaches, but do not see clearly; my vision is fixed elsewhere.

'William, William Constable, is it you?'

I lift my head and see a face I know, framed with flowing yellow hair.

'Who?'

'William, it is Charles. I bless the good fortune of this meeting.'

'Indeed, no more than...' I close my eyes tight and open again to make certain this is no dream. 'Charles Wicken, is it you who has saved me?'

'What has happened here, William?'

I allow myself a few moments to calm my breathing and gather my thoughts before replying. I rise slowly and move away from the body at my feet. 'I... I was here with George Duckham. We stopped; Duckham to relieve himself in the trees, while I rested by the stream.' My mind is fuddled and it takes an effort to arrange events, so recent, but which feel far-off and faint. 'I heard naught, except a rustling in the trees. My senses were spiked and when I looked back, Duckham was fallen and four men had me ready to be killed and robbed at their leisure.'

'Duckham is dead; his throat slit.'

'It is as I feared. I pity the poor man. He accompanied me on the orders of Captain General Hawkins.'

'But why – why are you here in this quiet place? I had thought you were safely lodged in Plymouth educating our ships' masters in the use of your instrument of navigation.'

'I was. I confess our delays have stretched my patience with confinement in that town and I sought a period of retreat from its noise and commotion. I had promised a friend, Doctor John Foxe, that I would visit the ancient church of St Loda. He holds fond memories of the church, which was founded before the first King William.'

'It seems that your prayers were well-received. Good fortune is a meagre way to describe the happenstance of hearing your calls.'

'Forgive me, I have not thanked you properly, Charles. I owe... my life...' I embrace him strongly and he pats me on the back with reassuring 'coos' and 'tushes' as though soothing a babe. I break quickly and must hope that my face does not redden with the discomfort I feel. His age is only one year in advance of my twenty-six and we are the same height, but his bearing and manner make me feel callow and soft. My body is unsteady and I am hesitant in my next words. 'The church... had a holy air, although my prayers were for... others and not my safekeeping here.'

'Ha, put yourself at ease, William. I see that you need some time to recover from this cruel disruption to your peace. It is God you should thank for his careful watch over you.'

'Nevertheless, I am deep in your debt.' I pause to catch my breath. 'How... how are you here, Charles?'

'I am returning from Dartmouth with my man, Stack, up there. I have been to survey the state of repair of our other ships in that harbour, and to pass a message to Sir Humphrey from Captain General Hawkins.'

'This would not be your usual path back to Plymouth?'

'No, we took the Ivybridge road to Dartmouth, but I had a fancy to investigate this lower way through Loddiswell on our return, lest it offer more discretion and speed in our correspondence between the towns.'

'I am thankful that you did.'

His eyes narrow. 'Those men up there we have killed; I have seen them in the inns at Plymouth. They will have waited for an opportunity to follow a likely prey into a quiet place such as this. Duckham was a sturdy fellow and handy with his sword, but you should have taken more men to guard your person.'

He mentions killing the attackers as though it was a small, everyday matter. I should be grateful that my rescuer is so proficient at soldiering. His fierce reputation is well-earned. Yet, he is also scholarly and I have come to welcome our discussions on politicking, mathematics of the stars and lighter diversions over the past few weeks. It is an unusual mix of attributes in a man I have come to regard as a friend.

I say, 'We must take Duckham's body back.'

'Yes, and the fuckwits who attacked you we will leave for scavengers to have their little picks. We will report this foul murder to the Justice in Plymouth and someone will recover their remains in the coming days.'

I bow my head in agreement and start to make my way back up the slope. I feel a hand on my shoulder and stop. Have I forgotten something?

'William.'

'Yes, what is it?'

'You cannot return to Plymouth in your present state. Children will take fright and hide behind their mothers' skirts. Even grown men will quail at the appearance of a devil on their streets.' He laughs and claps me on the back. 'You are covered in blood and soft, black earth, with the appearance of a monster escaped through the gates of hell. You must wash in the stream while we examine the bodies for any trifles and marks to bring us their names.'

*

Back at my lodgings in Plymouth town, I have had bowls of water and cloths brought to my chambers so that I can rinse away all remaining traces of the attack from my body. Mistress Gredley stared open-mouthed at my appearance at her door and I was obliged to offer a brief account of the incident. She will hear soon enough, in any event. Her concern for my person soon transformed into much 'tutting' and head-shaking over the trouble it will take to wash my soiled dress. She is a good woman who keeps a tidy household, and I fear I was abrupt in my ending to our conversation. I will make amends when my disposition returns to its normal state.

My head is full of thoughts of Helen. I wrote her a letter only two days past but will set myself to another. I must be circumspect and dance around the details of today's misadventure, but the writing may help to free up a tangle of thoughts about my unexpected reprieve from a sudden and violent end to life on this earth.

Finally, it is finished. Helen may wonder at the frequency of my communications and I hope that she will take this as a mark of my devotion or a filling of idle time as we wait for the sailing of our great adventure to the New Lands.

My Dearest

I trust this latest note finds you and your household in good health.

Tomorrow will be the ninetieth day since our parting and I hold tight to the memory of our last embrace. I took heart from your most recent letter in which you fancied your father was softening his position and may, after all, allow you to accompany him to this town to mark the despatch of our fleet. My motives are selfish. I know the journey from London is long and arduous, but Sir George will ensure your party is well-guarded and will secure whatever small comforts he can for you, if his decision falls in our favour.

There are further delays here due to ship repairs and disputes over ownership of cargoes. The patience of all our number is stretched and Captain General Hawkins has had to make examples of ship men and soldiers as drunken brawls become more frequent. I know some of the townspeople will be glad when we sail as our nuisance bears down on their profits. Yet, I am told that the town will quieten as the time for our departure draws near and thoughts of our task ahead settles a calmness on the men.

Today, I visited the church of St Loda. You will remember I promised John I would call there while I am lodged in the West Country. It is a holy place with a quiet air holding memories of older and simpler times. I confess my thoughts and prayers were coloured with images of you, rather than John and his kindly, but austere, manner.

I happened upon Charles Wicken on my return journey. He is a fine man – hard and much admired for his braveness, but with good learning and a gentler side. In these short weeks, I have come to consider him as a friend and, together with Oliver Tewkes, I find pleasure in our conversations, which help to enliven the days of inactivity.

This next day, I will meet with Captain General Hawkins and other notables when we will learn more of the readiness of our ships and expected date for sailing. I am impatient, not for the adventure itself, but for its ending, so that we may state our vows before God and begin our lives together.

Do not delay in your reply. I am eager for your written words, so that I may dream of our closeness to come.

With fondest love
William

Two

We are gathered at the house of Captain General Hawkins. It is a large building with many chambers and a hazardous collection of timber, bricks and ropes at one side, where an addition is under construction. A short walk from the quayside, it also has enough distance from there to afford relief from its raucous activities and strong odours. There will be fifty or sixty of us in his dining hall: ships masters; secondaries; traders; and soldier captains. I see Oliver raise his hand in welcome. He comes to greet me and claps my shoulders.

'William, it is a joy to witness your good health. I have heard of your attack and rescue – you must recount the circumstances.'

This is not the first and it will not be the last telling, but it is to be expected. I am almost finished a brief account of the affair when the room quietens and Hawkins enters, accompanied by his muster master. The latter is called Pennes - a dark man from Maroc. He is large and heavy, with no head hair and a belligerent set to a finely trimmed beard on his chin. We have not spoken, but I have witnessed his treatment of men in need of correction and it was not pretty. Still, I suppose he must be brutish to keep Hawkins' men in order.

Hawkins bangs a fist on the table for our attention and ushers forward the small figure of Pastor Gadge to bestow God's blessing on our proceedings. When he is done, Hawkins begins his oration. Normally an erect and vigorous man with ruddy complexion, his slackened bearing and greyness on his cheeks betray the strain of our troubled preparation. There is good news and bad. Steady progress is made on the repair of five ships damaged in a storm during their passage from Sandwich. One of our fleet, a carrack named *Divine*, has withdrawn from the venture and will instead ply her trade in Flanders. Her owners have taken fright at our delays and fear the value in their cargo may be diminished or lost. Hawkins dismisses their concerns and presses us to be firm in our resolve. Nevertheless, it is a loss to be deplored as it is one of the largest carracks and well-armed. We are strongly urged not to allow critical and sniping news to leak from our messages to associates and families. I will not be the only one experiencing a sliver of guilt at these words as I recall my letters to Helen and Mother. Hawkins pauses and scans the room before continuing.

'Gentlemen, you will all be aware of a growing unruliness in our men. I know that idleness and impatience will breed intemperate action and black humour, but it cannot be excused. I have received representations from notables, here and in Dartmouth, about thievery, stabbings, assaults and ill-mannered behaviours in sight and hearing of local goodmen and goodwives.' He takes a breath clasps his hands behind his back. 'Punishments will be harsh and, at my choosing, wrongdoers may receive quick and severe ship's justice in place of gentler and slower considerations in the town.'

Oliver mutters to me that Hawkins intends to hang a few by the neck on ships' yards as an example to our men and to satisfy the townsfolk. That would not be good. I do not like the thought of disregarding fairness in favour of a show of prompt action.

Hawkins adds that it would be a welcome relief if ships could be exercised out of harbour more frequently for the further testing and training of crews and soldiers. He ends with a deduction that the fleet should be ready to sail in four or five weeks. The hum of conversation returns as those assembled take their leave or mingle to share their opinions with others. I am about to depart when Hawkins catches my eye and approaches. He takes me by the shoulder and leads me to a corner.

He says, 'I am sorry for your trouble the last day, Doctor Constable. I trust you are recovered?'

'Indeed, I am unhurt and in good health, thanks to the action of Captain Wicken and his man. Thank you for your concern, Captain General.' Although we have conversed many times these past months, our exchanges have not progressed beyond the formal. I am sure he is an admirable man, but I do not warm to him.

'Captain Wicken tells me you were brave and persistent in your killing of one of the attackers.'

'It was… it had to be done and there was an element of good fortune, but my recollection is hazy.'

He hums a little and nods his head slowly as if expecting me to relate a more heroic tale. When I do not respond, he says, 'I would have you accompany some of our ships' masters on their sea trials to ensure they are proficient in the working of your instrument of navigation – the shadow-staff. It is vital that all our ships are consistent and accurate in their routing.'

'Yes, I will be glad to do that. It has been done already, but I understand…'

'Also, I would recommend that you accompany a small party on their journey to Dartmouth on the morrow. I have a message for Sir Humphrey there and intend that travel should be by the lower, Loddiswell path. It will benefit your spirit by revisiting the scene of your triumph, so that you do not brood on the darker aspects of that encounter.'

I mumble a reply of assent, although this is not a diversion I welcome. No doubt he has my interests at heart, but I fear revisiting that place so soon will bring memories of the terrible death struggle into sharp focus.

*

It is a short time past noon and I am with Oliver at Charles' house where we have been invited to dinner. It is only a short walk from our lodgings on the east side of town, in a fair neighbourhood. The house is not as grand as Hawkins' but is fine enough, and it is clear that Charles is a man of substance to afford temporary accommodation on this scale. He has charge of three ships for Jeremy Sindell, a wealthy merchant from the North. Two are Sindell's ships, but the other is Charles' own galleon, *Hawkwind*, which he has leased to the merchant for the venture. I have heard of his reputation as an adventurer and swaggerer out of the ports of Biscay and Brittany. His reported success in taking treasure from Spanish ships is no doubt why Sindell sought him out as his commander. Charles himself is coy about telling of his earlier days and I know only that he has family in Lincoln.

We are taken into the dining room by his housekeeper and find Charles sat at the table examining a chart. He rises as we enter, rolls up the chart, bids a welcome and pours each of us a cup of claret. We take our seats and enjoy a quiet moment as we savour the wine.

Oliver says, 'What do you make of Hawkins' new estimate of our sailing date?'

'Sindell will not like it, nor will the other backers,' answers Charles. 'I fear our planning has been found wanting and the preparations are haphazard.'

This is a little harsh on our leaders and I suggest that mischance and the unusual magnitude of the venture have played their part. Oliver is in agreement, but I see that Charles is unwilling to absolve Hawkins and Gilbert of blame. Two house servants enter with dishes of steamed codfish and pickled oxtails. We murmur words of appreciation and set to with our first mouthfuls. I wait until the servants are gone before I return to our subject.

'You do not have a high opinion of Hawkins and Gilbert then, Charles?'

'Both men have earned credit for their valour, but I believe this venture has stretched them.'

'It is plain to see in Hawkins that responsibility bears heavily,' says Oliver. 'I do not wonder if he receives badgering notes each day from his backers and the money men in London. Do you know how Sir George takes news of our delays, William?'

'He does not like it, but he is a practical man and will understand the complexities of such a large undertaking. We have lost two ships since our arrival here, but the fleet still numbers forty-three in its two parts and there are over two thousand men to keep in check. It is no small thing.' Helen has said little of her father's humour in her letters; it is my mother who has written of his impatience, but also that Sir George accepts we cannot risk a hurried and disordered sailing.

'I share William's opinion,' says Oliver. 'This is not only a simple matter of trade with settlers in the New Lands. Our venture will be regarded with indifference if we do not succeed in wresting treasure from Spanish ships on their passage back to Castile.'

Charles drains his cup and leans forward. 'It is true that the fighting capabilities of our fleet is the thorn that pricks most. Some of our ships are ill-suited to offensive action and the fitting of extra guns is problematic. Demi cannons and sakers cannot be set on the broadside of older trading ships without reinforcement, and this, in turn, will bring disruption to speed and agility.' He uses his hands to illustrate his point. 'All this should have been foreseen and contained in the planning.'

'Do you share your concerns with Hawkins and Gilbert?'

'Ha, I have tried, but they consider themselves beyond the reach of advice from one such as me.'

I am no authority on ships and warfare, but I find this troubling and recognise the traits of vanity in our leaders that Charles voices. 'It is known that you have experience and some success in these matters, Charles. Why would they not pay heed to your anxieties, and do you fear for our competence in the fighting to come?'

'I suspect they regard me as an irritant and competitor for their glory-seeking. I believe they would be happy if I was gone from this place.'

Oliver breathes deeply and spreads his hands on the table. 'I am one of those with little knowledge of fierce action at sea. I have mastered trading ships with a need only for small defensive guns on bow and stern. It is a worry if you consider we will be short-practised for the climax of our venture.'

'I cannot offer comfort now; only hope that improvement will come. It is the men as well as ships that require advancement. I do not trust that man Pennes, the muster master for Hawkins. He has recruited a low character of man for soldiering. Many are cutpurses, thieves, scab-ridden beggars and worse.'

His words dampen spirits and conversation for the remainder of our dinner is subdued. Charles has confirmed some of my misgivings, especially about the type of men I will sail with for the next two years. I have thought for some time that I will not, after all, be suited to a prolonged confinement aboard a fighting ship, even though my berth is on *Justine*, one of the newer and larger galleons. My senses are a mix of excitement, revulsion and anxiety. I am eager to visit the mysterious and faraway lands of Hispaniola and Venezuela, but disturbed at the thought of our first call on the coast of West Africa. Our trade there will be for slaves. I have been assured that these poor unfortunates will have good care on our journey to the New Lands, but I remain unconvinced and uneasy at this commerce in human misery. Then, there is the climax of our venture – the raiding of Spanish treasure ships off Hispaniola. Part of me recognises the thrill and glory to be gained from a battle on the high seas. My body is strong and I will not shrink from a fight, but neither do I seek combat and the status of a warrior. I am a scholar of astrology and physic, not an adventurer and soldier. I have promised Sir George that I will be an eager and active member of our grand venture to the New Lands. I dare not disappoint its chief sponsor and my future father-in-law.

*

I am at Hawkins' house mid-morning to find a group of four horsemen waiting for my arrival. We are all cloaked against blustery, cool weather and there is promise of rain in the skies. Muster Master Pennes is at the head of the party. He does not speak a welcome; instead, bows brief recognition, turns his horse's head and leads us on our way to Dartmouth.

We ride in silence, save for a few muttered exchanges between the men. As we approach the place of my attack, I urge my horse alongside Pennes.

I say, 'Are the bodies already taken back to Plymouth, Master Pennes?'

He grunts, 'It is for us to do the necessary.' He sees my look of surprise and continues, 'We are to examine their likenesses, so names and positions can be placed, and then we will take the remains to Dartmouth.'

'To Dartmouth?'

'Plymouth and Dartmouth towns are of a distance.' He shrugs. 'I doubt the dead will show a preference.'

His manner shows he is unwilling to prolong this line of conversation and I let my mount fall behind as the path narrows.

Why have we not brought extra horses for the bodies? I am uncomfortable at the thought of close company with those who so recently sought my end. Still, as long as I do not have one of the stinking cadavers slung across my horse I will leave this concern unspoken.

The skies lighten and glimpses of sunlight break the green canopy sheltering our progress through a wooded valley. As we near the place of the attack I say, 'It is there, fifty paces ahead.'

I take a lead to where the three bodies were laid by the side of the path. But – they are not here. Perhaps I have mistaken the spot. There are many twists and turns with a similar aspect along the path. No, it was here, I am sure. I dismount and examine the ground. I gesture to the area around my feet. 'It was here, but they are gone.'

The expressions on the faces of my mounted companions suggest doubt.

'Look – here – the ferns are broken and the earth disturbed.' I search for other indications, but find none. 'They have been taken by others.'

Pennes glances at his men, mutters to himself, says, 'Well, 'tis no matter,' and spurs his horse forward. I am left behind to wonder at this strange turn of events. Who would take them? Friends or confederates perhaps, so that their identities may not be discovered? I clamber up again and follow with conflicted thoughts. A revisit to this place has not unbalanced me and I am glad that I have not had to stare at those dreadful faces again, but I am troubled at the vanishing and Pennes' apparent indifference.

We have reached the parish of Townstal and have a grand view of Dartmouth harbour beneath us. There is a steep track down to the main cluster of buildings, but we turn upriver and make our way down a gentler slope to the ferry crossing that will take us to Sir Humphrey Gilbert's home. I have visited here once before; it is a large, comfortable country house atop a rise, which affords a commanding view of the estuary.

Our approach has been observed, as stable hands wait to take our horses at the frontage. I am taken inside with Pennes, while his men are led around to the rear for nourishment in the kitchens. We enter a receiving room to find Sir Humphrey standing with a lady of middle years that I do not know. He steps forward with outstretched hands.

'Doctor Constable, it is a joy to meet again. Do you know my wife and mother of my children, the Lady Anne?'

'I have been denied that pleasure to now, Sir Humphrey.' I bow to her and she returns with a demure smile.

Gilbert beckons to Pennes and leads him to a corner where he is handed a note. I am left with the Lady Anne, who is a small woman with startling blue eyes and an industrious aspect to her bearing.

'I have heard of you, Doctor Constable, and you are handsome as in the telling.'

'I thank you for the compliment lady, which I repay with advantage. You have a fine house and I hear you are blessed with six vigorous children.'

She shuffles her feet and colours a little. 'I understand you are betrothed to Sir George Morton's daughter. She is indeed a fortunate young lady.'

'I can assure you that the balance of providence weighs heavily on my side, lady.' This is amiable enough chit-chat, but I am thankful to note that Pennes departs and Gilbert re-joins us before my fund of dainty words is drained.

'Doctor Constable, you will join us for supper and rest here this night. Master Pennes will accompany you the morrow back to Plymouth.'

'Thank you, Sir Humphrey; that is kind.'

'We have heard of your recent trouble near Loddiswell and thank God for your deliverance from such cruel mischief.'

I dip my head and mutter some mild words in my reply, which highlight the brave actions of Charles and his man. I have no plans for an evening back in Plymouth, so I will try to take pleasure in supper here, although my expectation is low.

I pass time before supper in the company of Sir Humphrey and his eldest son, who is also named Humphrey. For reasons that were not explained, this son is referred to as 'Or'. He is a lanky youth of near fourteen years with a good mind and a keen interest in ships and our venture to the New Lands. He is eager to learn about the mathematics of the heavens and the working of the shadow-staff, which we will use for navigation in the wide expanse of seas away from sight of land. We retire to Sir Humphrey's chamber of business and I draw a few schematics, which the lad receives with delight, promising that he will study them with diligence.

I am called for supper and sit with Sir Humphrey at the dining table, while the Lady Anne busies herself instructing on the preparation and serving of our dishes. At last, she joins us and we can begin. Gilbert appears edgy, as though something preys on his mind. In our early discussions, he is at pains to explain that his ships in Dartmouth are near ready and will join the fleet in Plymouth as soon as matters there are settled. He picks at a leg of boiled fowl and wipes his beard with his napkin.

'You keep Sir George informed on our progress, Doctor?'

'My correspondence to now has been with Helen, his daughter. I have assumed that you and the Captain General keep Sir George supplied with details of our preparations.'

'Indeed, and no doubt the Lady Helen will share selected snippets from your letters with her father.'

I murmur my agreement, although I am not certain that Helen does as he surmises. In fact, I would hope that she guards the intimate nature of our exchanges closely. Lady Anne turns the conversation to her children and thanks me for the brief tutoring of young Humphrey Or in mathematics. I am not surprised to learn that he is eager to join with our venture. Sir Humphrey was in two minds, but his wife argued for a delay because of his youth. Her view has prevailed with a promise that he will be blooded in the next endeavour. There are a few moments of quiet before Sir Humphrey drains a cup of wine and clears his throat.

'There would be an advantage if you could use your influence with Sir George to explain that rumours of calamity and ill-fortune here are unfounded. It would be a great favour if you would write and encourage him in our near-readiness.'

So, this is why I have been treated gently and dined in his house. They are fearful that delays and reports of chaos may lead to more withdrawals from the venture, or even its cancellation. Hawkins has passed the burden of this request to Gilbert and I suppose this has been done because of Gilbert's easier manner.

I say, 'I will be glad to write to Sir George expressing the excitement and impatience here for our sailing. The Captain General has given an estimate of four or five weeks for our departure.'

'And we would hope for a shorter delay.' He pauses. 'There has been some talk that Lord Burghley may accompany Sir George here for the start of our enterprise. That would add lustre to our parting and calm some of the baseless misgivings that circulate.'

'I can see how that would benefit and I will encourage Sir George in that direction.' This adds to the discomfort I am placed in, but it would be churlish to deny his request or appear reluctant to accede. I suspect my influence with Sir George in this affair is lower than their expectation. I have not heard any talk of Burghley attending and deem it unlikely that any entreaty by me in this respect will make a difference. It is a further sign of the unease that plagues Hawkins and Gilbert.

Our supper proceeds with dishes of eel pie, roasted duck and sweet jellies. It is an unusually grand meal for a singular guest, especially a scholar of only middling reputation. The Lady Anne leaves us to attend to household affairs. Gilbert broaches the subject of astrology and questions whether a star chart could be drawn to provide guidance and comfort for our adventure. I am wary and on safer ground in deflecting this enquiry.

I answer, 'My casting of stars nowadays is either for the navigation of ships or to help with my practice as a physician in an understanding of the nature and susceptibilities of patients, Sir Humphrey. I do not hold with a view that astrological charts can foretell the success or otherwise of complex situations such as our intended mission.'

He clicks his tongue and shakes his head with disappointment but appears to accept my assertion. I am relieved when our conversation ends and I retire to the chamber set aside for my night rest.

Three

Back at the Gredley house in Plymouth town, I have taken a cup of claret to my chambers where I must find the words to frame a letter to Sir George. It is a puzzle and a far greater stretch of my ingenuity than I imagined when I gave careless agreement to Gilbert's request. I have some sympathy with our leaders' concerns, but I cannot litter this note with untruths. Sir George will not treat me lightly if I mislead him about our state of preparedness. Margaret, one of the Gredley servants, raps my door, bobs a curtsey and announces that I have a visitor. She offers his name as Captain Tewkes, although he is generally known as plain 'Master'. I understand her confusion as a number in our party have styled themselves with military terms such as 'Captain', 'Gunner' or 'Sergeant'.

'Good day to you, Oliver, do you arrive to tempt me with dinner or some other diversion?'

I see he has a serious face. I offer him wine, which he refuses at first, then demurs. I pour him a cup and wait for what is to come.

'There has been a murder.'

'What – who?' This is unwelcome news, but there have been other killings of our sailors and soldiers over the past weeks. 'Is this one particular in unpleasantness?'

'It is not one of our crews. It is a young notable from town named Walter Tremayne. He is the son of Robert Tremayne, who has substantial property and is well-connected.'

'I do not know him, but this will likely heighten the ill-feeling towards us by the townspeople. It is not good.'

'There is more.' He shakes his head slowly. 'Charles has been confined under suspicion.'

'Charles?'

'The watchmen and justices were brought to the scene. Questions were asked, first testimonies taken and Charles was named.'

'When was this?'

'It was early this morning. The body of young Tremayne was found by a midden in the back quarter of a house that lies close to Charles' lodgings.'

'But why was Charles named? Surely, he cannot be at fault.'

'I was with him the last night. We were at a table in the *Seven Bells*. Tremayne was with us.'

'Did you witness any quarrel between the two? The Charles I know would not be muddled by strong drink or the instigator of a conflict over trifles.'

Oliver relates the limited extent of his knowledge. There were four at their table for supper. Tremayne was raucous with too much wine and Charles assisted him in a visit to the privy for heavy spewing. This failed to quieten Tremayne and he continued with drinking and unruly behaviour despite the advice of his elders. Oliver departed with his secondary, Henry Fincham, leaving Charles with the care of a drunk Tremayne. He heard no more until the news was brought to him by his housekeeper at breakfast.

I ask, 'How was Tremayne killed?'

'That aspect, I do not know.'

'There must be more to this than the naming of a man who took supper with the victim.' Oliver shrugs with an admission of regret at leaving Charles with the charge of a soused and naïve youth and is unaware of any other indications.

'Where is Charles kept?'

'He is restricted to his house under the watch of a town constable and one other.'

I ask Oliver if he would go with me to visit him, but he cannot as he is sailing his ship with three others in a short sea trial this day.

*

Two men guard the frontage of Charles' house. One is a wide, brutish looking fellow, who is scraping his boots with a dagger. The other lolls against the door with folded arms. I approach and address the one with a dagger.

'I have a message for Captain Wicken.'

He grunts and answers, 'Who are you?' He pauses to survey my figure and adds, 'Sir.'

'I am Doctor William Constable, his friend and physician.'

I am a head taller. He stretches himself and rolls his shoulders to confront me. 'There is no entry to this place without the authority of the justices.'

The other man straightens and adds, 'Wicken is kept here for a most foul killing. We have orders.'

'I understand his confinement was done in haste while full enquiries are made. This is no prison and there is no certainty of his part in the killing.'

The thickset one places his dagger in his belt and folds his arms in a gesture of rebuttal. 'No paper of authority; no entry.'

'It is an urgent matter. I do not bear arms and my visit will be brief.' I pause and see their belligerence remains. 'But if that is your way, then I must report back to Captain General Hawkins that his message cannot be delivered. He will be displeased and wish to learn your names so that he can confer with the Justice.'

The thickset man shuffles his feet, then moves to the door and exchanges low words with his fellow. I see their resolve is weakened. Despite the growing ill-feeling in the town about the nuisance of our men, Hawkins is an important and feared notable here. I have used his name, perhaps unwisely, as Charles had admitted that he is held in low regard by our leader.

'A physician should be harmless enough.' He stands aside while the other opens the door. 'But it must be quick.'

I enter the hall to see the trailing skirts of a servant scurrying through a doorway. She will have been listening to our encounter at the front. I wait for a few moments and when no one comes, I hail Charles by name. And again, with more force. A door opens and Charles appears with long hair uncombed, blouse flapping loose and his bearing shrunk a little.

'Ah, William – good day to you.'

'There is no redeeming goodness in finding you in this state, Charles. What is this pickle? Surely, you are caught in some hurried misunderstanding.'

He answers with a faint smile and begs me follow to the parlour. I see he is already set here with a seat, footstool, jug of wine and the half-eaten carcass of a roast bird. He pours me a cup and I take a seat waiting for his words.

He says, 'Did you know Walter Tremayne?'

'No, I have only heard his name spoken.'

'He was a good young man. He had his foolish ways, but a kind heart and useful mind. He did not deserve an untimely and cruel fate.'

'Oliver says you both supped with him the last night.'

'Yes, we were with him. He did not hold his wine well. He became muddled and unsteady.'

'You were left with his care?'

'Oliver and his man left us and Walter seemed to recover most of his senses. We left a short time after the midnight bell. I accompanied him a distance and tried to hold him steady, but he came to resent my attentions and insisted that he was left to make his own way to his house.'

'Where did you leave him?'

'We parted some twenty paces past my front door. That was my last sight of him.'

'So, you have been named simply because you left the *Seven Bells* in his company?'

'It will be that. There can be no other cause.' His manner is subdued. He lifts his head and meets my eye. 'You must know that such a foul act is not within my inclinations.'

'Of course.' I reach over and clasp his shoulder. 'Do you know how he was killed?'

He shakes his head. 'There has been no mention…'

'Charles, you must gather yourself and raise your spirits to meet this challenge. If there was no sight of you at the killing or other damning testimony to follow, then you must be cleared of any suspicion.'

'The hearing must be fair.'

'Why would it not be?'

'Walter was the nephew of the Mayor and Justice of this town, one Stephen Shanning.'

'Then, he should be eager to seek justice for his loss.'

'Yet, I fear that men of influence would be happy to prolong my discomfort.'

'You cannot refer to Hawkins or Gilbert?' He shrugs. 'This has naught to do with our venture, Charles. An arraignment for trial would add further disruption to their plans.'

'Well, I can only hope that you have it right.'

'Do not doubt it, Charles. You must ground yourself in an understanding that our world is not such a devious place.'

I speak with more confidence than I feel. A conspiracy against him is too fanciful, but I know that sometimes fevered emotions can override logical thinking and fairness. I leave Charles with another plea to lift his mood and an assurance that I will seek out Hawkins and request that he use his good offices for an even-handed hearing.

*

Hawkins has a place of business on the quayside. It is a modest, two-storey building originally used for storage and has little in the way of homely comforts. He is harried by merchants, ships' masters and other men from boats and carts as I stand and wait patiently in a small anteroom. I am surprised to discover from overheard talk that he concerns himself with everyday trade in this harbour as well as the preparations for our venture. It is no wonder that his humour is stretched and he is short in some of his exchanges. His attention is free at last, and he beckons me into his chamber.

'God's blessing on you, Doctor Constable. I trust you had a pleasant stay with Sir Humphrey?'

I return his greeting and confirm my enjoyment of Gilbert's hospitality. He sits heavily in his chair and points me to a stool by his table, which is scattered with papers and charts. He passes a few comments about his troubles dealing with mundane matters of trade, then raises his eyes and inclines his head, inviting me to speak.

'I am concerned about the treatment of Captain Wicken. He is named in a killing and confined to his house when there appears to be little justification.'

He breathes deeply and sets his jaw firm with a grim expression. 'Ah, Wicken, I have a report on this low affair from

Justice Shanning.' He pauses and sits back in his seat. 'What do you know of the matter, Doctor? You are recently arrived back here and will have missed the actions around the discovery of the body and Wicken's detainment.'

'I know only what I have heard from Master Tewkes and Captain Wicken himself. There was little in the telling, other than the young victim was at the *Seven Bells* in their company and became muddled with wine.'

'You have seen Wicken this day?'

'It was a brief meeting only a short time ago. He is guarded and kept in his house.'

He fixes his stare at me and makes a low noise in his throat. It is clear he disapproves of my entry to Charles' house. He reaches across his table and picks a piece of paper between his thumb and forefinger as though it is unclean. 'This report suggests there is more to it.' He pauses and scans the note. 'Wicken was seen having fierce words with young Tremayne on two occasions after leaving the inn. Also, a clump of yellow hair was found in a closed hand of the victim.'

My body stiffens at this news. 'I... I did not know of these testimonies.' I recall now that Charles said Tremayne became fractious before departing his company. That would be an easy misunderstanding, but perhaps now is not the time to debate this point. 'Is it known how Master Tremayne died?'

'It is written that he was strangled by the throat. The face was purpled and there were marks on the neck indicating a severe constriction.'

'Was a physician or surgeon called?'

'Doctor Millard attended. You know him a little, I think.' I mutter an agreement, with thoughts distracted by the trouble now faced by Charles. Millard acts as Hawkins' physician and we have met twice, both times in his presence. He continues, 'Justice Shanning will hear the facts and depositions this next morning in the Guildhall. If it is decided to refer the case to the next quarter session then you can be sure that Wicken will not be treated so kindly.'

These last words are spoken with a trace of malicious pleasure and reinforce Charles' opinion that he is strongly disliked by

Hawkins. I leave with a heaviness of spirit. I cannot believe that Charles is guilty, but the dice do not roll in his favour.

I retreat to my lodgings where Mistress Gredley scolds me for missing the dinner I had requested. She offers a plate of cold meats to take to my chambers, but I decline politely as my appetite has gone. I dabble a while with my letter to Sir George. The words will not flow. There must be an exactness, which encourages an eventual success for the venture, but does not hide current problems. The bells strike five and I desert my chambers for some air leaving my scribblings unfinished. The late afternoon is warm, the sun is bright and the streets take on a cheery aspect as I stroll west towards the quays. There is an unhurried quality to the comings and goings in the shops and houses and the background hum of voices provides a pleasant accompaniment to my thoughts. I started with no clear purpose in my walk, but it seems that my instincts have taken me in the direction of Doctor Millard's house.

I am here in front of a whitewashed house of middling size in a quiet lane located between the busier quarters of Plymouth town. I tap the handle of my dagger on the polished brass doorplate, which dazzles in direct line of the falling sun. A young maid servant answers the door. She bobs a greeting, mentioning my name, which is a surprise as I have not visited here before. I am taken through to a receiving room with advice that Doctor Millard will join presently. The door opens and Millard enters. He is a small, sparely-made man of middle age, but his stoop and thinning grey hair confer the impression of an older figure. Oliver has told me that he suffers from aching bones and that I should be wary of his temper.

I say, 'Doctor Millard, please forgive this unplanned intrusion. I was taking the early evening air and thought to pay my respects.'

'Doctor Constable, you are welcome and there is no necessity to excuse your visit here. I should like the opportunity to converse with a fellow physician, most especially one with a reputation for a wider learning.'

I thank him for his words and he bids me follow him to his study where he offers a cup of sweet wine. It is a middle-sized room and somewhat cramped with tables spread with books and charts. The musty odour of paper, vellum and inks provide an immediate sense of my own home and a longing to be back with my household in West Cheap. I recognise some of the books and there is familiarity in the schematics.

'I see from your charts that you also have an interest in the stars and navigation of ships, Doctor.'

'Indeed, the safe journeying of ships is a vital interest to all in this town. I have seen your shadow-staff, Doctor, and it is well done. You are to be congratulated on your quick mind and invention. I know that Captain General Hawkins has a great regard for your instrument and places trust that its service will aid a successful venture.'

We spend a pleasant time discussing the shadow-staff and the development in my thinking that led to its creation. His fascination is genuine and his learning enables him to pose perceptive questions. We are started on our third cup of wine and I have found difficulty turning our conversation around to the subject of my visit. Eventually, there is a quiet moment as we sip wine and reflect on our exchanges.

I say, 'I heard that you examined the body of the unfortunate Tremayne.'

'Yes, I am physician to his family. He was an agreeable young gentleman; foolish and headstrong in a way that often marks one of his years; but good-hearted. It was a most undeserving death.'

'Were there marks of violence?'

'It was my opinion that he was strangled by the neck.'

'It can often be troublesome to know the exact cause in such cases.'

His eyes widen and he snaps his head to meet my gaze. 'Do you have experience in such matters, Doctor? I had thought enquiry into circumstances of those passed from this life was beyond the inclinations of London physicians.'

I must be careful. He is defensive about his expertise in this affair and the supposed easy living of his profession in our capital. 'Yes, I have been called to offer estimations on the causes of death, but I am sure that your knowledge in these unpleasant situations far outweigh mine.' My words are honest as I have given testimony on only three such incidents.

He bows his head and hums a low noise through closed mouth. I hope that he is placated. He hesitates with a thoughtful expression before continuing. 'The face was blue and purple; the eyes unnatural and bulbous; indications of a severe and unusual constriction of air to the lungs was apparent.'

'Was the tongue protruding?'

'Indeed it was. Why do you ask?'

'It is only that I have known one or two incidents where a blow on the head from a fall caused the tongue to be swallowed. If it is not retrieved quickly from the throat, the air is blocked and the unfortunate becomes throttled until death.'

He mutters an agreement, sits back in his seat and clasps his hands over his middle. 'There was bruising around the neck. You would accept that as a signal of strangulation?'

'Yes, you are right, although it can be problematic to identify bruising when head and shoulders are purpled from a desperate seeking of air.' I pause to sip wine, hoping that my further questioning will not offend. I commend the quality of the wine and he adds more to our cups.

'Do you have a particular interest in this case, Doctor Constable?'

He has seen through me. 'I count Charles Wicken as a friend and would not wish to see him unjustly named for the crime.'

'It is as I thought. I suspected this was at the heart of your visit and I wonder it took you so long to broach the subject.'

'Please do not misunderstand, Doctor, I have enjoyed our conversation on diverse topics this evening. I trust you will not think I am here to gain unfair advantage for the hearing tomorrow. The involvement of a friend does not disqualify my interest in the facts.'

He shifts in his chair. 'Yes, you have it right. I am sorry if my last words appeared unkind. I too, have enjoyed our discourse and would regard it as a favour if we could be more familiar in our exchanges. May I refer to you as William, and you must use my informal, Jacob?'

I am relieved that our discussion has returned to an easier

arrangement and I agree readily to a relaxation in our naming.

He sips his wine and says, 'Do you have more questions on the situation of the body and the way of killing?'

'There is only one, Jacob. Did you note whether young Tremayne was lying by his vomit? It is known he was befuddled with strong drink and that he had spewed his supper with some force earlier that night.'

'It is a reasonable enquiry and I see where your thinking is directed. There was some dribble and puke from the mouth, but not an excess. Some ejection would be expected from distress to the innards.' He pauses and fixes his gaze on me directly. 'This was not a blameless death, William. Tremayne's hands had wrenched yellow hair from the attacker in a struggle. The hair was clamped firmly in his hand when I was called to the scene.'

I am discouraged, but there will be naught to gain by prolonging this line of conversation, and so I turn to a lighter topic and enquire about his practice of physic in the town and its environs. His humour lightens immediately and he is eager to share his experience of perplexing ailments and learn of my opinions. He mentions his aching bones which have worsened in recent times. I have known others with painful and misshapen knuckles, hips and other joints. I know of no curative, but offer a suggestion that oil of olives, taken in moderate and regular dosage, may serve to ease the pain and loosen movement. He accepts my recommendation in good heart and avers that he will put it to the test. We depart on good terms. I have taken a liking to Jacob in our brief convention. He has a keen and insightful mind, which I would applaud under different circumstances. I have a foreboding that a time may come when I will have to question his capability in the next quarter session if my friend Charles is to be found innocent of the killing.

Four

We arrive at the Guildhall in good time. It is a new building, with parts unfinished, located in an open space with rows of some of the finer houses of west Plymouth either side. It is a large, squat and plain construction, lacking any fine decoration, although no doubt there will be plans for future improvement. I am with Oliver, who tells me that a good part of the funding for the Guildhall has been furnished by the victim's father and the Tremayne town house is less than a hundred paces distant. There is jostling and raised voices from a crowd waiting to enter. A strong interest is shown in the killing of a prominent young gentleman in the town and the opportunity to spread scandalous gossip. We are ushered away from the general mob by an attendant who leads us through an anteroom to the side of a large hall where the customary business of the Guildhall is done. We are in an area reserved for gentlemen and other notables where two rows of stools are already occupied. We are obliged to stand at the rear. Opposite is a raised platform with an empty seat and stools below. To our right are vacant stools, which I surmise are for those who will make up the jury. There is an empty space to our front and a roped enclosure to our left where townsfolk gather. It bulges already with the crush and will not be sufficient to hold all those clamouring for entry.

A quarter-hour has passed and there is an air of impatience in the hall. Finally, a door opens and a group of gentlemen and yeoman take their places on the jury stools. There is a pause until a short fellow with overlong cloak enters bearing a staff, closely followed by a proud, erect man in fine robes. He must be Shanning. The man with a staff bangs it thrice on the floor and orders quiet. Oliver mutters in my ear that Shanning has the appearance of one that will not tolerate even the smallest trespass. I bow my head in agreement. I have attended only one such hearing before in Cripplegate, but that was some years ago and a less crowded affair. Oliver has more experience and has already advised on the outcome he expects for Charles. I share his misgivings.

A scribe seated near Justice Shanning shuffles over to the jury and takes their oath. Three are led into the open space; roughly-dressed, with the appearance of workmen or labourers. Two are grown men and the other a lad of no more than ten years. The men stand still, facing the platform with heads bowed, while the shoulders of the lad heave. He is crying. Shanning states their names in a loud, clear voice and declares they are accused by a landowner of stealing a sheep, which was found, butchered and ready for eating. He reads the testimony of a watchman and the landowner who avers they are from a corrupt family of idlers who are well known for their mischief. I anticipate more, but Shanning has finished and turns to the jury, who answer, 'Aye' as one voice.

I say to Oliver, 'That is too short. Surely, there is more for these poor unfortunates?'

'That is the way for their kind,' he answers in low voice.

One of the men speaks, although I do not hear his words.

'They plead the clergy,' says Oliver.

I have heard of this relief for trivial offences but did not expect it for stealing a sheep. The first recites a passage from *The Book of Leviticus* beginning with, 'Do not seek revenge or bear a grudge against anyone among your people, but love your neighbour as yourself...' That appears to satisfy and the next man offers a different passage, in which he is slower and less exact, but completes in a fashion. The lad, however, is halting and unsure in his exposition and it takes long, agonising moments before satisfaction is achieved. Shanning pronounces that they shall not, after all, be hanged, but must undertake heavy work for the landowner to the value of three sheep.

I ask Oliver, 'Was all that done according to law?'

'No, but it will serve.'

Charles must wait a little longer as the next to appear is a bent old man in rags. He is named for vagrancy and lewd gestures to a goodwife, causing her alarm and recourse to a calming preparation from the apothecary. The poor man utters a few desperate words, but the outcome is quickly reached and he is led away to be branded on his cheek.

There is an air of hushed excitement as Charles is ushered into the open space by one of the men who guarded his house. I am pleased to note that he has a steady bearing and is dressed well with hair neatly tucked under a dark velvet cap trimmed with discreet coloured edging. Shanning glares around the hall until all is quiet, then begins a lengthy discourse on the untimely and evil taking of a promising young life. The history of Walter Tremayne is sketched in some detail with glowing praise of his Godly devotion, obedience to his father and balanced humour. It seems the victim was near sainthood.

'Charles Wicken, you are named as the one who took the life of Walter Tremayne.' He pauses and glares sternly at Charles. 'I understand you are a gentleman of property and the intended principal master of three ships that will sail with the adventure fleet close-harboured here and Dartmouth town.'

Charles affirms these facts and Shanning continues, 'You were seen with others plying the young victim with strong drink in the *Seven Bells*. Thereafter, Goodman Hagger and a serving maid named Amy Wearing sighted you in a fierce argument with the victim on leaving the inn. The maid testifies that this confrontation continued into the night outside for fifty paces or more.' He directs his gaze to the jury to ensure he has their attention, then returns to Charles. 'Goodwife Langley gives testimony that she spied you holding and shaking young Tremayne with some force by the side of the house where she is employed. That house is neighbour to the one where Watchman Sykes discovered the lifeless body of Walter Tremayne, a much loved and respected young gentleman in this town. The watchman reports that the victim clutched a handful of yellow hair.' He strains his neck to peer closely at Charles. 'I see that, despite an attempt to hide under a cap, you have hair that matches this last testimony.'

Shanning sits back and allows the buzzing and humming of muttered disapprovals to circulate before turning to the jury. ''Well, is this man to be tried?'

He is answered by a chorus of, 'Ayes' from the jury and angry cries of assent from others in the hall. The short attendant rams his staff on the wooden floor so that Shanning may speak.

'Charles Wicken, you will be detained until the next quarter session. That will be held here in fifteen days from now on the twenty-fourth day of June, when you will be put on trial for the murder of Walter Tremayne. You will be judged by High Justice John Downish of Crediton and twelve gentlemen of property.' He sits back in his seat and surveys Charles with barely-disguised contempt. 'I trust that you have the means to avoid detainment in the cells?'

Charles answers with a simple, 'Yes.'

'In that case, you will be guarded in your lodgings at the rate of two crowns for each day of your confinement. This will be sufficient to pay for your guarding and other inconveniences.'

There is a gasp among those gathered at the extravagant amount Charles must pay to escape the foulness of prison, but that will have low standing in his worries.

*

'Did you know about the sightings and the hair?' Oliver passes me a cup of claret. We have retreated to his lodgings after finding the inns close by the Guildhall full of men eager to pass opinion on the hearing.

'Charles told me of his company with Tremayne part way to his home and that he felt obliged to allow him to continue on his own after he became indignant with his care. I knew of the yellow hair from Hawkins.'

'Hmm, drunken men can often be contrary in their ways. The belligerence may be explained, but the hair is damning.'

'I agree, the prospect appears grave for Charles.' I hesitate as though considering, but my mind is firm. 'I cannot have him as the killer. He is a fine man and, even if it was a death through mischance such as a fall, then his character would not allow an unworthy concealment.'

Oliver sips from his cup. 'You must not let your friendship and recent rescue muddy your thinking, William. I am with you on the matter of character and he is also my friend, but... but we men can be strange beasts when the heat is up.'

'Heat? I have not seen Charles too quick in his temper.'

We are quiet for a few moments, each of us staring into our cups with our own thoughts. Am I over-eager to see Charles blameless because he saved me? I have known him for only a few months, but I count myself a fair judge of men and he has given me no cause to doubt. Oliver is more circumspect.

I say, 'I think we have both been close to Charles for the short interval of our joining here. Do you know his history?'

'Only that his family own property near Lincoln and that he has good learning. He has a strong reputation as a commander at sea and has accumulated considerable wealth from raiding the Spanish in Biscay. It is also rumoured that he has a high connection at court; perhaps, even Walsingham, himself'

Walsingham, now that is news to me. I wonder if this association might save him. No, it cannot be relied on.

'I must find a way to help Charles. I will make enquiries these next few days to establish whether the testimonies can be trusted and if there are other aspects not yet disclosed.'

I return to my lodgings determined to free my mind of the coming trial for the remainder of the day and construct a letter to Sir George. Once again, the delicate formulation of the letter defeats me.

Five

I must have a plan. I have scratched a few notes this morning after a short breakfast. I will visit Charles again and construct a more detailed account of his memory of that night. I will also seek out those that testified to the sightings of Charles and Tremayne upon leaving the inn. I am cautious in the matter of the body. I would not wish to offend Jacob or the family, but should not overlook the possibility that an examination may yield further intelligence or contrary facts. The weather is not warm and corruption of the body will not have progressed beyond the state of informing on the manner of death. I rise from my table and walk to the window overlooking the activity in the street below, which is called Lockyer Lane. This scheme is all very well but will come to naught unless I have free access to Charles in his confinement and am not obstructed in other enquiries. I must seek a note of permission and I suppose this will be from Shanning. It will not be easy.

The weather today is no friend. It is June, but the rain is swept in biting-sharp flurries of a wind that has no sure direction. I take my horse to Shanning's house for the sake of his exercise and also to escape the mud which abounds in the marshes on my short journey. The house is old, spread wide and built in stone over a single storey for the most part, with a brick-built, two-storey wing to one side. It is an odd assortment, but well-tended and speaks of some affluence. I am received with courtesy and ushered inside, while my horse is taken to the courtyard at the rear. A man servant takes my wet cloak and bids me wait in the hall. Shanning appears in short time.

'God's blessing to you on this unseasonal morning, Justice Shanning. I am William Constable, trusting that I do not disturb important business.'

'Doctor Constable, welcome to my house. I have been told of your accomplishments by the Captain General.' He returns my bowed greeting with an expression of mild surprise. 'Your mission will be urgent to call on a morning such as this.'

'Indeed, it is on a matter of justice that I call.'

He raises his eyes and beckons me to accompany him into the next chamber. It is a long room with a low ceiling, decked with tapestries of industry at sea and on land. I am offered a seat at a carpeted table, which I take, and refreshment, which I decline with politeness. His bearing and accommodation speak of wealth and authority. I remind myself that I must choose my words carefully in this exchange.

I say, 'Thank you for receiving me with such good grace. I mentioned the subject of justice and I will declare my status as a friend of Captain Charles Wicken.'

He stiffens and attempts to hide an immediate show of distaste, which fails. 'You will know, I am sure, that Wicken is detained for the quarter session. The matter is out of my hands and I wonder that you would wish to concern yourself with a man of such low character, capable of a foul and terrible act.'

'Yet, there can be no certainty of guilt until the testimony is tested.'

'You will have been at the hearing, no doubt? It was a damning catalogue.'

'There can be no absolute firmness in cases where the killing is not observed and the offender not arraigned at the scene.'

He narrows his eyes. 'Why are you here – Doctor? There is naught I can give you or would wish to.'

'I would visit Captain Wicken. I should also like to examine those who have given testimony – not in any strong way, but simply to determine if there were other aspects, forgotten or mistaken.'

'Ha, those who bore witness are free to speak – if they wish. As for Wicken, he is closely guarded and will not be disturbed.' He folds his arms in a gesture of finality.

'Justice Shanning, I applaud your caution and correctness in this affair. However, I am here to request a note of permission in your hand, so that I may go about this business unhindered.'

He is indignant and about to rise from his seat. I reach out with a hand and say, 'The primary motive in my asking is not to satisfy idle curiosity, or even for the benefit of Captain Wicken. I must answer to a higher authority.'

I have stayed him, for a while. 'What higher authority?'

'Do you not wonder why I, a scholar from London town, one plainly unsuited to the rigours of an adventure to the New Lands, is placed here among the brave and hard men soon to sail?'

'I... I had heard of a new instrument to aid navigation.'

'There are other interests I must watch – interests of concern to those in the highest authority in Her Majesty's state.' He is perplexed, still and brooding. I do not want to dig deeper into half-truths that may come back to haunt me. Still, it seems he is not inclined to accede based upon veiled generalities, so I will be more open. 'You have said that my name has been mentioned in conversation with Captain General Hawkins.'

'Yes, it may...'

'And was there reference to a high connection in the matter of our state's security?'

He shakes his head slowly as if sifting through his recollection. He gets closer, but is not there, yet.

'I have been charged to keep a keen eye on the gathering here by Sir Francis Walsingham himself.' There, I have said it. It is even less than a half-truth as the obligation he placed on my unwilling shoulders ended some months past.

'Secretary Walsingham? Why... why would he have an interest... in this local and vulgar affair?'

'I have said too much already.'

'But...'

'The forces that control the security of Her Majesty have a long reach and their functioning will not be easily understood by those without a close association.' I have said little of substance, but I see that it has an effect. 'You will know from your exalted position here in Devonshire, that large gatherings of men attract malcontents and others who seek ways to sow unrest and sedition.' I pause to add weight to my final words. 'There is more to this killing than may be supposed and we trust your discretion and cooperation in our request.'

It is done. He has weakened and will comply. Perhaps my use of the collective was enough to satisfy that Sir Francis is the hidden hand in this demand. He reaches across the table for a roll of paper.

I say, 'There is another, more delicate, aspect that should be included. I would wish for a brief examination of the body of Walter Tremayne before it is interred.'

He shifts uneasily. 'That will cause some upset to the family. You know that he was my nephew?' I bow my head in acknowledgement. 'But if it must be done, then let it be with God's grace and due deference. His body lies in the church of St Andrew in Sutton, to the East.'

I concur and move to dictate the words to be written. He is meek in following my narration, but I see that he is troubled and will search out the truth in my telling. I must hope that I am gone from this place before my overreaching is exposed.

The note is sealed and I depart Shanning's house with uplifted spirit that there may be some small prospect of saving my friend from the rope.

*

Nature has calmed, the rain ceased and there is a glow in the sky that promises a brighter interlude. It is a short distance to Charles' lodgings and I ride through puddled streets taking a longer route than necessary so that I can collect my thoughts for the conversation to come. I will be firm in my questioning, so there can be no doubt in my mind before I progress with an investigation. I should also be wary that I do not offer him hope which may be dashed. He must prepare himself for the worst as the likeliest outcome.

I have encountered one of the guards at the front door before. He recognises me, rolls his wide shoulders, and then places his thumbs in a low-slung belt to meet me with an attitude of firmness.

He says, 'You have been before, but there will be no entry this time – Master Constable.'

'God's morning to you, goodmen. You have the advantage of me. You greet me by name, but I do not know yours.'

He takes a half-step back. 'I am Larkin and this fellow is named Fleck. But a cheery manner will do you no good.'

'I have a note from Justice Shanning that permits free access to Captain Wicken and this house.' I dismount, pass Larkin the note and hand the reins to Fleck.

I cannot be sure that they read all the words there, but there can be no mistaking his seal. Following a brief scan of the note and exchanged glances, Larkin opens the door and touches his cap, while the other takes my horse around to the rear. The housekeeper stands in the hall with an expectant and worried face. I tell her there is no cause for alarm and enquire where I may find Charles. She leads me to the parlour door and opens it but does not enter to announce my presence. Charles is sat, hunched forward on a stool beside an empty fire. He is still for a few moments before turning his head.

'William – yes, it is William Constable. You are welcome. I had thought all would be barred entry, save the guards and the servants here who scurry from me like frightened mice.'

'Good day to you, Charles. I have succeeded in obtaining a permit to enter from Justice Shanning.'

'Shanning – why that is well done – and a surprise. Do you think Stack may also be allowed to converse with me? He has been denied up to now.'

'It would be wise not to strain the limits of Shanning's patience. I will pass messages between you and Stack if you wish.'

He rises from his stool and bids me follow to a seat at a small table. His appearance is neat enough, but there is a sunken greyness around his eyes that signifies a sleepless night.

'If only... if only you were with us that eve, William. You have the coolest head and would have steered away from carousing and over-indulgence in strong drink.' He pauses and eyes me directly. 'But you were not here, at your lodgings. I found you had gone to Dartmouth with Hawkins' man, Pennes.'

'Yes, I was dined and rested there by Sir Humphrey and his wife, Anne.' I hold for a moment and think back to that visit which was only two days past, but feels distant. 'It was a strange journey. We travelled via Loddiswell and passed the scene of my rescue to pick up the remains of the attackers. But they were gone.'

'Gone – how?'

'It is unknown, but it appeared to be a matter of indifference to Pennes; as though it was somehow expected. The meeting with Gilbert was arranged to recruit my encouragement in a letter to Sir George for his continued enthusiasm and forbearance of delays to the venture.'

He is silent for a few moments, then shakes his head, leaves his seat and wanders the chamber. Does he ponder the significance of this short tale, or is he simply distracted by more urgent concerns? He stands, framed against the dull light from a window and clasps his hands behind his back.

'There is a subject I would discuss with you, William. It is not something I do lightly, but what you have told me deepens my suspicions to near-certainty.'

'What is it, Charles? Surely, there can be no topic more pressing than your arraignment for a killing?'

'There is a connection; please be patient.' He strides to the table and resumes his seat. 'I do not think you were the intended target for the assault near Loddiswell.'

'You must explain.'

'There is a malign force in this place. I believe it is at the heart of my false naming for the murder of young Tremayne.'

I am confused. 'How could the settling of blame on you for a killing, aid a wider conspiracy? And what has this to do with my attack and rescue?'

'Ah, forgive me, William. I run too fast with my reasoning.' He fidgets with his fingers and rises from his seat once more. 'My business here is more than the management and sailing of ships.'

There is space for more questioning, but I am silent and wait for what is to come.

He has some trouble in finding the words. 'I am charged to watch and report.'

'Watch – what? Report – to who?'

'You are known to the high office that receives my reports. It is the one that cares for the safety of Her Majesty's state.'

I am bewildered; amazed. He tiptoes warily around the name in the same way I did with Shanning less than an hour before.

The correlation is startling. But, do I believe him? It is as though his ears were pinned to the walls at Shanning's house.

I say, 'I am known to Sir Francis Walsingham. Let us do away with this guarded talk and speak openly. You say you are working for him?'

'A man named Mylles approached me at the turn of the year. I attended Sir Francis at his house at Barn Elms. He had a concern at the collection of many men and ships in the West Country. It is also known that agents from Spain and the Catholic League mingle here. I have connections in France and Corunna, which could be helpful in informing on either the misuse of our fleet or its endangerment from foreign militaries.' He spreads his hands in a gesture of helplessness. 'I could not deny him my assistance, and so here I am; sailor and intelligencer – now humbled and without value in both employments.'

I know Mylles and there is some truth in the concern over the congregation of men and ships, but I had thought that was done with last Christmastide. 'How is the attack on my person bonded with this talk of spies and danger in the ports?'

'The assault was planned against myself and Stack. Two men on a lonely path through the woods are easily mistaken for others.'

The pieces start to come together. But I am not wholly convinced, yet. 'The complexity in your story and the multiple attempts to put you aside, lead me to surmise that you have some intelligence of great value that our enemies wish to keep from Walsingham.'

'Indeed, and I know you will wonder at the honesty of this wild story. Master Mylles offered some advice to be used if there is peril to my mission and reports cannot be sent. He said that you could be relied on, William, if I had occasion to need assistance. Further to this, he said that I could use the words "unknowing maid" to aid in persuasion. I do not know what this signifies, but hope that it will give you comfort in your stretch to accept my account.'

All doubt has vanished. Those two words are among those I uncovered from a cipher as a reluctant helper in an earlier conspiracy. They were part of a false claim about a hidden, bastard child of our monarch. He could not have known this without being taken into confidence by Walsingham and Mylles. I rise from my seat and embrace Charles, begging to be forgiven for my circumspection. He holds me strongly and kisses my cheeks. He is near to tears; breaks to turn away and wipe his face on his sleeve. I hope this outpouring of relief at my support and strong trust in his innocence is not misplaced. How can I extract him from this pickle? Walsingham is many day's ride away in London. He must be warned. But of what? And how?

I say, 'Why can you not inform Hawkins or Gilbert and have faith that they will report your intelligence to Walsingham. They will also surely use their influence to ensure there is no hasty outcome at the quarter session for one in his employ.'

'You know that they have no love for me.'

'But I understand that is in respect of professional jealousies. They will be obliged to attend to information which has an impact on our state's safeguarding.'

He makes to respond, then withdraws and becomes thoughtful. He begs forgiveness for not providing refreshment and leaves to obtain wine and cups. He returns in short time carrying a tray himself. It seems he cannot rely on his house servants for close attention. He pours our wine, drinks greedily and places his cup on the table with unusual firmness.

'I cannot rely on Hawkins or Gilbert. They are too bound up in the venture to pay proper regard to warnings of a wider danger, even those most perilous and imminent.'

'My dear Charles, this is fanciful talk. Surely...'

'It will be my urgent news that is the cause of my present trouble and I cannot discount the involvement of Hawkins.' A puff of air escapes my mouth. His imagination runs wild and in unpredictable directions. He sees my scepticism and continues. 'Any suggestion of a foreign danger to these ports will be unwelcome news to our leaders. It may bring about a royal command to divert ships and men from their venture to a defence of this realm.'

'It is true that they are eager to overcome any influences that may harm the success of the venture, but they would not dare go so far.'

'You have told me of Pennes' strange reaction to the missing bodies. Perhaps this was done so that they could not be identified as men taking instruction from Hawkins.' He pauses to let this statement take hold on my thoughts. 'I grant, that this may not be the likeliest motive, but it must be considered with care.'

He pours more wine in his cup and moves to the window, leaving me to sift and measure these tangled assertions and suspicions. It is true that I considered whether the secret removal of the attackers' bodies was done to spoil any chance of identification. There is also a desperation in the attitude of Hawkins and Gilbert to maintain the viability of the great adventure. Would they stoop so low to attempt the removal of a renowned master of ships and raider of Spanish treasure? And the murder of an innocent young gentleman of this town? I have come to know Hawkins as a hard man, capable of an easy cruelty; Gilbert less so, but sly, resolute and unbending in his aims. Stop – I should not allow mistrust of these men to colour my thinking. It is too terrible to contemplate and plunges me once more deep into a world of treachery and peril; one that I had hoped I had left behind in London.

I twirl the cup in my hand. I have not supped since the wine was poured. I sip slowly and gather my thoughts. I have come around to the idea that Charles may have been set as the innocent victim in a deadly game to quiet him and keep intelligence from Walsingham and his coterie. But the movers in this conspiracy are more apt to be the Catholic agents he talked of, rather than Hawkins and Gilbert. What is this intelligence? He has not disclosed it, and the answer to this riddle will be bound up in its nature.

I break a long stretch of silence in this small chamber by asking, 'Can you divulge the character of the vital information that you believe is behind your detainment, Charles?' In truth, I would prefer not to know and stand distant from this intrigue, but it seems I have no choice.

'Please leave me to ponder how this may be best handled,

William. I do not doubt your discretion and honesty, but it is a matter of sensitivity that should not be rushed.'

There is no more to be done here for the present. I take my leave, promising an early return and my best endeavours to uncover facts that may help his cause at the quarter session.

Six

The air has warmed and the sun struggles through breaking clouds on my journey to Sutton. I am slow in my progress, taking a gentle plod through lanes, cloying mud in the marshes and finally into the streets of Sutton, a sprawling outpost of Plymouth town. My thoughts are scrambled from all that I have heard from Charles, and it will take some time before they settle. I dismount at the porch to the church of St Andrew and tie my horse to a mounting stage.

The door is open. I remove my cap and step into a cool stillness with subdued light. It is a large church with scattered areas of whitewashed walls and fragments of old paintings still in evidence. Some of the smaller windows are glazed, but the larger ones are bare and open to nature. A bird flaps and flutters its way to a fresh perch in the transept. It is otherwise empty from my view. I go to the altar, kneel and mutter a short prayer for His assistance in my quest to unravel the threads of this mystery.

I am done, rise and brush dust from my cap. There is movement to my right side. A man stands there gazing at me with clasped hands and tilted head.

I say, 'I am Doctor William Constable, come here to show deference to the mortal remains of Walter Tremayne.'

'I am the keeper of this holy place, named Gilles. The body lies in the chapel through the north transept.'

I thank him and turn away.

'Your name is not known here, Doctor. Observance in the chapel is restricted to those authorised by the father, Robert Tremayne. The funeral will be held here two days from the present. You are welcome to attend here at that time.'

I should not be surprised as there was challenge in his manner from the start. I take the note from inside my doublet and present it to Gilles. He doesn't like it, and there is much 'tutting' and shaking of the head before he leads me to the chapel. The body is laid on a carpeted table with sprigs of lavender on the chest and two candles, near-burnt down, either side of the head. It is dressed in fine clothes and the head is tightly wrapped under the chin with a linen tie to stop the tongue protruding. The colour has drained with settling of blood. The face is pale with some mottling around the eyes and cheeks. I use finger and thumb to gently pull aside the ruff and inspect the neck. I ignore the noises of disapproval from Gilles who stands watching by the door and move to examine the other side. The hands are clasped over the middle. I lift the icy flesh a little and peer under them but can see no hair.

I turn to Gilles. 'Was the body washed here?' He bows his head. 'And was a clump of hair in the hand kept aside with other possessions?'

'The clothes and boots were returned to the family. There was naught else.'

'No purse?'

'The purse was empty. It was returned with belt, dagger and other trinkets.'

It has been cursory, but I can do no more. It seems Jacob had it right. There are round marks suggesting a fierce pressing of the gullet and neck by thumbs and fingers. He was strangled. I anticipated that the hair would be discarded and that is a pity as matching the shade of yellow would weigh heavily in a verdict. The empty purse is significant. He may have been robbed by the watchman or another after death, but in a court they would swear against this. A man of wealth such as Charles would not have reason to steal a few pennies.

*

The letter to Sir George is maddening. I have laboured for over two hours on the words, and still I am not satisfied. I have not mentioned the naming of Charles for the killing as this would be seen as a strong indication of chaotic and unruly behaviour in the fleet. But this news will surely reach him and he will wonder at my withholding.

A door opens and Oliver enters. He asks if I will take supper with him at the *Seven Bells*. I accept gladly and hand him the letter for his opinion. It is closely written and he studies carefully, running a finger along the lines to ensure he has the full sense. A shake of the head and he reads again. Finally, he passes it back and says, 'It is a clever note and I do not have an impression of you in its writing, William. It contains many half-truths, evasions and generalities. I have an idea of what is behind the note. It cannot have been easy.'

'I am sure you have seen the essence of it. I have been pressed by Hawkins and Gilbert to encourage Sir George in our eagerness and readiness to sail on the great venture. They fear other backers waver and the project will fail.'

'I see you do not include any reference to the murder of Tremayne and the naming of Charles.'

This leads to disclosure of my visit to Shanning, the consultation with Charles and examination of the body. I tell all, excepting the suspicions of Charles about the complicity of Hawkins and Gilbert. He blows a whistle through his lips at the extent of my efforts.

'You tread a dangerous path, William. It would not go well if Charles is found guilty and the extent of your meddling becomes known.'

'Do you doubt his innocence?'

He is quiet and takes a longer time to consider than expected. 'No... no, he must be free of blame.' He pauses, then continues, 'He is our friend and it is, therefore, a short stride to the mark where he is innocent, but there has been talk of his quick temper and unnecessarily fierce handling of captives.'

'But that will be in times of battle. Such inclinations cannot be transferred to conversations with allies over a peaceful supper.'

He accepts my view and we move to lighter conversation about the sea trial of his ship and the successful handling of the navigation instrument by his secondaries. I am glad to hear this news, but a part of my mind has stayed with wondering about the letter to Sir George. I will send it. When it is sealed and ready for the morning courier, we adjourn for an early supper.

The *Seven Bells* is one of the largest inns I have encountered, spanning the width of three houses in the busiest street of

Plymouth town. It caters for all classes, from working men through to the gentlemen's area where stone floors are swept clean and wood-panelled nooks with benches and tables afford a degree of privacy. Familiar faces in the latter section bow their heads in greeting as we take a table in the centre of this space. It is quiet around us, but there is a merry hum from greater numbers in the other parts. Oliver points to the niche bordering ours, as the place where he supped with Charles and Tremayne on that night. I ask if he knows the serving maid named Amy Wearing and he inclines his head to a figure lolling against the door to the kitchens. Oliver beckons her to our table. She is very young - perhaps no more than fourteen years - with pleasing face and dainty figure, neatly dressed with crisp, white bonnet and grey skirts. Oliver requests a flask of claret wine and a bowl of oysters to tempt our appetite for more. She offers a quick smile to each of us in turn and hurries to do his bidding.

'You will question her, William?'

'Yes, and I know it must be done gently. She has the look of one who will take fright easily.'

We sup for a while and talk of Hawkins and Humphrey. Oliver admires both men and sympathises with their frustrations at delays beyond their control. Activity in our area increases as men seek refreshment after their work. We request a plate of cold meats and pickles for our supper. We eat well and it is soon gone. The maid comes, bobs a curtsey and enquires if it would be our pleasure to taste the jellies. Oliver shakes his head.

I say, 'We will have sweet wine, but no jellies. You serve us well, young maid. Do you enjoy this work?'

'Indeed sir, I am fortunate and happy to oblige good gentlemen in this place.'

'I hear you witnessed a distressing event here a few nights past.'

She is on her guard quickly and bows her head. She does not answer and I persist. 'I see you recall the incident. Did you know the gentlemen involved?'

She mutters a reply, which I do not hear. Oliver begs her to repeat.

'Master Tremayne was a fine young gentleman. He was well-liked.' Her words are barely audible.

I say, 'The loss of one so young is a deep shame. Did he pay you particular attention?'

She lifts her head and I see that she is near to tears. They were of an age and there must be some truth in the closeness suggested.

Oliver says, 'And the other man; was he known to you?'

Her lips tremble, then she speaks with some force. 'He is a tough bully who intimidates. I feared for... Walter.... I...' She stops, turns and hurries to the kitchens.

Oliver sits back and places both hands on the table. 'Well William, it seems you will not get any relief for Charles from that quarter.'

He is right. Perhaps I was too direct and clumsy in my approach, but I do not think it will be worthwhile to continue with her questioning this evening. Oliver does not know Goodman Hagger, so I must find him through some other association.

We depart the *Seven Bells* as a red sun throws its last light over a pink sky. I take my leave of Oliver outside the inn, intending to wander the streets for a short while in search of the watchman who found the body.

I see a man on the corner of Union Street carrying a staff and unlit lantern. I approach, offer greetings and enquire after his name. It is not the right man and he advises the one I seek may be found in Cumber Street.

I am here and spy a group of men gathered outside another inn. There is a flickering glow from within the group and there will be a good chance he is there.

'God keep you all safe this fine night, goodmen. Is Watchman Sykes among you?'

A man steps forward, bangs his staff on the ground and says, 'I am Sykes. Do you have mischief to report - sir?'

'I am Doctor Constable, attached to Captain General Hawkins. There is no mischief this night that I know. May I talk with you – quietly?'

I walk a few paces and he follows. A big, heavily-bearded fellow of middle years, he lifts his lantern to my face and says,

'I have seen you before, Doctor. Men speak of your clever mind and… an instrument… of sorts.'

'I would ask you a question, Goodman Sykes. It is a delicate matter and I would not wish you to misunderstand my motives.' He grunts and I continue. 'I hear you discovered the body of the poor unfortunate Tremayne who was killed near here.' He grunts again. 'Did you consider that he was robbed? I understand his purse was empty.'

His eyes widen and he puffs air. 'Why do you find that killing of special interest, Doctor? It is a strange question to put to someone you do not know.'

'It was a chance remark at a meeting with Goodman Gilles at the church of St Andrew. I am simply a seeker of truth and would know what evil design was behind the killing of one so young and well-regarded.in this town.'

'Ha, I see why you would use pretty words to soften your question, Doctor. I am no thief. I am steadfast and honest in my work in this town where I have lived all my forty-two years.'

'I did not mean to offend and I do not doubt your word.'

'This is the first mention of a purse. My only concern was for the life of young Walter. I raised a cry and men came. There was no time. I paid no heed to a purse, his pockets, or baubles. Other men were there… came quickly…'

His voice trails away and I see indignation has given way to thoughts that he may have to defend himself against accusations of thievery.

He says, 'Wait – I remember his dagger was in his belt. His purse was close by and… I did not put my fingers inside, but… it did not hang as though heavy with coin.' He lifts his head trying to recall the scene. 'It may have been empty.'

'Goodman Sykes, I believe you. There is no stain on your good character. It is plain to me in this short exchange that you are an honest man with pride and diligence in your occupation.'

He bows his head in appreciation. My words were extravagant, but I do, in fact, think he speaks true. His manner is straightforward and I have the sense of a man who would not find it easy to be devious.

A NECESSARY KILLING

Seven

I am at a late breakfast when Mistress Gredley calls to give me a letter. I thank her and compliment her on the frumenty, which is highly spiced and laden with stewed fruits. She has a deserved reputation for keeping a good table and shows pleasure at my words. Before she leaves, I ask if she knows of Goodman Hagger. Her expression changes and she wrinkles her nose as if scenting a fart. He has a tannery by Rope Walk and the manner of her telling suggests she holds him in low regard.

The letter is from Helen. It has a date six days past and speaks of good health and contentment in the household excepting her father who is apt to break into bouts of ill-humour when reading notes about our slow progress in the West Country. She regrets the time has not been right to press our request to join his journey here. The decision hangs in the balance. She has visited my mother... together they viewed a royal procession on the river... it ends with a declaration of her love. I miss her company. I delight in receiving her notes, yet their reading leaves me empty and adrift; regretful of my decision to join this fleet on the great adventure.

I am promised at a meeting of ship's masters at noon when I will answer questions about the handling of the shadow-staff. I am told by Oliver that some grumble at its unfamiliarity and intend to revert to the cross-staff on the voyage. Still, Hawkins and Gilbert appear well-pleased with its functioning. My interest in the device I invented has paled, but it is the reason for my presence here, after all, and I must not be indifferent to its use. I will visit Hagger on my way to the quays and plan to call on Charles again before supper.

The noxious odours from the tannery reach me some way before I arrive there. It is a messy collection of huts and pits where a half-dozen men wearing heavy aprons are at work. The stench is too much and I cannot hold back a bout of coughing. I ask for Hagger by name and a man points to a brick-built house some fifty paces away. I take an embroidered lined cloth from inside my doublet and hold it to my face. It was given by Helen and its faint perfume helps to move my senses from the overpowering odour. I dismount outside the house frontage. Before I can knock, the door opens and a stout man confronts me. He has little hair on his head but compensates with an impressive beard. I introduce myself and wait for his answer as he surveys me from top to bottom.

'I am Hagger. What business do you have here, Doctor?' His delayed reply is followed by a satisfied belch. He places his hands in his belt and wriggles his belly as if allowing food to settle.

'I have been to see Justice Shanning with a view to examining the mystery surrounding the killing of Master Tremayne.'

'Ha, there is no mystery in that for me, nor the Justice from all I hear.'

I put the cloth to my face to stifle another cough. A smile twitches at the corner of his mouth.

I say, 'You gave testimony on sighting a disagreement between young Tremayne and Captain Wicken.'

'I did, but why should that concern you?'

'Do not bother with my concern. I have a note of permission from Justice Shanning to assess the testimonies.'

I hand him the paper. He inspects it for only a moment, then passes it back. 'Well, it is no bother to repeat the scene I witnessed that night. My account will not change.' He pauses to take a breath and fold his arms across his chest. 'They were at it for some time in the inn. I was at a table close by. Wicken was browbeating the youngster over some matter – just words at that time. I followed them as they left. Wicken had his arm tight around Tremayne's shoulder. Later, they stopped; Tremayne pleaded to be left alone and Wicken shook him fiercely. I would have intervened, but they quietened and continued on their way, close-coupled like a pair of sodomites.'

This is much the same sequence of events told by Charles, but there is a marked difference in interpretation. According to Hagger, Charles is an aggressor rather than a protector.

'Was young Tremayne drunk?'

He shrugs. 'He had been drinking and was loud from time-to-time, but it was a late night.'

'It was reported that he spewed with violence, yet continued drinking 'til he was near senseless.'

'Not that I saw.'

He is firm in his answer and I see I will get no change in his story. I leave him with only cursory thanks and relief to be gone from his stinking business.

*

Our meeting at noon is set as a working dinner in a chamber adjoining Hawkins' place of business on the quayside. There are near thirty of us at a large table with Hawkins at its head. I am seated to his right with Pennes on his left. Oliver is here, but I do not sight any of Charles' secondaries. We finish plates of eel and boiled fowl before Hawkins opens our discussion. There is more opposition to the use of my shadow-staff than I had envisaged. The cross-staff has problems of taking readings from the top and bottom of the transom in the full glare of the sun on a rolling deck. My invention uses a shadow cast from the sun at the rear and a sighting vane that allows this and the horizon to coincide with a single sight. Of course, it cannot be used when clouds obscure the sun and in this case, they should return to the older, but less exact, methods of readings from a cross-staff with the moon and North Star. I am overlong in my exposition and have to hold tight to feelings of exasperation when questioners show little understanding of simple mathematics. I remind myself that these men are adventurers and soldiers, not scholars.

Our meeting ends a short time before the sounding of three bells. I have it mind to ask Hawkins why no one was here to represent the interests of Charles' three ships. He is busy in conversation with others, so I save my question for a later time, and after I have visited Charles.

They are ready for me at the front of Charles' lodgings; my horse is taken and the door opens without comment from either of the two guards. I call his name and wait in the hall for an answer. A maid brushes down her skirts as she enters and bobs a curtsey. I am surprised to learn that Charles is in the courtyard and the maid leads me through the kitchens to the entry at the rear of the house. He is sat at a table in a small area in the corner of the yard bathed in sunlight, away from the shadow cast by the house. He rises from his seat and welcomes me with a strong embrace.

'Why are you here, Charles?'

'The day is fine. Inside, the four walls press too narrow and remind me of my status as a prisoner. Out here I can feel the warmth of the sun and taste the air.'

He has anticipated my visit with another chair and a tray with two cups and a flask of wine that cools in the shadow. He arranges my seat, fetches the wine and moves aside the paper and writing materials on the table. It is clear that his spirits have lifted since our last meeting. My news is mixed and I will offer what little encouragement I have before disclosing findings that offer no reassurance. But he is eager and speaks before me.

'I know what must be done, William. In this town, there is a plot to put me aside and keep vital intelligence hidden. Walsingham will be my salvation. When this information is brought to him and he hears of my plight he will have no option but to stay the hanging ordered by the court and set me free.'

This is a quick turnaround from Charles and on my first assessment, it is too fanciful. The intelligence will need to be of high significance for Walsingham to act as he expects, and once he has the information, why would he need Charles? Walsingham is not known for nostalgic attachment to his agents or sympathy for those facing a rope.

I say, 'Are you convinced then, that you will be found guilty at the quarter session?'

'Yes, I am grateful for your efforts, William, but I cannot rely on them. There are men of influence here with an interest in ensuring the hearing goes against me.'

He refers, without naming, to Hawkins and Gilbert, but I am not yet settled on their part. I do not warm to either man, but it stretches credibility too far to suppose they conspire in this tawdry and complex affair. Or, does he have others in mind – Shanning, for example? I will hear what he has to say about Walsingham in due course, but must try to bring his mind back to a straightforward understanding of his position here and how to argue for his innocence.

'Nevertheless, Charles, it would be wise to prepare yourself for the trial and how to refute harmful testimony.'

'Yes, forgive my impatience. What have you found, William?'

'There may be significance in Tremayne's purse. It was empty when the body was washed for its funeral repose and I am certain the watchman did not have his pick when he discovered the killing.'

'So, you suspect thieves?'

'Indeed, this will spread doubt among the twelve who will sit at the quarter session. You are a man of substance and reputation. It would be absurd to imagine you capable of killing for a few pennies.'

I see this prompting takes hold and he is quiet while contemplating its worth. He has a striking appearance with clean-shaven face and olive skin presenting an unusual match against flowing, yellow hair. A large, handsome man who would be difficult to mistake for another, except in the darkest streets.

I say, 'As to the clump of hair reported; it was discarded at the rinsing of the body and cannot be produced at the trial. You should argue strongly that there are many men in Plymouth town with hair of lighter colour.'

'This is most heartening, William.' He twirls a lock of his hair. 'As you can see there are no missing strands or bare, white scalp showing here.' He makes light of it, but he knows it will not be easy to shake this testimony away from his striking appearance. To cut his hair or hide under a hat would only serve to deepen suspicion. 'Do you make progress with the other testimonies?'

'I have examined the body of Tremayne and it appears Doctor Millard was right in ascribing death to strangulation of the neck. I had hoped there may be evidence that he simply choked on his own vomit, but that possibility must now be discarded.'

'Hmm, and the others?'

'There will be no comfort from the testimony of the serving

maid or Goodman Hagger. They are firm in their witnessing of you as a forceful companion to Tremayne; not one who tended his drunken incapacity.'

He breathes deeply and purses his lips. 'It is simply untrue, but I can expect no softening from Hagger. He disliked my correction some weeks past.'

'You quarrelled with him?'

'There was no argument with that fuckwit. He insulted my person with veiled comments and I had cause to chastise him.'

'Was there some violence in your correction?'

'A touch with the back of my gloved hand - no more.'

'Then I will not approach him again. I plan to visit with Goodwife Langley on the morrow and must hope that she will offer some relief. I trust you have had no spat with her?'

'Ha - no you can rely on that. I do not know her. You are a good friend, William, and I am humbled at the endeavours you undertake on my behalf.'

The shadows are chasing us and we move table and seats to a shrinking area of light. He pours the wine and we sit quietly for a time, contemplating all that has been said. I wonder what these papers on the table are. Letters to Walsingham, perhaps? I wait for enlightenment.

He clears his throat and says, 'I know I can trust you, William, but must request that you will disclose what I will tell to no other, at least until the trial is done.' I murmur my assent. 'You have heard of a man named Stukley?'

'Yes, he is notorious as a rabid opponent of Her Majesty's rule.'

'Indeed, he has been conspiring for some years with Rome and Spain to obtain the funds for an invasion.'

'There have been rumours, but is he…'

'There was a gathering at Lisbon the last year. Word had reached Walsingham's agents and a close watch was kept. Stukley led a small fleet to Maroc where there was fighting and a battle at Alcácer Quibir, the site of a grand castle. He was reported to be killed there by a cannonball, which cut off his legs.'

'So why do you concern yourself with Stukley?'

'It was a feint – do you see?' There is a spark in his eyes as he gestures with his hands. 'The expedition to Maroc was a diversion to lull the defenders of these shores into false contentment.' My murmuring is noncommittal. I understand why such trickery may be employed, but I do not see where this leads. 'Stukley lives and continues to conspire with Nicholas Sanders, a confidante of the Pope and the King of Spain. Through connivance with a papal nuncio, large funds have been obtained for ships and men. They are marshalled in the ports of Corunna, Gijon and the Bay of Santander – scattered to hide their magnitude.'

'And what is the intention of this fleet?'

He sits back in his seat and drains his cup. He seems to delight in telling this complexity, as though he has forgotten his plight here. I am wary, for although I can understand Walsingham's keen interest in the intelligence, I fear I may be caught up somewhere in the mix.

'They scheme to invade the ports here in the West Country. When this is done there will be signals made for barges and other ships to take Spanish soldiers and mercenaries from Antwerp to the eastern coast. It is a grave threat.'

I am stunned at the extravagant extent of this design and have no immediate response. I know little of politicking between nations but cannot imagine a more severe danger to our realm. It will be of vital interest to Walsingham, but surely, he will have some inkling of this from his network of intelligencers.

'How have you learned of this scheme, Charles?'

'I have allies and confidantes in Corunna and the Biscay ports. There has been suspicion for some months and I had confirmation from the master of the carrack, named *Falkin*, who discharged his cargo of sweet wine in Dartmouth a few days past.'

'So, that was the reason for your journey to Dartmouth that day.'

'Indeed, the intelligence is irrefutable. Stukley was seen in Corunna and other murmurings verified the true intention of the preparations.'

'Do you consider that Walsingham may already have this

news? It will be difficult to hide such a grand scheme from prying eyes.'

'The whole understanding will not be with Walsingham. There is more to this plot. There is another name. He is one of the Geraldine lords in Ireland, called James Fitzmaurice Fitzgerald.'

'What part does Ireland play in this? I had thought all the Irish earls had pledged their obedience to our queen in exchange for considerations of land.'

'Stukley and Sanders have been involved in the planning for many months. They have the cunning and the ear of the Pope. James Fitzmaurice is estranged from his superior, the Earl of Desmond, and it is his dearest wish to wrest the earldom and take Munster for himself. Fitzmaurice is a simple man with a gabbling tongue who does not have the wit to understand how the other two lead him by the nose. Any suspicions about the gatherings and preparations will reach an understanding that the assembled forces are for a small landing in Munster. That is the way it is played to those who snoop and listen. Walsingham will have little concern for a quarrel between two minor lords over a province in Ireland and will not be readied for the true menace that faces England.'

Our cups are empty, the shadow has had its way with the courtyard and so we retreat to the house where he promises more wine and light refreshment. I am troubled. It is clear that Walsingham must learn of this conspiracy – and quickly. But why did Charles not declare this earlier? His naming and confinement were directly after his return from Dartmouth. Others must have learned the intelligence was received by Charles and acted promptly to confound him. It is plain there is a malign influence with a broad reach here.

Charles has brought his papers with him. When we are settled I ask if they contain the message to Walsingham.

'Indeed, I have prepared two identical letters, together with a note for Stack. I would ask that you pass these to Stack, but do not do this openly. You should be circumspect and conceal your true intentions.'

'You will send two messengers?'

'Yes, Stack will choose reliable men who will take diverse routes from this town.'

'They should make haste. The journey to London is five days or more and the quarter session will be in twelve.'

'I understand there is little margin in the timetable but will rely on Walsingham to act quickly.' He hesitates a moment. 'And that the court will not order an immediate execution of their decision.'

I have accepted the sense in his plan, but misgivings remain.

I say, 'Would it not be wise to inform Hawkins and Gilbert of the threat? They would not dare to stand in the way of such crucial correspondence and they must be readied for the threat.'

His eyes widen and he gazes at me directly. 'Your mind is too good, William. You see the balance of right and wrong but are too willing to accept the honourable path will carry the day. I may be wrong about Hawkins and Gilbert and they are blameless in my condition, but I must guard against the alternative.' He senses my uncertainty and continues in lower voice. 'I do not say that they conspire with Spain and Rome – that would be too much – only that their interests in this great adventure overwhelm all other considerations. They would be ready to believe the threat is overstated and there is a more mundane end to the plotting. A small incursion to Ireland would not halt their sailing, but an invasion of these ports would signal an end to it; an end that would damage their finances and reputations most severely.'

He has stated his case clearly and with conviction. Perhaps he sees through to the heart of me; that I am too trusting and unwilling to acknowledge the dark nature in men. I am fortunate to have moved in scholarly circles where such matters had trivial consequences – at least until recent times. It would be churlish to continue an argument against his strategy. I know he is innocent of the killing and his plan offers the likeliest solution to saving his life and restoring his position.

We talk more of his proposals and I am thankful when he arranges a light supper, which offers an interlude to this dizzying intrigue and we talk of lighter matters. Mention is made of Sir George and Helen and I am filled with guilt that my activities this day have not left space for thoughts of my dearest love. I retire to my lodgings and go directly to my bed, hoping to banish this disagreeable tangle of deception and dream only of her. It is too much to expect. I am restless and occupied with imaginings of Walsingham, an invasion of our shores and the body of young Tremayne. The next dawn draws near.

Eight

I am woken by a door closing and footsteps outside my chamber. There are sounds of industry in the house and in the streets outside. My eyes are grainy, my limbs sticky and aching from a fitful sleep. I have woken late and must hurry to be about my business for this day. I open the door and ask a maid in the corridor to bring me a bowl of water and linen cloths, so that I may rinse away the dullness in my body.

My breakfast is a mash of eggs, honey and dried fruit, but I cannot do it justice. I pick away and wait for Mistress Gredley to appear with her expected playful scolding of the late hour of my rising. Eight bells have chimed before she enters with 'tuts' and shaking head for my poor appetite. I greet her warmly and excuse my meagre eating through a griping belly from sour wine the last night. I enquire about Goodwife Langley and she embarks on a tale about childhood friendship and their continued closeness. The goodwife is married to a man named Able who farmed sheep and traded in wool until his brain became addled with age. They have sold their small landholding and she occupies her days tending her dribbling husband and relaxed duties around the house for another childhood friend named Hurst. For the sake of politeness, I let the story run its course until I learn that the Hurst household is on Union Street, no more than eighty paces from Charles's lodging.

I am about to leave the house when a boy arrives with a note for me. It is from Hawkins and he requests my presence at his place of business at noon. I calculate that I may have sufficient time for my first task this day. I bid the boy wait until I write a note and hand him a penny for prompt delivery. The note is for Stack who I say he will find on the quays by his ship, *Hawkwind* or in his lodgings at the nearby inn, *The Maid's Head*. I have arranged to meet with him between ten and eleven bells on Rope Walk at a deserted and ramshackle hut in sight of Hagger's tannery. It is a quiet spot away from town, but close enough to meet my later engagement with Hawkins.

The day is warm with little movement to stir the air. I have arrived at the hut in good time, so tether my horse to the branch of a tree and rest my back against the trunk to seek refuge in its shade. Three cartmen and a drover pass by at a leisurely pace with none paying great attention to my idling. There is a gentle lulling in the birdsong and hum of insects. My eyes are heavy...

'Doctor Constable.'

My neck is crooked and stiff and I wince as my head jerks back. I turn and see a man's face close to mine. Who? It is... Stack. I have dozed. I am clumsy with first movements, then pull myself up and brush twigs and dirt from my arse. How long have I been here?

'Good morning to you Master Stack. Forgive my daydreaming, I have...'

'No matter, Doctor. I have your note. It speaks of an urgency.'

'Yes... do you have the hour?'

'It is near eleven.'

'Good, there is time enough.' I remove the papers from my doublet. 'I have important letters written by Captain Wicken, but first you must read this.'

I hand Stack his note of instruction from Charles. He breaks the seal, peers at it closely and takes some moments to complete his understanding of the plan. He looks up, meets my eyes directly and then returns to reading again. Eventually, he folds the paper and stuffs it deep inside his jerkin.

I say, 'These letters are for Sir Francis Walsingham who will likely be at the Palace of Whitehall or his house in Seething Lane. You will pick two trustworthy men with good horses so that they deliver in quick time. It must be done now and in secrecy with the two men taking different routes from the town.'

It is clear that he has a good appreciation of the task entrusted to him. Nevertheless, I repeat the importance of speed and circumspection. He looks at me queerly as though this extra emphasis is not required. A fierce man, with sour face and few words, he is a strange choice for a close secondary, but Charles has faith in him and he assisted bravely in my rescue. He receives the letters without further acknowledgement and departs briskly, urging his horse into a canter. I mutter a quick prayer for the safe deliverance of at least one of the letters, then ride in his wake.

*

Hawkins is waiting outside when I arrive on the quay and he beckons me to follow him into his workplace. Gilbert is there, seated on the edge of a table with folded arms. Hawkins closes the door and bids me take a seat. There are no words as we take our places and my senses are pricked by a heaviness in the air, which suggests this will not be a happy meeting. Am I to be admonished on some matter? Do they know of my enquiries about Charles and the visit to Shanning?

Hawkins says, 'You had a supper with Sir Humphrey in Dartmouth, where there was talk of a letter to Sir George.'

'Yes, it was a most pleasant evening and the Lady Anne arranged a fine table. I trust the Lady and your children are well, Sir Humphrey?'

He mutters thanks for my concern and asks, 'Was the letter written and sent?'

'Yes, I wrote in the way of encouragement for our readiness as you suggested. I handed it to Master Nance who has been diligent in arranging our correspondence through his couriers. That was two days past.'

'Indeed, Nance has enjoyed good business from our regular communications here.' He pauses and glances at Hawkins. 'Was mention made in your letter of Wicken's position?'

'No, I considered that would cause alarm.'

'Good,' joins Hawkins, 'I knew we could trust your good sense, Doctor. And, of course, you would not wish to sully the reputation of a friend.'

'No, but the news will certainly find a way out in time. Do you know how Master Sindell will take the news?'

'Sindell will not present a problem. I understand he knows Wicken's reputation, rather than the man himself and will not be firm in his attachment. I am sure we will have his confidence and authority to handle the arrangements for his ships and cargoes. Pennes and other competents will take on their management and sailing. It is the disposition of our other backers and partners in this great venture that gives us cause for deep concern.'

He hesitates, peers at Gilbert, who nods a form of approval before continuing. 'We have come to know that scurrilous and untrue rumours circulate in this town and Dartmouth about a threat to the security and good management of our departure to the New Lands.'

Does he refer to the danger of invasion described by Charles, or some other more trivial affair?

I say, 'Might I know the nature of this danger to our venture?'

'It will not bear repeating. We trust your discretion, Doctor Constable, but must guard against an inadvertent leaking.'

So, why have they told me this? There are moments of silence in which I could pose further questions but wait to hear more.

It is Hawkins who follows. 'We have set up strong controls and limitations on the correspondence that passes from these two towns. These have been told to all ships captains, masters, clerics, surgeons and other men of letters in our fleet. All notes must go unsealed to the hands of Master Nance. These will be read by the Reverend Penrose and Pastor Nancarrow before they are sealed and sent to ensure they are free from unsettling untruths and other statements that may threaten our security.'

I had not expected this. It is a swingeing and unwelcome curtailment of our freedom. How will my complicity in bypassing this measure with Charles' notes be viewed? It was less than an hour before this news and they will be severe in their disapproval if my part is discovered. Would they dare to tamper with a message to Mister Secretary Walsingham? I cannot be sure. It seems Charles' caution in keeping his plan from these two men is justified. Still, I must hold fast and keep this secret for his sake.

I say, 'Am I to be included in this restriction? You will know that I have regular correspondence with Helen Morton, Sir George's daughter. I would not have the delicate words that pass between us open to prying eyes and those who may scoff and prattle at our expense.'

Gilbert bows his head in understanding. 'We understand your

feelings and have made special arrangements. If you would take your unsealed letters to the Nance place of business, they will be sealed without inspection and risk of embarrassment. We have devised a special seal in the name of our great adventure that all correspondence must bear.'

'Thank you for that consideration.' A possibility occurs and I speak before thinking. 'What of the townspeople? Your carefulness is to be applauded, but there may be those with devious intentions in our number who pass messages to folk in the towns to evade your measures.'

'That has also been managed. We have posted guards on all roads out of the towns to challenge those who may be acting as couriers and examine their pockets and bags.'

'Is that lawful? It may antagonise the literate men in the towns.'

'These processes will only be in place for a short time. We will be ready to sail near the end of this month. Besides, we have the agreement from men of substance in the towns and have made arrangement similar to yours for their correspondence.'

Fuck! What damned ill luck. I cannot imagine a more destructive turn of events for Charles' plan. His notes will surely be discovered and I will be fingered as the likely conduit for their despatch. I can bear their displeasure, but what of the intelligence to Walsingham about the scheme to invade these ports? And Charles? Without Walsingham's intervention, it is probable that he will be tried unjustly and hanged.

*

My mind spins and I cannot settle. I had it in mind to call on Goodwife Langley but will postpone this now. A first thought on leaving Hawkins and Gilbert was to seek out Stack and enquire on his progress with the notes. But I may have been followed and this meeting reported. Instead, I went to Oliver's lodgings, but was informed he was with his ship. Then to the quayside only to discover his ship was alongside another in mid-harbour practising some manoeuvre for boarding. I cannot discuss the full detail of Charles' plan with Oliver, but he may know more on the substance of the rumours and have an opinion on the limitations set on our communications.

I retire to my chambers in the Gredley household and start to read a volume of the French Translation of *Arte de Navegar* by Pedro de Medina. I have borrowed this from Hawkins who confessed he found it difficult reading. I can see his point. It is a moderate translation and appears to be written by one who may have navigated ships but did not fully understand the mathematics of the stars. Whether this is the fault of the author or translator I cannot be certain. This diversion will not work. I call Mistress Gredley and beg for an early supper.

The air is damp and warm with thunderclouds gathering, but I must be free from the confines of my chambers. I wander the street towards Charles's house and stop at an inn to quench my thirst with ale. I have watched carefully and cannot see that I am followed. I fall into conversation with two local merchants about their trading in cloth and the dangers of French corsairs in the Narrow Sea. They have heard my name spoken and enquire about my invention of a navigation instrument. Pride will not let me deny an exposition; I drink too much ale and I depart the inn when the sky is dark and the streets are puddled with the aftermath of heavy rainfall.

I will not call on Charles this night; my humour is too dark and I have no encouragement for him. I turn back the way I came and call at Oliver's lodgings to leave a note inviting him to dinner in my chambers the next day.

Nine

Oliver arrives shortly before noon and we retire to the chamber that serves for both my receiving and dining. He enquires on the progress of my investigations on the testimonies against Charles. I admit that the serving maid and Hagger will not speak in favour of Charles and seek his opinion on the empty purse and the possibility of thievery. He is mildly heartened by the discovery, then proceeds to imagine other circumstances that could have drained Tremayne's purse. We are agreed that it may sow a sprinkling of doubt but will not clinch the hearing in his favour.

Oliver says, 'You have heard of the restraints imposed upon our correspondence?'

'Yes, do you consider them reasonable?'

'I can understand why they are jittery now we are close to our date of departure.'

'It is extreme and I have never heard of such measures imposed by those without the force of law behind them.'

Mistress Gredley and a maid bring in plates for our dinner and we pause in our discussion. It looks as though we have a generous helping of oysters to work through before a pie, which we are informed contains mutton soaked in claret with a rosemary crust. I see Oliver is eager to eat and my appetite is recovered. We are half-way into our oysters before Oliver responds to my last remark.

'It is a temporary measure and will not be the cause of too much displeasure. I would assess there is general contentment, among those who would write in our fleet, that it is prudent to adopt such a procedure.'

'Did you know that guards are posted on the roads to intercept messages that may have avoided examination at Nance's place?'

'No, I was not aware of that aspect, but…' He shrugs as though it is only a minor inconvenience.

'Hawkins and Gilbert told of hurtful and untrue rumours in

the towns. They must have a vital bearing on our sailing for such extreme measures to be put in place.'

'Indeed.'

'Do you know their character?'

'Not for certain - I suppose they gossip about our state of readiness and continuing quarrels among the merchants on the value of their cargoes.'

So, I am no further forward in understanding the reason behind this ploy. I will arrange a further meeting with Stack to determine if the notes were safely despatched or taken. First, I will call on Goodwife Langley. It may be wasted effort, but I should try to learn more of the testimonies in order to prepare a defence for Charles. If word does not reach Walsingham, it will be his only hope of escaping the rope.

When our dinner is done I call Mistress Gredley and request that she finds a reliable boy to send a message within the town. In short time the boy runner from yesterday appears eager for his penny. I may wish to use him again and learn that he is named Huckle. I hand him a note for Stack with coin and a promise that I will use him again if he continues to provide good service.

*

A young maid answers the door at the Hurst house and I enquire if I may speak with Goodwife Langley. I enter a hallway, which is small, but well-tended and with a pleasant scent of lavender from sprigs arranged in two bowls on a table. A short, round woman with ruddy complexion enters. Assuming this is Goodwife Langley, I doff my cap and offer my name.

'Why, Doctor Constable, you are well known to me in telling by Erith Gredley. You are as big and handsome as she describes.' She hesitates. 'This is not my house. I am housekeeper here for Goodwife Hurst. Is it me you wish to see?'

'Yes, if it please you. Can you spare me a few moments to assist with my enquiries?'

'Of course. My duties here are not onerous and I will not be scolded for welcoming a dashing young scholar into this house. We will use the parlour. Please follow me.'

She has a cheery aspect and there is no sign of mistrust at my request. The parlour has a carpeted table and two stools. She begs me take one and offers refreshment, which I decline because of a full belly from dinner. When we are both seated she smiles and inclines her head to indicate she is ready for my words.

'I will declare first that I am a friend of Captain Wickham, who is named for the killing of Walter Tremayne.' I pause, but her expression does not change. 'You gave testimony that you saw a commotion between those two persons close to this house.'

She folds her hands across her skirts and wriggles on her stool for greater comfort. 'That is not exact. I was arranging the house for the night and was in the hall when I heard raised voices outside. This is a quiet street away from the inns in the coarser sections of the town. I opened the door and spied two men outside the neighbouring house. Loud words were spoken; some most vulgar and profane.' She stretches her mouth with distaste at the recollection.

'Was any name spoken in this uncouth exchange?'

'No, not that I recall. I recognised young Tremayne. The other man was bigger – perhaps your height, but also wider.'

'Did you identify the other, from his dress or hair colour perhaps?'

'No, it was dark and I was faced with only his back.' She shakes her head. 'The argument was no match. The bigger man had Tremayne gripped tight and shook him fiercely.'

'How long was the confrontation?'

'A count of twenty, no more. I shouted, "Stop" or some such word then began to retreat inside in case they turned their rage on me.'

'Did they stop?'

'Yes, when they heard my words, they stopped and the big man dragged Tremayne away. That was the end of my watching. I closed and bolted the door, then retired to my bed.' She spreads her hands. 'As you can see, Doctor, I was born to cosset and coddle babes, not to calm the violent tantrums of drunken men.'

I smile acknowledgement at her little jest. She has answered my questions willingly and it is plain that Shanning has added his own refinement to her testimony. She did not identify Charles. This is promising and must be exposed at the quarter session where she confirms her attendance. I thank her for her time and am about to leave, but she stays on her stool and would say more.

'Might I detain you here for a short while, Doctor?' I murmur my assent and hope that she will not compromise her statement thus far. 'My husband, Able, is an older man. His mind is addled, he does not have full control over his bodily functions and he has strange habits which require my regular attention.'

This is an unexpected turn. I offer my sympathy and wait for what is to follow.

'I know we must live with his incapacities and strangeness until his days are done on this earth, but... he has recent pains and discomfort which make him most distressed.'

'What is the nature of the pain?'

'He has severe headaches and blurred vision. These bouts of agony make him loud with ranting and raving, which cause upset and agitation throughout the household.'

'You would have me examine your husband?'

'It would be a kindness. Doctor Millard has seen Able but can offer no remedy. Erith tells me that you practice as a physician in London and may bring a wider understanding.'

I agree out of consideration for this likeable woman who is straightforward, kindly and showed no reason to hide or embellish what she saw that night. I hold no great hope that I can help but must appear willing. I am led to the kitchens where a shrivelled old man is sat in the corner rocking gently to and fro. She introduces me to her husband who gazes briefly at both of us without interest. He is humming a tune; vaguely familiar; perhaps a bedtime lullaby. The goodwife stands back so that I can inspect her husband.

I say, 'Why does he sit here?'

'We do not know, but he stays here the most part of every day until I take him to his bed. He has a fondness for cheese and will always have a piece to hand.'

I see there is a wooden plate on a small table by his side with a broken slab of crumbly white cheese. He reaches over, picks a piece and places it in his mouth. I move closer and watch as he chews. He works the cheese carefully on one side. The other cheek is swollen. I open his mouth. I blink and shake my head as I am met with a noxious smell. I use my fingers to open his mouth further. Some teeth are missing and there is a tender area around two teeth on the top of his left side that is blackened. I gently push and pull at these teeth. He winces but is largely passive and compliant.

I say, 'Two teeth must be removed and that will ease some of the pain.'

'But he will not leave this place to visit a surgeon. We have tried before and he struggles so that we relent and leave him.'

I say that I will try and extract them here. They are loose so it will not require too much force. The goodwife scrabbles around the kitchen looking for a suitable instrument. She can find naught, but I say that two strong metal spoons will do and ask if she can bring some brandywine. Able Langley is unperturbed by the activity and sits quietly with his swaying and nibbling.

He drinks the brandywine offered, smacks his lips and holds out his cup for more. He has three more cups before his expression shows signs of its effects. His forward rocking has stopped and he rolls his head trying to fix his eyes on his wife.

'Why do you ply him with so much strong drink, Doctor,' she says with worried voice.

'It is to ease the pain. It is thought that it may also counteract some of the noxious fluids that will flow in the blood when the teeth are pulled.'

I must do this quickly before he struggles. I request that she holds his head while I open his mouth and clamp the spoons either side of his teeth. I take a firm grip and pull hard. One tooth is out. Again. It has slipped. He raises his hand and makes a gargling noise. Once more and… the other tooth is out.

The goodwife releases hold of his head, puts her hand to her face and closes her eyes as though horrified at what has been done. I stand back, then take her arm and bring her around to face her husband. He stares at us with wide, amazed eyes and a grin of delight on his face. I hand him another cup of brandywine, which he drains in quick time.

I say, 'He must stop there; no more strong drink. He would benefit from an infusion of nettles and cloves if that can be made here. I regret I have not brought any potions with me to this town.'

'Thank you, Doctor. I know it is not the practice of physicians to do a surgeon's work and I bless you for the relief you have brought him.' She is beaming with joy at the transformation in her husband.

'He may have a sore head with the brandywine, but that will pass and I am confident that his longer-term pain will be eased.' I hand her the spoons, which she wraps in linen cloth. 'The teeth may not be the complete solution. I have come across a case of head pains and disturbed vision before and there was a similarity in that too much cheese was eaten. You should try to keep the cheese from him for some weeks, or at least ration his amount. If it calms him to peck and nip at food, then try to substitute apples or pears.'

She is overcome with gratitude for my brief attentions. She mentions coin and when I refuse, offers to supply pies, sweetmeats and other delicacies whenever I should fancy. She is quietened when I remind that her friend, Mistress Gredley would not welcome competition for the fare she provides at my lodgings. I leave with spirits uplifted at the reassuring news for Charles from the genuine testimony of this warm and caring woman.

Ten

I am waiting by the hut on Rope Walk for Stack. I have chosen the same meeting time, hoping for a quiet part of the day when most are at, or near, their dinner. The weather is not so kind this day with a strong breeze and a grey sky. Still, I will not have long to wait as I note a horseman, who has the look of Stack, following only a quarter mile behind.

He dismounts and joins me by a wall sheltered from the wind.

'Good day to you, Stack, I trust you are in good health?'

He answers my pleasantry with a grunt.

'Was all well with the sending of the notes?'

Another grunt with a nod of the head, which I take to be an affirmative.

'I did not know at our last meeting that certain restrictions had been placed on correspondence from the two towns.'

'I knew.'

Then, why he did not bother to inform me at that time? 'So, how was it handled?'

'Do not concern yourself, Doctor. It was done. That is all.'

'Nevertheless, I should like to know. I was fearful that you were not aware of the measures and that your couriers would be detained.'

He takes a breath and heaves his shoulders as though resenting the effort he must make.

'We took a ship to the mouth of the estuary. Two row boats were sent with the couriers to the East and West shores, where we had horses waiting.'

'So, they intended to take wide circles around the town and join the roads to London after the blockades?' A simple solution, which I confess had not occurred to me.

'Indeed.'

'It will add to their journey time.'

'Yes, perhaps an extra day.'

'Do you have news if they evaded the guards on the roads?'

He shrugs. 'There has been no return and we know where

guards are posted. At least one will reach their destination.'

'Good, I will pass this information to your master, who will be heartened at the success of your ingenuity. Do you have any other message for him?'

He shakes his head. It is clear that he does not want more conversation, so I thank him and he departs. It was a perplexing meeting. Why was he reluctant to report detail to me? Why not make more of his resourcefulness and show happiness at its realisation? Well, I must not complain; he has served Charles well and I do not have to suffer his company for lengthy intervals.

*

Charles opens the door himself. I raise my eyes in question and he explains that a maid has left his household. I ask the reason and he confesses that a fierce reprimand for spilling wine was the cause.

'Forgive me, William, I have been in a foul humour these past days. It is as well that I am near alone in this house; I would be poor company for you, Oliver or other educated men.'

'Who do you have to tend for your needs here?'

'There is only my housekeeper and the stable man who skulks around the courtyard trying to escape my attentions.'

'Others have left?'

'Two left when I was named. They could not bear to share a roof with a monster.'

I see his mood contains self-pity as well as anger.

'Do you need me to find servants to replace them here?'

'No, my requirements are slight, contained as I am.'

'Well, I have some news that may cheer you.'

He hesitates as though undecided about some matter. I suggest that we move to a more comfortable chamber and lead the way to his parlour. Now, I see why he was reluctant to move here. The chamber is a battleground: table, stools and a chair are broken; bottles are smashed; the walls are stained with red liquid; the remains of a dinner are scattered on the floor. I reserve comment and guide him back through the hall and to his receiving room. He takes a seat and I go to find his housekeeper for wine. She is in the kitchens, cowering in a corner and folding linens. She looks relieved to see that it is me. I ask her for a jug of wine and two cups.

Charles has the look of a child caught at some mischief. I pour wine and he mutters an apology for his poor welcome and show of violent temper.

'Do not worry yourself, Charles, I can understand your frustration and impatience to resolve this unfortunate situation.'

He sups the wine quickly and pours more. His eyes are red, underlined with dark shadows and he has not shaved since we last met. I must encourage him to take better care of his health and tidy his appearance – but later.

I say, 'Your notes have been sent and, God willing, they will reach Walsingham in time for his intervention on your behalf.' I decide not to mention the restrictions on correspondence in case that angers him further and deepens his suspicions of Hawkins and Gilbert.

He smiles and offers his thanks. 'Do you have any other word from Stack for me?'

'No, he has a good appreciation of the situation and will continue to act in your interest.'

'He is a good man, William, and you should not be disturbed by his abrupt manner.'

Does he read my thoughts? 'I have other news that may offer some cheer. I have visited Goodwife Langley and it would seem that Shanning embellished her testimony. She did not identify the man she saw with Tremayne, only that he was a large man who appeared to be bullying him. This should be exposed at the hearing.'

He raises his eyebrows. 'That is helpful, but I must not rely on the logic of testimony to secure my freedom. As I said, there are forces at work here which may overcome rational consideration.'

I understand his feelings, but I will continue my endeavours to discover any frailties in the case against him. Our discussion moves to the state of readiness of the fleet and he enquires whether there is news of the attendance of notables from

London for the grand departure. I am surprised at the question, but remember that he serves Walsingham, so may be acquainted with others at court.

'I have no further knowledge on that score. Gilbert requested that I refer to this in my letter to Sir George, but any answer will not be due for some days.'

I see his mind wanders and our conversation becomes stiff and empty of meaning. I take my leave with counsel that he should care for his health and that the quarter session will look more favourably on an orderly, well-presented man of substance. He is gruff in his response and I fear that my gentle advice will have little effect.

Eleven

The days pass quickly. I have little to do, but also too much. It is only four days until the quarter session and there is no message from Walsingham. I have tried to question the serving maid at the *Seven Bells* again, but she refused to talk to me and kept her head bowed as she scurried to serve in the gentlemen's area. Hagger was more forthright in his denial, taking a broad stick in his hand and gathering his men around him to threaten violence unless I left his property. This morning, I was reduced to standing in the middle of town and counting the hair colour and height of men as they passed by. I was met by many stares and looks of mistrust as I stood scratching marks on a paper. I enlisted the help of the Huckle lad in my survey. He was timid at first and begged me not to send him with another note to Stack, who he admitted made him quiver with fright with his fierce manner. He was bemused at my instructions to stay by my side holding paper and ink while I scribbled away in the street but delighted at his reward of two pennies for a simple task. I hold no great hopes that my findings will bear much weight in the court's decision. Nevertheless, it yielded interesting results.

I have had no reply from my letter to Sir George, but there have been two letters from Helen. The second was written after receiving mine sent immediately after the attack. She must have sensed my unease as the first part was full of declarations of love and her wish that we should be joined once more before our sailing. The latter part held news that was both hopeful and concerning. She was more confident that her father was disposed to allow her to accompany him for the celebration of our departure, but she had disquieting words about her father's health. It seems he had been suffering from bouts of dizziness and shortness of breath. She averred that he was somewhat recovered after rest and herbal potions mixed to aid relaxation. Her careful words could not hide the worries that coloured the general impression received from her message. Letters have been sent to Sir George, other merchants and backers of the venture that our departure date is set and that they should journey here to witness our sailing. I know Sir George is eager to add splendour and pageant to this occasion. As the principal architect and financer of the great adventure, he plans a grand oration to the crews of the assembled ships. It will be a severe disappointment if poor health means he cannot fulfil his dream of proclaiming the start of a historic and profitable enterprise in person.

There has been a change in Charles. I have had no new intelligence to bring cheer, but contrary to expectations, his mood has lightened. He is more like the old Charles, with bearing and appearance improved and it seems that I am the one whose humour needs lifting with his small jests and confident talk about the success of our great adventure.

He greets me at the door with a hearty welcome. The day is warm and bright and he has arranged a dinner for us in his courtyard. It seems he has made peace with his stableman, who assists in the transference of table, seats and even small ornaments into the yard, then helping the housekeeper in presenting our fare. All is set and we take our places.

'Eat well, William. You have the look of someone who needs a good belly-full.'

'Yes, Mistress Gredley shows disappointment that I do not do justice to her servings. You, on the other hand, Charles, have the appearance of one who is well-fed and carefree.'

'I am resigned to whatever may come. If the court cannot see my innocence, then surely Walsingham will investigate and uncover the truth in my warnings.'

'Do you receive comfort from prayers, Charles? It seems a divine spirit has provided you with assurance.'

'I pray, like most men – regularly, but not to excess.'

'I have not questioned you on your faith. Are you content with the new religion, or do you hold fast to the old?'

He shrugs. 'I care little for labels and am happy to commune with God in the way that causes the least offence.'

My questions were out before I had time to consider if they were wise. It is a delicate matter to enquire into the way of worship these days and I know in the West Country many hold to the customs of Rome. His answer is much the same as I would give in private conversation.

I say, 'Does it worry you that we have not heard from Walsingham? A quick return on your message would have been received here by now.'

'Walsingham is not a man to act in haste. I trust we will see his intentions before too long.'

'There are four days only 'til your hearing.' He takes more wine and does not answer. 'You are uncommonly self-possessed for one in your position. I confess that I would fret and stew to distraction if it were me.'

'I follow your advice, William. Inside I am fevered, but I must show my innocence to the world with a calm and righteous exterior.'

Of course, he has it right, but he convinces in a way that is beyond my understanding. I relay the outcome of my survey of the height and hair men in the town. He has a bemused expression and asks that I repeat the assessment.

'Why, William, it is your training as a scholar and expertise in mathematics that led you to undertake such a task.' He raises his cup to me and laughs. 'The jurors and others in the court will not understand your tinkering with numbers. They will think you conjure up some magic to confound their reasoning. Your findings must be presented in a way that common men will understand.'

His words make me pause to consider. I had thought that this was a simple matter of counting categories and expressing ratios as in games of chance. Could the results be expressed in a way that makes them easier to comprehend? 'Perhaps the exposition could be in everyday terms instead of abstracting numbers into fractions and ratios.'

'Yes… yes, I can see…'

He hesitates, puts his cup down, then rests his elbows on the tables and steeples his fingers as if contemplating prayer. 'Would you be willing to speak for me at the quarter session, William? You have questioned witnesses, gathered facts and have come to know more than I about the events of that night.

You would convince in a way that I could not. More, you are a renowned scholar with experience of expounding your theories and arguments to learned men. Can you not adapt your expertise for a humbler audience and put your opinions and contentions in plain words?'

'But that would not be... usual in a hearing.'

'Why would it not be allowed? I might claim a soreness in my throat or some other incapacity, but surely that will not be necessary. Come, William, it would be the act of a true friend and the natural culmination of all your efforts on my behalf.'

I cannot refuse his plea. I have sufficient vanity and reasoning to assume that my presentation in the court would be more persuasive than his. I am no expert on the operation of our laws. Nevertheless, I must prepare his case with diligence and be ready for all forms of accusations and counter claims.

*

Now, there is one day until the quarter session opens and still, there is no sign from Walsingham or return of the men sent with Charles' notes. I have had another meeting with Stack but cannot read the man. He had the air of one unconcerned about the men he charged to act as couriers. If they had reached their destination safely, then there would be ample time to complete their return journey. Both Stack and Charles appear to hold confidence in Walsingham's knowledge and imminent action against the invasion plan that I do not share. My worries have increased with the realisation of the nature of the task I have taken on as an advocate for Charles. I do not have any substantial experience of common law or the procedures of quarter sessions and there are no books or source of advice I can rely on in this town. I called on a man named Trenance who I heard was a retired lawyer from one of the London Inns, but he was an old and ill-tempered fellow who did not have the patience to listen to my requests.

There is a small parade in town. High Justice Downish is here on a horse with colourful trappings, flanked by two outriders bearing pikes with royal pennants. Behind, follow a disparate collection of ten or so riders. Those in black and greys will be the court attendants and clerks, while men in finer apparel will be jurors. Oliver tells me that the Sheriff of Devonshire appoints a number of jurors short of the twelve required. Each town must also offer jurors qualified by status and property to make up this number. Normally, these will not be sought after positions, but the notoriety of Charles' case ensures that there will be plenty in the Guildhall later this day anxious to be chosen.

I call on Oliver shortly before three bells and we walk to the Guildhall.

'Have you heard of the hangings today, William?'

'Today? No, I have not'

'Whatever the outcome at the next day's quarter session it will at least offer some recognition of a system of justice. Early today, Hawkins had two men hanged at the yards of his ship, *Gallant*. At the same time, Gilbert had one hanged in Dartmouth. I know naught of the crime in the other town, but here one was accused of thievery and cheating at dice, while the other lewd calling and showing his arse in the streets.'

'Was there a hearing on the ship?'

'In a fashion. It was done quickly. Both men protested their innocence, but with no clear testimony or prospect of judging fairly, I cannot say if they were to be believed.'

'Even so – a hanging for a bare arse. It is…'

I cannot find the words to express my revulsion. Hawkins and Gilbert had promised as much to reinforce discipline and fear in the crews, so I should not be surprised, but taking men's lives so freely is distasteful in the extreme. I wonder again if I should have thrown in my lot with these two men.

There is a crowd gathered outside and their mood is merry. Stalls are selling ale, codlings and sweetmeats, while entertainers juggle and exhibit their tricks and skills to claps and cries of delight from children. What will the scene be like tomorrow if this many assemble merely for the selection of jurors? Shanning is at the frontage. He sees me, mutters an aside to one of the guards and disappears inside.

We weave through the bustling masses to the front door of the Guildhall. Other gentlemen are guided through a door as a guard approaches us with outstretched hand. He asks our business. We offer our names and state our wish to watch the selection of jurors. I am prepared for his reply, which is that only men of property from this town may enter. Oliver is ready to argue the point, but I pull him away. Let Shanning have his little victory. We do not want to be linked to a disturbance now in case our names in this regard spill over into the trial on the morrow.

Twelve

It is a dreadful thing to have the life of a man you admire teeter on the edge while you have a tenuous hold on his trailing hand. It has affected me physically as a dull ache in my chest which I cannot shake. I woke early and have written down all that I must say and remember in the quarter session. The case for a finding in his favour is stronger in my mind than it appears on paper. I can do naught about the testimonies of Hagger and the serving maid. I fear they may hold more sway with the jurors than my attempts to sow doubt on the identity of the killer. Oliver called late last night to inform that five jurors were chosen from this town to balance the seven travelling with Downish. I do not know whether this mix serves either cause, but much will depend on the clear thinking and fairness of these twelve men.

The masses are out by the Guildhall again, but I am in good time and ushered inside. The hall is laid out much as it was for Shanning's hearing, save that the gentlemen's area is enlarged, while there is less space for the commons. My section soon fills. I see Oliver enter, but there are too many bodies between us to join him. The commons section remains empty and I suppose that will be loaded in a final scurry shortly before all is ready for Downish.

Our wait is near done; there is pushing and shoving as the commons packs in short time and the doors close. The jurors enter from a door behind me and take their places on two rows of six stools to my right. When they are seated a loud banging of a staff announces the entrance of Downish and his attendants from the doorway opposite. The High Justice has a hawk-like appearance; sparely-made, of middle height with large, hooked nose, thin lips and keen eyes set under dark, heavy eyebrows.

An attendant takes the oath of all twelve jurors as one and announces that the first hearing will concern the killing of Walter Tremayne. I am in two minds on whether I should welcome this early hearing or have more time to settle into a better understanding of the working of the court. Well, I have no choice. Charles is led in and stands in the centre of the hall. I am pleased to note his neat appearance and composed manner. Downish reads the testimonies from Shanning's hearing in a quick, disinterested voice as though scanning a list of trifling possessions. He puts down the paper, fixes his gaze on Charles and states that Justice Shanning concluded the testimonies pointed to Charles as the killer. There is a pause as he sits back in his seat, clasps his hands across his middle and asks if Charles wishes to speak against the testimonies.

Charles bows to Downish and says, 'If it please the High Justice, I should like my friend, the renowned scholar, Doctor William Constable from London, to speak on my behalf. He has my words but will present them for a better and clearer understanding. I am a mere ship's captain without his practice and capability at oration.'

It is nicely spoken, but Downish frowns as if disliking his request. After some moments' consideration, he replies, 'Very well, I will allow this. I have heard a little of Doctor Constable's quick mind and should welcome the opportunity to observe his talent.'

He instructs an attendant who comes and bids me stand by Charles. I glance at him, but he remains unmoved with head bowed and hands hung loosely by his side. I clear my throat and begin.

'Thank you High Justice Downish for permitting me to offer information and opinions to this court on behalf of my friend Captain Charles Wicken. I am convinced – nay, I know him to be innocent of this terrible crime against an admirable young man from this fine town.'

I hold a paper as if reading notes. 'First I should like to mention the testimony of Doctor Jacob Millard, who I see is in attendance here.' I turn towards Jacob and bow my head in recognition. 'Doctor Millard attended the killing and ascribed the cause of death as strangulation by the throat. I had occasion to examine the body of Walter Tremayne while it was in repose at the Church of St Andrew in Sutton. This was done in the presence of church warden Gilles with due care and deference. I concluded that Doctor Millard was indeed correct and

Tremayne was killed by strong hands pressing on his neck to constrict the passage of vital air to his body. I do not, therefore, challenge the assertion that the victim was murdered, only that Charles Wicken was not the man who committed this foul act.'

There is murmuring and a few raised voices which the attendant silences with two sharp raps with his staff.

'While I was in the church, Warden Gilles mentioned that Tremayne's purse was empty when his body was received there for rinsing and preparation for holy rest. Later I spoke with Watchman Sykes who was quick to attend the scene of killing and summon assistance. I see that Watchman Sykes is in this hall and should like to bring him forward so that he may speak.'

Heads turn to the common area where there is movement. An attendant lifts a rope and Sykes joins us with an air of some reluctance.

'Watchman Sykes, I know from our brief meeting that you are a steadfast and honest man. Your concern at the scene was for the victim and you did not disturb his body or tamper in any way with his dress, dagger, belt or other trinkets about his person.'

I gesture with my hands to prompt a response.

'Yes – yes, that is right.'

'When I questioned you about his purse, you remembered that it was on his belt close by the dagger. Further, you stated that it did not appear to be heavy with coin and there was a fair chance it was empty.'

'Yes, those were my words.'

I thank him and he returns to his place behind the rope. There are more blows of the staff and I wait until there is quiet before proceeding.

'It would seem, then, that this was murder in the act of thievery for coin in the victim's purse. Charles Wicken is a man of substance, with no need to thieve pennies from a purse. He is a married man with his wife settled in his freehold land near Lincoln. He owns a large fighting ship which he has leased for the great adventure to the New Lands. His exploits in relieving Spanish ships from their treasures in Biscay are well known. He has become a man of some wealth with notes of credit in

London and Paris based on bankers' promissory. In all, he will have a worth in excess of two thousand pounds.'

There are gasps and whistles in the room. I have exaggerated a little, but if all is true that he has told me, then I calculate his fortune is near that mark.

'Let me come to the clump of yellow hair found in the victim's grasp. Justice Shanning made great play of Charles Wicken's fair hair in his summary. As you can see, my friend has no cap and his hair is indeed, fair. It was also said that the attacker was seen by Goodwife Langley and he was taller and broader than the victim.' I turn to face the jurors. 'If these facts are to be used as signs of possible guilt, then some of you gentlemen must take care to account for your actions that night. I see that three of you have fair hair and ten of your twelve are larger than Walter Tremayne.' I pause before adding, 'I beg forgiveness for my rudeness in examining you each as you entered this hall.'

There is some laughter and muttering at these last words. Downish bangs his hand on the table.

'Doctor Constable, your tone is impertinent and offends this court. You will not make reference to the jurors in this way.'

'I beg your pardon, Justice Downish. I had intended to use all the men in this town as an exemplar, but there may be some difficulty believing my findings. I have stood in the middle of this town and observed men as they go about their business. I hazard there will be at least six thousand grown men in this town. If that is the case then my mathematics suggest there are near one thousand men with fair hair and over three thousand that are bigger than Walter Tremayne.'

I let these numbers take hold for a time as I shuffle my papers. I see jurors turn and whisper to each other. I hope they did not take offence at my staring and that there is none among them to question my mathematics. My calculations are not in error, but they do not tell the whole story. It is a small piece of trickery, but I excuse this from my conscience through certainty of Charles' innocence. I see Shanning whisper to one of his associates. He glances quickly to me and then Downish with an expression of puzzlement. I am sure he would wish to challenge my last statements, but perhaps he does not have the wit to see through the numbers.

Downish says, 'Are you finished, Doctor Constable?'

'I beg your forbearance; there is a little more. I mentioned the testimony of Goodwife Langley and I should like to seek clarification from her.'

She is standing at the front and lifts the rope herself to come and stand by me. Once there, she looks around, smiling and acknowledging her neighbours and friends. It is clear that she is not overcome by the importance of this occasion. She eyes me, nods her head and folds her arms under her bosom to signify she is ready.

'Goodwife Langley, the testimony spoken by Justice Shanning tells of your sight of a man struggling with Walter Tremayne near the front of the house where you are the housekeeper. It was said that you identified the man with Tremayne as Charles Wicken. Is that the testimony as you gave it?'

'No, it is not. I have not seen Captain Wicken until this day, so I did not give his name in my testimony.'

'Perhaps there was confusion or misunderstanding when you gave your account to Justice Shanning?'

'Indeed, I saw only that he was tall and wide from my view of his back and could not offer any other particulars. It was dark.'

Downish turns to Shanning who sits to his side. 'Is that your recollection of the Goodwife's testimony, Justice Shanning?'

'No, there was definite mention of Wicken's name.' He is quick with indignation in his answer.

I say, 'But if Goodwife Langley has not seen Captain Wicken before this day, how could she state his name?'

Downish slams his hand on the table and eyes me fiercely. 'Doctor Constable, your conduct becomes ill-mannered. You may not question the Justice.' He addresses the jurors and states that they must disregard my last remark and he will allow Justice Shanning to say his piece again, without interruption.

Shanning is overlong and complex in his narrative. Clearly, he does not wish to offend the Goodwife who is well-liked in the town, but he will not lose face by altering the testimony as he wrote it. In the end, he tries to compromise by suggesting that she described the man in such a way that there could be no doubt it was Charles. Any fair-minded man would take her telling as the truth, but I cannot determine if the jurors lean this way from their expressions. Goodwife Langley was my principal card in the deck designed to set Charles free and I must hope that my intemperate riposte to Shanning has not spoiled its presentation.

I conclude my part in this case with Charles' account of the events that night: Tremayne's over-indulgence in strong drink; his spewing; his continued state of drunkenness; Charles' care of an unsteady young man; and their parting long before reaching the scene of killing when Tremayne insisted on being let alone. I thank Downish and the jurors, with exaggerated politeness, for their patience in hearing my exposition and return to my place in the gentlemen's area.

Downish requests Shanning step forward and offer evidence of Charles as the killer. He stands in the front of the table brandishing a paper, which he states contains the names of eighteen persons of good standing who swore they witnessed a strong argument between Charles and Tremayne inside the inn and outside on leaving. He speaks the names, one by one, slowly and with deep emphasis on their qualities of reliability and honesty. More, he avers that all these persons swore that Charles was the forceful party with Tremayne meek and obliging for the most part.

I raise my hand wishing to protest. Downish dismisses my signal with a wave of his hand and says to Shanning, 'There are but two names on your list of testimonies in this regard, Justice Shanning: a Gooodman Hagger; and a serving maid from the inn. Will they be heard?'

'There were many who witnessed the bullying and only those two names were selected for written testimony in order to save repetition, which would have made the deposition stretch to unnecessary length.'

'Nevertheless, it would be prudent to hear confirmation from these two.'

'I regret that Goodman Hagger has an illness and has taken to his bed. He is unable to attend here but has sent word to affirm his written testimony.'

I raise my hand again. Downish sees me and this time, with a sigh of impatience, asks if my enquiry has any relevance to this last statement.

I say, 'Thank you Justice Downish, I only wished to add that Goodman Hagger has a known enmity to Captain Wicken. There was a minor quarrel some weeks past when Captain Wicken was insulted most severely.'

Shanning responds, 'Naught is known of this dispute. It would be contrary to the balanced disposition of Goodman Hagger to suppose that he instigated this disagreement. His family have served this town well over many years and he holds a good reputation for kindness and a calm manner.'

I was too quick with my challenge and should have kept silent. I must hope the jurors will not take the spat with Hagger as a sign of Charles' aggressive nature. Shanning does not describe the Hagger I have met, but I can say no more if the man is ill in bed.

Downish says, 'Very good, that is Goodman Hagger confirmed – and what of the maid, named Amy Wearing? Is she here?'

Heads turn, and there is a small commotion in the commons as the maid squeezes through the throng to the rope. She is guided to the centre of the hall and stands facing Shanning.

'Amy Wearing, you were a serving maid in the gentlemen's section of the *Seven Bells* on the night of the killing. Did you observe Master Wicken and Captain Tremayne closely?'

She speaks, but I cannot hear. Shanning begs her to repeat, but louder.

'Yes sir, I served those gentlemen at their table.'

'And did you witness the tormenting and mistreatment of Master Tremayne by this man?' He points an accusing finger at Charles.

She mutters some words, but again they are too faint. Downish interrupts Shanning to instruct Amy that she must speak so all in the hall might hear.

She says, 'It was not quite as you say. Master Tremayne was… he was drunk and played the fool. The other man… Captain Wicken tried…' Her voice trails away and Downish reminds her once again to raise her speech.

'It was as though… as though Captain Wicken tried to soothe excessive spirits.'

'That is not the telling from this testimony and against which you made your mark.' Shanning brandishes the paper, first to her and then to the jurors.

'There was… much excitement and…'

'Well?'

'Perhaps I misspoke. There were many gathered there with sympathy for Walter – Master Tremayne – and quick to name Captain Wicken.'

Shanning turns his back on her and shakes his head at Downish. She is dismissed and hurries back to her place with head bowed. Shanning tries to excuse her altered testimony through an unsteady mind brought on by fright at the stares of so many fine gentlemen. He reminds the jurors of the other witnesses who confirmed Hagger's account and finishes with loud accusations and jabbing finger at Charles.

Downish turns to his left and converses in low voice with his scribe who scratches on his paper. Downish watches this for some moments until the scribe cleans his quill with a cloth and bows his head to signify he is done. The High Justice sits back in his seat, surveys the hall and narrows his eyes as though considering his next words carefully. Much will depend on his advice to the jurors. He starts by summarising the case against Charles as stated in Shanning's written testimonies. 'But there has been some doubt cast on the identification of the killer and the nature of the quarrel between Master Tremayne and the accused. Is this doubt sufficient to persuade you of the possible innocence of Captain Wicken? It is finely balanced and I trust your good sense to reach a verdict that is just and fair in the eyes of God.'

He asks the jurors if they are content to continue their deliberations in the hall or if they wish to retire to their anteroom. After brief consultations, they are led from the hall by an attendant and Downish leaves by the other door.

The noise swells as men turn to their neighbours to voice opinions. I do not hear the sense of any words as my gaze is fixed on Charles, expecting him to look about for signs of encouragement or dismay, but he stands still facing the chair emptied by Downish. I cannot help but wonder how my belly would churn and roil if I were in his position.

This wait is too long. The crowd grows restless, there are shouts of 'hang' and others who profess their support for Wicken, but they are outnumbered; the mood of those in the hall is against him.

Still we wait. Eleven bells have rung and the jurors have not emerged.

At last, there is a sign. The attendant opens the door from the anteroom and crosses to make a signal to Downish in his chamber. They enter together; Downish from his door and the twelve jurors one by one from theirs. I watch closely, but can tell naught from their expressions, which, for the most part, are serious and fixed straight ahead. They settle on their stools, the staff is rapped for quiet and Downish peers with stern face around the hall to ensure all attend to his words.

He says to the jurors, 'It is fitting that you have laboured for some time over the testimonies presented here. This is a most serious charge against a man of property and reputation for the violent killing of a fine young gentleman of this town.' He pauses. 'Will you offer your decision with one voice?'

Most jurors respond with calls of 'Aye'. A few remain silent.

'What is your verdict? A declaration of "Guilty" will signify the accused was the killer and a call of "Free" that he is innocent of the charge.'

'Free,' is the word – spoken strongly by some jurors; muttered quietly by a few.

There are moments of quiet while the verdict takes hold, then a babbling and murmuring which grows. There are cries of 'Shame' and 'Wrong'. I hear a man close by say, 'There was no certainty' and another, 'Someone must hang'. Downish declares the case has ended and Charles is an innocent man, free to go about his business. There are calls for order and the next hearing to be brought forward. Charles has not moved. I walk to him and touch his shoulder. He turns and I embrace him muttering words of cheer and relief at his liberation. Oliver joins, slaps Charles on his back and says, 'That was well done, William. It was a close call.'

I stand back and look at Charles. He stares ahead in a daze, shakes his head and says, 'Thank you, William, may God bless you for this new life you have given me.'

Three of us push our way through the front of the Guildhall. The crowd outside have heard the outcome and there is some braying and shouting displeasure at being cheated of the opportunity to see a gentleman hanged. I have not prepared for our escape through a hostile mob. I hesitate to consider whether to retreat and seek a passage from the rear, then I see Stack approach with a group of his men. They surround us and break a path through to a more tranquil place in the next street. Charles speaks to Stack in low voice, who gathers his men and departs to the quays. Oliver says we should celebrate with good wine and refreshment, which waits for us at his lodgings.

This is a muted affair; not all as I had anticipated. We are sat in Oliver's place supping and picking at sweetmeats. After uttering words of congratulations and joy for the release of Charles on first raising our cups, we retreat into our own thoughts leaving our conversation broken and forced. Should I be surprised at the verdict? I am firm in my belief of his innocence, but realise only now that I did not expect others to share my opinion. I had steeled myself for losing a friend at the end of a rope and my spirits are strangely numbed at the outcome. I must not be fooled that it was my oratory that swayed the decision. Goodwife Langley will have spread doubt about the identification. Were the jurors persuaded it was the work of a thief and dazzled by Charles' wealth, or did my exposition on the hair and build of men in Plymouth muddle them? I wonder how the maid, Amy, summoned the fortitude to alter her testimony and deny Shanning's browbeating. All this, and more is unresolved in my mind as Oliver and I leave Charles to attend to our everyday affairs.

PAUL WALKER

Thirteen

We are four days past the end of the quarter session and the fevered atmosphere in the town has quietened. Shanning and his men have been stung into action and have taken vagrants and beggars from the streets for questioning over the killing. Two are held in prison for further investigation. I do not envy their situation or chance of a fair hearing, should that be the outcome. Charles has resumed his position as the commander of three ships and he admitted receiving a gruff welcome back into the venture from Hawkins. Despite my protests that he must now absolve Hawkins and Gilbert from any involvement in his discomfort, Charles retains his suspicions. One of Stack's couriers has returned and confirmed the note was given to Walsingham. The whereabouts of the other is not known.

I am troubled that there has been no news from Walsingham. Charles is adamant that the threat of invasion is real and imminent, yet is curiously detached from the subject and unwilling to advise Hawkins and Gilbert. I am pressed to keep this intelligence undisclosed and rely on action from Walsingham, which Charles is certain will be forthcoming. Well, it must be soon and before our fleet sails, or our ports here will have little in the way of defence.

It is the middle of the afternoon. I am with Doctor Jacob Millard at the Hurst household examining Able Langley with his goodwife and Mistress Hurst in attendance. My services as a physician have been in demand since my treatment of Able's teeth and headaches. Goodwife Langley has not spared my blushes in extravagant praise of my care and simple remedies to her neighbours and friends. I denied all such entreaties out of deference to Jacob as their competent and local practitioner. It is to Jacob's credit that when he came to learn of this gossip he invited me to join him on visits to his patients, rather than sulk in a fit of professional jealousy. I have spent two pleasant and interesting half-days with Jacob and it has made me realise how I miss my practice as a physician in London.

Able is much improved. His headaches are almost gone and his spasms of ranting and crying have stopped. He is addle-brained beyond repair but appears content. We leave Able in his kitchen seat and Mistress Hurst leads us through to her parlour for refreshment. Cups of sweet wine have been poured when the door opens and Master Hurst enters.

'Good day to you my dears... and doctors.' He kisses his wife and Goodwife Langley. 'We are honoured by the presence of two scholars this day, but must hope this does not indicate that anyone in this house has an ailment requiring a special curative.'

'Ha, I know you jest, Phillip,' answers Jacob. 'The only payment we require for this visit is a cup of wine. All here are in rude health.'

Mistress Hurst explains our examination of Able, but it is clear that her husband has news and he calms her gently so that he may talk.

He says, 'Three fighting ships have arrived in the harbour; one a galleon and the other two large carracks. They fly royal standards and are here on Her Majesty's business. There is much excitement on the quays.'

So, this must be Walsingham's doing, at last. He is known to dislike sea voyages and, if Sir Francis himself planned to come, I had expected him to travel here overland. I say, 'Do you know who commands the new arrivals?'

'I did not stay to observe their disembarkation, Doctor, but I heard the name of Sir William Wynter mentioned.'

I beg to be excused, saying I am required to attend at the quays.

*

On my way to Hawkins' place of business on the quay, I see Oliver. There is a commotion at the front where men hand out notes to a group of boys who set off at a run.

Oliver says, 'There is a meeting at Hawkins' house in town. Notes are being sent to summon certain captains and secondaries. I have not seen him, but Sir William Wynter is here and that will be the reason for our gathering. That is his ship, *Formidable*.' He points at a large galleon where the crew are busy tidying the decks and yards.

We walk into town to the meeting. I do not know if I am invited, but would hear what Wynter has to say and am sure I will not be denied entry.

I say, 'Do you know Sir William?'

'Only by reputation. He is a fine master of ships, has good control of his men and I understand he is a sober man of balanced humour.' He pauses for a moment, then adds, 'There is rivalry between Wynter and Hawkins.'

'What is its nature?'

'Sir William was expected to be offered the appointment of Treasurer to the Navy this last year, but Hawkins received that honour. Some say that Burghley intervened in favour of Hawkins.'

'So, his reception here will not be easy.'

'That will depend on the reason for his visit.' He touches me on the arm and turns to eye me with an enquiring expression. 'I wonder if you know something of the purpose of this meeting, William. Is there a connection with Charles or the guarding of outgoing correspondence?'

Why does he mention Charles? I have not disclosed his intelligence about the threatened invasion. I must be circumspect in sharing this information until I am sure that Wynter is here under orders from Walsingham. I shrug and say I cannot be sure but suspect it will be a matter of high importance that brings two royal ships here.

We are ushered into Hawkins' main receiving room where a dozen or more are already gathered. There is an expectant air and muttered speculation about the intentions of Wynter's arrival. Charles enters with Stack, nods a brief welcome and comes to stand behind us. The chamber fills until there are forty or more. Eventually, there is a lull in conversation, the door opens and Hawkins enters followed by Pennes and another man who must be Sir William. He is a tall, handsome man of middle years, finely-dressed in burgundy doublet and black hose. Hawkins stands at one end, a space is cleared to his front and we arrange ourselves in a semi-circle. He is brief in his introduction of Sir William, saying only that we are honoured to welcome him on urgent business.

Wynter steps forward and brandishes a paper in his hand. 'Gentlemen, I am here under royal warrant to investigate a report which has vexed Her Majesty and may compromise the security of her state.'

He pauses to let his statement take hold and the murmuring to cease.

'Secretary Walsingham has received intelligence on the marshalling of fighting ships in Biscay. The extent of this mustering is not known in its exactness but it may be considerable as we suspect the backing of Rome.'

He waits again to underscore what has been said and what is to follow.

'There are names connected to this scheme that give grave concern and may be known to you. They are well-known for their evil conniving and wicked words against Her Majesty over many years. One is Nicholas Sanders and the other is Thomas Stukley.'

There is a mix of disbelief and derision at the last-named. More than one states that Stukley is reported dead.

'Indeed, there was news that Stukley had his legs shot away at a battle in Maroc. That would be a happy state if it were true, but there are strong rumours that this was false news spread mischievously to hide real intentions.'

Oliver says, 'And what are the objectives of this fighting force assembled by Sanders and Stukley?'

'It will come as no surprise to learn that harm is planned against Her Majesty's state. In its extreme potential, an invading force will attack these ports in the West Country with a corresponding assault from the low-countries in the East.' Hawkins scowls and emits a low growl. 'But there may be lesser mischief designed with raids upon our territories in the West or in Ireland.'

Hawkins says, 'This intelligence must be questioned. We have learned of no such threat from the comings and goings in these ports.'

'I understand your concern, Captain General. You will not wish any further delay to your sailing to the New Lands and I do not order the immediate surrender of your fleet to Her Majesty's defence. But if my investigations determine the threat is true and imminent I will have no option but to take that course. No affair, no matter how grand in its scale, can take precedence over Her Majesty's security.'

There can be no argument against Wynter's statement. He is asked how long his investigations will take and what this means for our ships during this time. Wynter only offers that he will undertake his task with as much speed as thoroughness allows. All ships in the fleet must seek his permission to leave the ports and they will not sail beyond sight of land. He is willing to answer other questions, but there are none. I note there has been no mention of Charles and I wonder if he intends to keep his name secret as the source of the intelligence from Hawkins.

We are requested to depart and introduce ourselves to Sir William on our way out so that he may know our names for future conversations. We form into a line and take our turn as each of us is presented by Hawkins. It is my turn, my name is given and I doff my cap to Wynter.

He takes my hand. 'Ah, Doctor Constable, I have a message for you from my friend, Sir George Morton. May I call on you later this day?'

'Why yes, Sir William, it will give me pleasure to welcome you and hear from Sir George. I am lodged in Lockyer Lane in Mistress Gredley's house.'

*

I am impatient for Wynter's news and idle away time with no purpose until after six bells. I have warned Mistress Gredley of his coming and she has laid out her best receiving chamber for my use. He is here. She opens the door to him and enquires on our preferred refreshment. Sir William pleases her with his understanding that she serves a fine table but begs to be excused with only a cup of wine. It is thoughtful of him and nicely done. She colours at his compliment, bobs a curtsey and fetches two cups and a bottle sweet wine in short time. We settle in our seats and sip our cups until we are alone. I am congratulated for my invention of the navigation instrument, which he intends to use on his ships in due course. I ask how Walsingham fares and he replies that he has an ailment in his belly which has prevented his travel to Plymouth.

He says, 'You must forgive my small invention about a message from Sir George, Doctor. I wished to find an excuse to converse with you about my consultation with Sir Francis.'

'So, you have no news from Sir George.'

'I regret that we have not spoken. I know only that Sir George journeys here in the company of his daughter, Helen. Sir Francis was particular that I mention the lady's name as he suspected that would give you great satisfaction.'

'Indeed sir, you have raised my spirits. Helen Morton is my betrothed.'

He congratulates me but wastes no more time on pleasantries and moves to the subject of his meeting with Walsingham.

'I am told that you have worked closely with Sir Francis and that I may trust you. He was fulsome in his praise for your quick mind and loyalty to Her Majesty's cause. You are the only person here that I will take into my full confidence, at least until my investigation has progressed further.'

'I am flattered that Sir Francis speaks so highly of me, but I am no practised intelligencer. Of course, I will assist in any way that I can as the threat is so severe.'

'Well, that is yet to be determined. I would ask you first for your opinion of Captain Wicken. He has many useful contacts, but is newly recruited to the service of Secretary Walsingham and his reliability has not been tested.'

'I count him as a friend. I have known him only a few short months, but to my mind, he is steadfast and true in his dealings. He gave me an account of the intelligence he has received on the threat to these ports and I believe him.'

'He was named for a killing of a young gentleman here, although I understand he has been cleared, due in no small part to your efforts.'

'I was convinced of his innocence, made enquiries and spoke

for him at the quarter session. He suspects that the killing and his naming was designed by conspirators to suppress his intelligence.'

'It would be a complex matter to construct a scheme such as that. Do you not consider that might be fanciful and his naming the result of simple misfortune or mistake?'

'Yes, I agree that his mind may have been overtaken and confused by the peril of his situation, but conspiracy cannot be discounted. His uncovering of the intelligence and his naming occurred within such a short time that it may not have been mere coincidence.' I pause to consider how to frame my next words. 'There is also another matter of mischance that should be taken into account. I was attacked with a companion near Loddiswell by a band of four cutthroats at the same time as Captain Wicken and his man were close by. I owe Charles Wicken my life as he killed the attackers bravely, although he was too late to save the life of my companion. The last piece of intelligence was gathered by Charles at Dartmouth before he set out on his journey and he asserts that he was the intended target of the assault.'

'I was not aware of this evil doing. You are to be congratulated on your escape, Doctor.'

'I should add that the bodies of the four dead assailants had disappeared in a strange and unexplained manner when I passed that way the next day. Their stealthy removal could have been designed to conceal their identities.'

He moves his mouth in a way that suggests he is chewing on a troublesome piece of gristle. It is clear that this news has surprised him and he deliberates carefully on its significance. Finally, he says, 'These two quirks of fate tip the balance of chance towards Captain's Wicken's telling, but I cannot say they are conclusive.' He pours more wine in our cups. 'Can you reveal more of the Captain's disposition and character? You are friends and he rescued you from a great peril, so you will have a good opinion of him. But I hear he has the reputation for fierceness and quick temper. Could the killing of young Tremayne have been at his hands, but accidental?'

'He is a fighting man and will need to summon savagery and

violence when the occasion demands, but I have not witnessed a foul temper in his everyday conduct. In general, I would say he has a balanced humour and my enquiries indicated that the killing may have been committed by a common thief.'

'Well, that is enough of Captain Wicken, except to say that I must ask you to tell no one of his part in this investigation for the present.' He sups the last of his wine and refills his cup. 'Your connection to Sir George Morton signifies that you have a vital interest in the great adventure. What can you tell me about the reasons for the delay to your sailing, current readiness and the temperament of the Captain General and Sir Humphrey? I understand it is no easy thing to speak frankly of great men, but I ask you to talk freely and can assure you that I will be discreet.'

There can be no denying that he is thorough and quick with his investigation. He has been here only a short time, has learned about Charles' freedom and puts probing questions about our principals and the status of our fleet. Do I trust him? Unguarded comments made here may return to injure my standing. But I think I must be honest. The matter is too important to cloak with politeness.

'I am not a nautical man and have reached an understanding of the reasons for our delays from the telling of others. Several ships were damaged in a storm on their passage from Sandwich and I am told that our carpenters here have been overstretched in their work. There have also been difficulties in strengthening some ships for heavier guns and attack decks for boarding.'

'Yes, this much is well known. There have been other difficulties?'

'There are many interests in the venture and it will be difficult to keep all content. There have been squabbles about the ownership and value of cargoes. I know that some cargoes have had to be returned or replaced while others have laid on the quays waiting payment before loading. I would hazard that it is delays of this nature that has exasperated our leaders here above others.'

'Are you on friendly terms with the Captain General and Sir Humphrey?'

'Our relations are cordial, but do not go beyond that. This may be because I am a scholar, not a sailor. Or, they could find my friendship with Captain Wicken problematic. It is plain that they do not hold him in high regard.'

'Why might that be?'

'I cannot be sure. Charles has a reputation as a brave raider of Spanish treasure and his experience and advice should be welcome, but…'

'But?'

'It may be envy and an unwillingness to share whatever credit and glory comes from the adventure. That is Charles' opinion, although it may be extreme.'

He inclines his head, hoping for more. I hesitate, trying to formulate my words so they minimise any offence. 'Charles – Captain Wicken – has been critical of our state of preparedness and planning, particularly in the recruitment of fighting men and the modifications of our ships for combat.'

He nods his head slowly, then sits back in his seat and clasps his hands over his middle. 'I see. How do you gauge the temper of Hawkins and Gilbert now and their handling of the delays?'

He is direct and I suppose I must answer in the same fashion. 'I have the impression that they are frantic for the venture to get underway and will call on all measures to ensure our departure without further harm.'

'All measures?'

'Discipline is severe and justice may have been bypassed to serve as examples to the men. I have been requested to write a letter of reassurance to Sir George and outgoing correspondence has been closely guarded to calm the anxieties of backers.'

I pause. He raises his eyes and asks if there is more. I will not mention Charles' suspicion that they had a hand in his naming for the killing as I am not convinced. I shake my head and answer that I can recall no more instances.

He says, 'Finally Doctor, have you heard mention of the names Stukley and Sanders in idle chatter in these ports?'

'No, I have not. The first mention in my hearing was when Charles outlined his intelligence of the invasion.'

'What of the other name in Wicken's message, James

Fitzmaurice Fitzgerald?'

'It is a name I have not heard before Charles' telling. I understand he is an Irish Geraldine noble estranged from his lord, the Earl of Desmond. I am not one for politicking and confess that I have paid little attention to Her Majesty's management of Ireland.'

'Good, good.' He raises his cup. 'This is an excellent wine and I thank you for both your hospitality and the direct, unfussy answers to my questions. It has been most helpful.'

I am relieved, but it seems we have not finished as he lingers in his seat.

'There is another small matter. I have attained my fortieth year and find that my aching legs are less steady on deck. You have a strong reputation as a physician and I wondered if you have a potion that will help me recapture some years from my youth. I would dance around the ship to encourage my crew to be merry in their work.'

A puff of air escapes my lips and I stare at him with open mouth. Can he be...

'Ha, wipe that worried look away, Doctor. I am teasing. You have such a serious countenance that I could not resist ending with a small jest. You will forgive me in time, I am sure.'

I relax at once. He has a genial aspect; quite unlike his rival, Hawkins. He is also a man who inspires confidence and I have no doubt that the intelligence received by Charles will be scrutinised in detail. Whether his actions will meet with approval from Hawkins and Gilbert is more open to question.

Fourteen

My thoughts on waking were of Helen. I wrestled to hold a vivid dream of tender and thoughtful moments as we lay in our bed, sated with our lovemaking. As with all dreams, there was a sharp edge to our happiness as we were flung into a state of weeping and mourning at the death of her father. I do not hold a belief that dreams foretell the future; rather they are a confusing mix of past events, thoughts and desires. The dream was a signal of my longing to be with Helen, coloured with the news in her last letter of the illness troubling Sir George. He is a large man with a great fondness for his roast hams and sweet jellies. When we next meet I should reinforce Helen's warnings to moderate his appetite and enhance his periods of relaxation.

Thoughts of careful eating are banished as Mistress Gredley serves a fine breakfast of eggs, ham, honey and white bread. Margaret enters with a jug of ale. She hands me a letter and its scent of lavender and other perfumes signify that it is from Helen.

My Dearest William

I am lost in a whirl of excitement as I prepare for our journey to Plymouth town. Yes, my love, father has granted permission for me to accompany him. The imagining of our meeting again in a few short days sends a shiver of pleasure through my whole being. I am a maddening mistress to Lucy and Rosamund, unable to decide on gowns, skirts, bonnets, jewels, scents and other trinkets I must have. They pack and unpack my chests as father scolds that I am too liberal with my baggage.

Yet, my joy is tempered by father's health. He avers he is much improved, but I note that he still gasps for air and will sit often to steady his gait. I suspect that he has allowed me on this expedition so that I may tend to his ailment. I have stored herbs and curatives from our drying room in our travelling bundles and I would welcome your advice on his condition and remedy when we meet.

Please excuse these brief and carelessly-shaped words. I am giddy and feverish in anticipation of our joining, my love. Save your sweetest kiss for our reunion, which should be in two short days after reading this note.
Ever your love
Helen

It is a short letter, but one that fills me with longing and resurrects recent memories of my waking dream. Two short days and we will be together. But only for a short time until the fleet sails for the New Lands. Would that I could extricate myself from the adventure – or, that Wynter commandeers our ships in defence of our shores. No, I should not summon thoughts for the threat of invasion to become reality, simply to serve my selfish craving.

*

I am aimless this morning and cannot shake thoughts of my love and our encounter here in the coming days. The air is fine and I stroll down to the quays, hoping to catch Oliver and Charles to discuss Wynter's investigation.

Activity on the quays is curiously muted, as though ships and men are biding their time waiting for instructions to sail or defend. This cannot be an easy stage for Hawkins and Gilbert to fidget and twiddle thumbs, wondering if their plans for riches and glory can proceed, or will be dashed by events beyond their control. I do have sympathy, but only a smidgeon.

I see Oliver, lolling against a cart on the quayside, talking to two of his secondaries. He sees me approach, comes to join me and we agree to adjourn to an inn for a jug of ale.

'Did Sir William visit with you, as promised?'

'Yes, we shared a cup of wine and conversed for a short time.'

'Was good news conveyed from Sir George?'

'He confirmed my dearest wish; that Helen accompanies her father to this town. With good fortune and fine weather they will be here on the morrow.'

'Then it must be hoped that the great adventure will be

permitted to sail. It would harm Sir George's ambitions severely if the expedition, so long in the planning, is cancelled on Her Majesty's orders.'

I voice agreement and keep my inner thoughts hidden.

He says, 'I have a conference arranged with Sir William in two hours. He has settled at Hawkins' house and I believe that all captains, masters and other principals in the town have been called there for private discussions.'

'He will be a busy man, but his diligence and industry is no revelation to me.'

'How did you find him on your consultation?'

'I took a liking to him. He is a serious and thoughtful man with a gift to put others at their ease. He is direct in his questioning and encourages openness.'

'So, he posed questions as well as offering news from Sir George.'

Did I speak too quickly? Well, he will know soon enough when he meets with Wynter. 'Yes, he asked my opinion on the state of readiness of our fleet and the temper of our leaders.'

He raises his eyes in mild surprise and pauses, perhaps expecting me to elaborate.

'I should say no more of Wynter in case it influences your meeting with him.' I take a draught of ale and switch the topic of our conversation. 'Have you talked with Charles? He keeps himself close these past days and I suppose it is no wonder he seeks a quiet space to recover from his ordeal.'

He shakes his head, makes to speak, then withdraws as though considering his words carefully. 'The outcome of the hearing was... difficult to comprehend. I was amazed that the finding was in his favour and had resigned myself to losing a friend at the end of a rope.'

'I was of the same mind, but we must be glad that our fears for the waywardness of justice were unfounded.'

'Indeed.' He twirls his cup and retreats from our conversation, gazing around the inn for distraction.

'Does something trouble you, Oliver?'

'Ah, it is simply our predicament. Our destiny hangs in the balance while we wait for Walsingham and his men to unravel yet another supposed peril to Her Majesty.'

I forget that Oliver will be eager to get the venture underway and does not share my misgivings. He will stand to benefit in large measure if it is successful and no doubt he has imagined this future enhancement to his wealth and standing. 'Do you doubt the veracity of the intelligence disclosed by Wynter?'

He shrugs. 'There will be many warnings proved false for one that is real. It seems a menace of such large scope that it would be difficult to hide from these ports, but... it must be examined.'

We drink and chatter idly for another half hour, then I depart saying I will look for Charles. I roam the quays, stopping to converse with two gentlemen of my acquaintance, but cannot find my intended target and return to my lodgings for dinner.

I have been keeping a journal since the start of the New Year. Many of the entries are missing or only contain a few words, signifying the tedium of the majority of my days in this town. The past few weeks are blank as my disposition would not settle to the task of writing and the events in this interval, though unsettling, deserve to be recorded. I spend over three hours scratching at my table and when I am done, resolve to take the air for a stroll before supper. I open the front door to see a lad hurrying towards me. It is the Huckle boy. He is breathless and gulps air before handing a note to me. His face is bruised and he carries his arm strangely.

'Are you injured, boy?'

''Tis naught, sir. I will mend.'

'Who did this to you?'

He bows his head and will not answer. I put my finger under his chin and lift his face to mine. His forehead is badly grazed and swollen. I ask again.

'Sir, it was that fellow with the grim look who is named Stack. He and his master with yellow hair cuffed and kicked me for disturbing their peace with the delivery of a note from Captain General Hawkins.'

His words shock me. I can believe it of Stack – but Charles? He must have been in high temper to take part in such a disgraceful assault on this poor boy.

I read the note. It is from Wynter, who requests my urgent

attendance at Hawkins' house. Well, that must wait while I take Huckle inside to clean and dress his wounds.

*

Wynter is with Hawkins and Gilbert at the dining table. They have finished a supper. Wynter is seated with Gilbert while Hawkins paces the chamber with arms behind his back. I am welcomed politely and take a seat at the table. Hawkins pours me a cup of wine and at the same time squeezes my shoulder. It is a strange gesture – of reassurance, sympathy or some other sentiment? He continues to pace and appears unsettled, while the other two are composed and raise their cups to mine.

Wynter says, 'Thank you for answering our call, Doctor Constable. May I refer to you as William for this conversation?'

'Indeed, I should be flattered by such warm consideration.'

'I have met with a number of captains and principals in this town today and regret that they do not point me in a direction for or against the prospect of danger to these ports. It is a knotty subject, which I have discussed with the Captain General and Sir Humphrey.'

Hawkins mutters some words, but I cannot catch their meaning.

Wynter continues, 'I have disclosed the position of Captain Wicken in this affair as an intelligencer for Sir Francis Walsingham.' He pauses and adds, 'I have also named you as a trusted associate of Sir Francis and told that I have taken you into my confidence.'

Gilbert says, 'We were not aware of Wicken's role in the employ of Walsingham and that may be the reason behind some of his peculiar behaviour.'

'How was it peculiar?'

'He has kept his ships and crews close guarded from the rest of our fleet and has declined offers to participate in our practice manoeuvres.'

Hawkins takes a seat next to mine. 'His manner has been aloof and uncooperative at the consultations with our captains and masters. His experience in boarding ships would have been…

helpful.'

'Could this not be an unfortunate misunderstanding or conflict between men of strong temperaments? I understand that Captain Wicken feels his offers of advice have been rebuffed.'

Hawkins growls his discontent at my words. 'He is a man I do not like.'

'Do you still believe he was the killer of Tremayne even though he was cleared at the hearing?'

'I give it no thought. That is a minor matter when set against our great adventure... or indeed, the security of our state.'

'Gentlemen, let us not become diverted from our purpose here,' says Wynter. 'We have reached a critical point in our deliberations.' He pauses to ensure he has our full attention. 'We must settle our opinion on the intelligence received of an extreme peril to our nation. It may be possible to obtain indications by sending scouting ships out to Biscay and perhaps a landing at one of the ports.'

Hawkins continues with muttering and I see that Gilbert shakes his head in disapproval.

'But there may be another way.' Wynter gazes at Hawkins and Gilbert in turn before proceeding. 'The Captain General and Sir Humphrey consider that this method would take several weeks and would place their ships in danger. Your venture would be... compromised.'

'It would be the end of it,' says Hawkins. 'We cannot countenance further delays, our backers would withdraw and our standing as a seagoing nation seen to be flimsy as a maid's petticoat.'

'Yes, Captain General, your view is known.' Wynter is sharp in his retort. This is my first sign of a taut relation between these two men. I suspect there would be harsh words to follow if I were not present. 'Fortunately, Sir Humphrey has an alternative suggestion on how we could unpick the threads of the intelligence.' He turns and bows his head so that Gilbert can explain.

'I am familiar with one of the names mentioned in the conspiracy. I have served Her Majesty in Ireland and have come to know many of the Irish lords. In particular, I had the fortune to prevail in bloody encounters against James Fitzmaurice Fitzgerald. He sued for peace, was granted his life and surrendered his sword to my hands these six years past. He swore fealty to the crown and wished to mend his broken trust with the Earl of Desmond in order to regain his standing as the Geraldine most likely to succeed to the earldom of Munster.' He takes up his cup and drinks slowly, leaving me to wonder why I am being told this tale of intrigues in a land I do not know. 'He was in my care for some months and when his estrangement from Desmond became certain he retreated to France with his family.'

I feel a need to drive this discourse from history to the present time and enquire what manner of man is Fitzmaurice.

'He was misguided in his rebellion against Her Majesty, but he is a brave and honourable man. Although he was a fierce adversary we became familiar in a way that was akin to companionship. He surrendered his eldest son, Maurice, as hostage and he is under the care of Sir John Bold at Greenwich, together with other young nobles. He is a fine young man who would now be in his fourteenth year.'

I say, 'This may be a useful background to one of those named in the conspiracy, but I cannot see how this will help to validate the intelligence from Captain Wicken.' I keep my thoughts unsaid on the diverse opinions on Fitzmaurice held by Charles and Gilbert.

'Have patience, William, Sir Humphrey will get there in due course.' Wynter gestures with a calming hand.

'Fitzmaurice has a house in the French town of St Malo. He is known to have travelled widely through France, Italy and Portugal, but his wife, Katherine, is settled in that port and has raised other children there.' He places his cup on the table and clasps his hands as if to stiffen the meaning of his next words. 'I visited young Maurice six months past and received a token from him to pass to his mother. I had intended to visit her in St Malo but pressing business with the venture has prevented this courtesy.'

All three steer their gaze to me as though I should comprehend the significance of this final episode in tying together all that has been said before. I wait for more, but when the quiet becomes uncomfortable I say, 'I understand that St Malo is but a short distance across the Narrow Sea. Do you have a proposal to consult with Fitzmaurice or his confederates there?'

'You have it, William,' declares Wynter. 'You will sail to that place and introduce yourself to the Lady Katherine, wife to Fitzmaurice, while others journeying with you will confer and listen at the inns and quays.'

'Me... you would have me...' My thoughts are too scrambled to finish the protest. Helen will arrive this next day and I should be here. It is not in my nature to be devious in extracting intelligence. St Malo is known to be a dangerous and lawless town. 'I am flattered that you think me capable for such a task, but surely there are others more suited.'

'You are too coy with your talents, William. Sir Francis has told me of your accomplishments in foiling a conspiracy only a few months past.'

'But I am not acquainted with the lady. Sir Humphrey has a close connection with Fitzmaurice, so would appear to be well-matched for this engagement.'

Wynter turns to Gilbert for his response. 'I regret that, although I am on good terms with Fitzmaurice, the same cannot be said for his wife. She condemned me as cruel for quelling the rebellion in Ireland with no quarter and I was never easy in her company. Besides I am known in St Malo and my arrival there would silence wagging tongues.'

I am in a daze imagining how I could handle this commission that they appear set on thrusting on me. If not Gilbert, then perhaps...

'What of Charles – Captain Wicken? He has pieced the threads of this plot together from his observations and contacts. He would be the person to confirm the true nature of the scheming.'

The other three exchange glances and it is Wynter who replies. 'We are agreed that would not be a fitting solution. He is too close to the intelligence and his objectivity in reporting could not be relied upon. Also, he will be recognised in that place. The Captain General confirms that he has used St Malo to harbour his ship from time-to-time. You, on the other hand, William, are a London scholar with no interest in trading, fighting or capturing ships. No one would suspect other than you deliver a message from her son in Greenwich to the Lady Katherine out of kindness and consideration.'

It seems I have no choice. I cannot refuse to assist in a matter which is tightly bound to our state's security and the fate of the great adventure. I murmur my assent. The others quickly straighten their backs and pull seats close to the table, eager to explain the arrangements.

I am to go in a small ship mastered by Pennes and our real intentions will be hidden by an excuse of trialling a slight modification to the instrument of navigation on a short sailing. There is much talk of the need to keep the matter hidden from general understanding and I am cautioned not to disclose the aim of our travel to anyone. There is more: I must take my horse as the Fitzmaurice house is some distance from the port; I should take my sword; Gilbert hands me a scrap of paper as the token for the lady; we will sail at dawn.

I depart with my senses in a whirl. Hawkins' final reassurance that Pennes can be relied on to assist if I should encounter trouble adds to, rather than soothes, my fears. Unasked questions surface from muddled thoughts as I journey back to my lodgings. What manner of woman is Fitzmaurice's wife? How do I address her? Will Fitzmaurice himself be there? Will our ship be welcomed into St Malo and will we encounter hostility in that place of pirates and brigands? And then there is Helen. She will wonder why I have chosen this time to be absent from her welcome into Plymouth. A short delay in our togetherness is a trifling matter set against the security of this country, but it rankles. I will write short notes to Oliver and Charles explaining that I cannot avoid a duty with the navigation instrument and request that they welcome her on my behalf and beg my forgiveness.

Fifteen

Uneven tips of grey crawl to edge the sea horizon as I reach the quays. I am not an early riser and it is a mild surprise to note there is already some activity on the ships, quayside and storehouses. I dismount and lead my horse to the far end of the quay where I am told a carrack, named *The Griffin*, waits. A lantern is lit ahead and I see that Wynter, Hawkins and Pennes are huddled there in conversation.

'God's blessing to you all on this new morning. I trust we are set fair for an easy passage?'

Hawkins and Pennes return a muted greeting, while Wynter is more welcoming in his tone. 'Ah, William, you are near set to sail. We have removed all but two demi-canons and two culverins from the ship to show we have no aggressive intent to the harbour guards there. If the wind remains fair you will be dining at St Malo on the morrow.'

A man takes my horse and leads it with some urging across wide planking and on to the deck. *The Griffin* is one of the smallest ships in our fleet and I must hope for a light swell so it does not bounce and dip overmuch to upset my belly. Wynter puts a hand on my shoulder and leads me away a few paces for a private conversation.

'I sense you are discomfited with this undertaking, William, but have full confidence in your abilities and open-mindedness. I know you have a keen interest in ensuring the timely departure of the great adventure, but that you also have faith in Wicken's intelligence and care deeply for Her Majesty's security. Your inclinations will be finely-balanced.'

'You have seen through me, Sir William. I am uneasy with the responsibility you have laid on me, but… I will endeavour to repay your confidence.'

'I am aware that there can be no certainty in this expedition and you may find no intelligence of value. However, it must be tried to satisfy the misgivings of the Captain General and Sir Humphrey. Here – will you take this for your personal protection?'

He hands me an object crafted in wood and metal, about a foot in length, with intricate design. It takes me a few moments to recognise it as a hand-held firearm.

'Thank you, Sir William, but no, I have never used a weapon such as this. It would offer more danger to me than an assailant.' This act of kindness has deepened my unease and I return it to his keeping.

*

We are underway and once we have left the confines of the harbour our progress is fair with a helping tide and light wind from the north-west. I have brought only a small satchel with no books or other diversions to pass the time and, after a couple of hours on deck, resolve to recover my rest from the last night. I am directed to a small door on the quarter deck. It opens on to a narrow corridor with openings to each side where the spaces are stuffed with crates, carpenter's tools and bales of cloth. At the far end are two open bays with small cots. I had anticipated a cramped area, but this is too small. It must do. I remove my sword, boots and outer wear and lay down with my knees raised. I have no great hope that sleep will come, but the gentle rolling of the ship and my tiredness may overcome discomfort and offer a short relaxation.

There is a loud banging in my head and I am woken rudely as my body lurches to the side of the cot. I push against a wooden support to stop a fall. My head is sore… tender to touch. It must have hit the side of the cot frame. The ship pitches and crashes against a wave. It seems the sea has taken on a more vigorous aspect. How long have I slept? I pull on my boots and return to the main deck. Ducking my head through the door, my first view is a blue sky, patched with small feathery tufts of white. Pennes is standing near the main mast.

'What is the hour? I slept longer than intended.'

''Tis no matter, Doctor. There is naught for you to do here. Your work will begin when we are on firm ground.' He looks up at the sky. 'It will be past three bells.'

I lean against a barrel as the ship rolls. The swell is heavier, but the ship rides them well. 'Do we make good speed?'

'We are close to five knots. The wind carries us east and it will be slower progress when we make a correction. If the weather holds we should sight the coast early this next morning.'

He is warmer in his conversation than in our previous encounter on the road to Dartmouth. Perhaps he has been instructed to show more courtesy and openness as we are confederates on this important mission. He takes the eye with the sun glinting on his dark, bald pate; a formidable fellow, well-muscled and with good breadth to match his height. It is unusual to find a dark man from Maroc in a position of high status and with heavy responsibility, but his men are compliant and few would dare question his authority.

'What style of town is St Malo? It is said to be the haunt of corsairs who ignore the laws of the French kingdom and act as an independent state.'

He eyes me from head to toe as if considering if I am worthy of a full answer. 'It is a wealthy town and well-guarded. The French and Breton authorities have learned to keep their distance from the affairs there to fill their coffers and avoid a bloody nose. It is not certain we can tie up there. They will want gold and also to be sure of our harmless intentions.' He shouts commands at a group of men on the deck. I do not understand his words, but they scurry up to the yards on the foremast to do his bidding. 'It is a dangerous place. You must take care when you ride back from the Fitzmaurice house.'

*

The sun nears its peak and we are in the eleventh hour, anchored in the lea of a headland while Pennes is rowed to the quay in a small boat. The first sight of St Malo is an impressive one. A fortress with many guns stands at the entrance to the harbour and the walled town, which appears to be surrounded by sea, save for one narrow causeway. To my untrained eye, it presents a more formidable aspect to an assailant than either

Plymouth or Dartmouth.

The interval since Pennes' departure is over two hours, suggesting he has difficulty in obtaining a permit for our mooring and entry into the town. My attitude sways one way, then the other. A denial of entry would halt our plan, see our quick return to Plymouth and the likely abandonment of the great adventure, that once excited, but now I would willingly forego. I would be reunited with Helen and would be absolved from any blame in failure to uncover further intelligence. With so much in favour on one side, why do I feel a sense of disappointment that our plan in St Malo may be scuppered? Is it the knowledge that my future father-in-law, Sir George, will be crushed by the humiliating collapse of his venture, so loudly trumpeted to those in high office? His standing and finances would suffer gravely. Or is it an eagerness to confirm the veracity of Charles' intelligence and aid in our vital preparations to foil the cruel threat to our nation's security? Well, it seems as though I will soon know in which direction I should set my resolve; Pennes' boat returns.

I stand ready as he levers himself over the side.

'We can secure this ship in the harbour,' he says to me briefly, then turns to his crew and gives commands and signals on their readying and handling into our place on the quays.

'Are we free to go about our business here?'

'We have papers that allow our stay for this night and no more. We must be gone from this place before midnight on the morrow.'

That leaves meagre time for my visit to the Fitzmaurice house. His wife may not be there and if she is at home, there will be little scope for becoming gently familiar and subtle questioning.

'What reason did you offer for our call into the port?'

'Our real purpose – that you are solicitous in your desire to bring news and comfort to Lady Fitzmaurice from her eldest son. It seems the lady is well-liked here.' He grunts in his throat and bares his teeth, in what may be an attempt at humour. 'They would not believe a tale spun about a passing fancy to taste local wine and sample their whores.'

'Will I be unhindered in my short journey from town to the

lady?'

'You have a letter of passage from the commander's office.' He brandishes a roll of paper. 'Let us hope that our business proves worthy of the gold I have paid for our brief adjournment here.'

The quays are busy with at least twenty large ships and many smaller boats leaving scant space for our vessel or other arrivals. Our manoeuvring takes some time with two row boats guiding us to our station on the quay. We have a crew of thirty or so men. Pennes selects half to disembark with a promise to the others they will have their turn in the whorehouses and inns in good time. There is a final severe warning that they will be careful with drink, keep their senses and listen for gossip on Stukley and Sanders. They are obedient and meek in their acceptance of his orders; no doubt they understand the consequences if he is crossed.

The entrance to the walled town is through a bar with well-guarded archway. Pennes shows our papers and we are ushered into town of St Malo. I had imagined a narrow network of lanes, edged with dark corners and filled with a throng of sly cutpurses, brazen whores, drunken pirates and their masters flaunting their wealth in gaudy dress. My expectations are confounded with well-ordered, wide streets, fine houses and a steady mingling of gentlefolk, yeomen and goodwives conducting their everyday affairs.

The men leave us and Pennes guides me to an inn close by the bar I will exit for my short ride to the house. My horse is led away to the rear while we enter into a dark, but well-kept and roomy interior filled with the smell of roast meats and the hum of patrons taking their ease. We take stools at the end of a long bench table and Pennes beckons to a serving maid. He does not ask my fancy but orders a jug of ale and two cups with cold meats and pickles.

He shuffles on his stool and plays with rings on his fingers as though he is searching for words to stiffen my resolve for the task ahead.

He says in low voice, 'I will see you to the bar, but then you must travel alone to the house. My appearance as a fighting man may disturb those in the Fitzmaurice house and your approach should be soft. You will take the causeway to the east and then follow the coast path for some three miles. I do not know the house, but have heard it stands alone in fair acreage, is built over two storeys and has an aspect to the sea.'

It is strange, but now we are here he appears more fretful than I. This is a man I could never imagine suffering from a nervous disposition, but perhaps it is this place that holds particular fears in his mind.

'You have been here before. Do you know the lady?'

'My time in this town was short and some years past; before Fitzmaurice planted his family here. A short account from the harbour guard suggests that she is admired for her fair face and has a well-trodden path of visitors to her house.'

Our food and drink are placed on the table and our conversation becomes a series of short exchanges between mouthfuls. He emphasises that I must return in good time for our return sailing the next night. He will lodge in this inn and wait for me here. Finally, he hands the letter of passage and wishes me good fortune. I leave him at the table, take my horse and lead him through the east bar on to the causeway. Pennes has served his part well, thus far. Perhaps I have misjudged him and there is more to his character than simply a hard brute of a man with low sensibilities. His close presence in this place was reassuring and I have a sense of frailty without his company as I plod the path to Lady Fitzmaurice.

The short journey is uneventful. There is a steady flow of carts, horses and foot travellers on the causeway, which thins as I branch on to the coast road. My first view of the house is a homely one. There is a small lake at the front and a group of children are dabbling and splashing watched by a maid and a working man who leans on his staff. I ride up, bid them good day and announce that I wish to call on the lady. The children stop and stare, while the man takes my horse and the maid hurries ahead to the front door. The house is built of rose-coloured stone with high-peaked roof in the French style and an old round, whitewashed turret to one side. It is well-tended and speaks of modest wealth. The maid ushers me inside and bids me wait in a small hallway. A short and heavily-bearded man appears and declares he is named Vaisy, the intendant or steward of the house.

'Good day to you Master Vaisy. I am Doctor William Constable come from England to pay my respects and with a message for the Lady Fitzmaurice.'

He fixes his eye on my sword and says that he will take it for safekeeping. I am led into another chamber where he waves a hand at a seat by a table and requests that I should wait. It is a middle-sized room with no furnishings save the table, two seats and a large, faded tapestry with an industrious presentation of a harbour, which I take to be St Malo. I sit quietly, close my eyes and rehearse what I intend to say to the lady. Images of Helen intrude. In my mind, I can see her arrival at Plymouth where her expression changes from keen expectation to confounded disappointment as Oliver and Charles explain away my absence. She will forgive me, in time. Vaisy appears.

'My Lady begs your patience, Doctor Constable. She is resting with a light fever but has requested you join her for supper.'

I thank him for the invitation. He turns, clicks his fingers and a maid appears with a tray containing a bottle and delicate wine glass. It is a small thing, but I wonder if the glass has been offered in place of a cup, as a statement of her standing.

It is near two hours before a maid enters and bids me through to supper. The dining chamber is light with a high ceiling, centred with a carpeted table set with an array of silver: candlesticks; goblets; platters; and knives. Two places are set, but I am alone. I stand by a chair, flexing my shoulders and legs as I wait to be joined by the lady. The door is opened by a maid and she enters. A striking figure in deep green velvet gown trimmed with fur, her face is framed with dark hair worn under a black laced French hood and white coif. I doff my cap and bow low.

'Lady, I am Doctor William Constable from London. My thanks for this gracious welcome into your household. I trust your fever has calmed.'

She is still and gazes at me directly for a moment before

taking the seat held by her maid. She nods her head to indicate I should sit at a place to her right side.

'Doctor Constable, I have not heard your name. You are a physician?'

'Yes Lady, I practice physic at my house in West Cheap. Do you know London?'

She shakes her head. 'I have not visited that town, but I understand it is some distance and you have taken a deal of trouble for an unplanned visit to this place.'

'You are right, Lady, I should have explained that I am lodged in Plymouth town at present. I have designed a small instrument for the navigation of ships, which is being tested there.'

'Ah, I dislike sea travel. It is my husband who has an interest in ships, but he is not here.'

She is guarded in her conversation. I must be careful. As she lowers her eyes, I steal a glance at her face. Uncommonly lovely; she has fine features with smooth, pale skin and a slight blush on her cheeks. She has carried her children well, for she has the look of a woman in her early twenties.

'The message I have is for you, Lady.'

'You have a message? Is it from an Italian tailor with news of a new fashion in gowns or a London goldsmith with an offer of a jewelled brooch?'

She has a delight in teasing and her eyes spark with mischief as she will know what I carry.

'It is from your son, Maurice, in the care of Sir John Bold.'

'Ah, Sir John, I wonder how a man of his years has the vitality to care for so many sprightly young gentlemen. Is he still troubled by his gouty foot?'

'I am not acquainted with Sir John, Lady. The token was given to me by Sir Humphrey Gilbert in Dartmouth. He regrets his business with trade prevents him from delivering this token himself.'

She puffs air as a sign of distaste at his name. 'That man is not welcome in my house, as he knows. He has sent you as his tame kitten to avoid my displeasure.'

'I understand why you mislike him. He is no favourite of mine and I am not his puppet.'

The force of my words startle her and she eyes me with a fresh look.

'Indeed, you will forgive my rudeness, but mention of his name stirs my temper.'

Two maids enter with our dishes and a bottle of wine. We are served with a fish soup, soft biscuits and a honey-coloured wine. She clasps her hands, mutters a brief thanksgiving, crosses herself and raises her glass to mine. Our conversation is stilled as we sup slowly. The wine is good if a little sharp.

I say, 'You have a fine family of children, Lady. I spied their playful games in the lake at your frontage.'

'Thank you, Doctor, but they are not all mine. I have two sons and a daughter here, while you know my eldest is at Greenwich with Sir John.'

'And your husband, the Lord Fitzmaurice, do his affairs allow him intervals for relaxation in this delightful house?'

She pauses, puts down her spoon and is quiet for some moments before replying simply, 'He is here from time-to-time.'

Our bowls are taken and replaced by silver plates on which a steaming meat pudding is served.

'Tell me about yourself, Doctor. Are you married?'

'I am betrothed, Lady, to the daughter of Sir George Morton, who trades in wine and cloth from the London quays.'

'She is a fortunate lady. You have a pleasing face and vigorous aspect to your body.'

Her directness is a surprise and I can only mutter my thanks for the compliment. I must hope that she does not flirt with me for sport as I am ill-suited to such elaborate and pretty exchanges.

I say, 'Helen, my betrothed, has a keen interest in herbal medication and her learning has aided in the healing of some of my patients.'

She lifts an eyebrow and leans forward a little. 'I too have an interest in wellbeing promoted by herbal remedies and confess I own low opinion of near all physicians I have commissioned.' She sips her wine. 'Do you believe perhaps that the female sex is capable of men's learning and may one day practice physic?'

'I do, Lady. There have been ancient civilisations where female physicians were held in high regard. I do not hold to the belief that the intellect and temperament of women are inferior to men and therefore unsuited to the learned professions.'

'Hmm, it is a dangerous position, your views may be regarded as wicked and a denial of God's plan by some.'

'Only by those with closed minds. Do you stand ready to denounce me, Lady?'

She smiles, then continues with her pudding. I am mindful that there has been no opportunity to broach the subject of Stukley and Sanders thus far. She distracts me with her beauty and insightful words. Our conversation progresses on herbal remedies, her children and longing to return to her country of birth. As we are served with a sweet jelly, I am pricked with the thought that I have not offered her son's token. I delve into my satchel and hand her a roll of paper bound with yellow ribbons.

'My apologies, Lady, I had forgotten the purpose of my visit here. This is from your son, Maurice.'

She takes it from my hand and dabs her lips gently with a napkin; unties the paper and smooths the roll on the table. The chamber is stilled as she reads. I am near enough to catch the sound of her breathing. She has reached the end – and reads again. Finally, she rolls up the paper and ties the ribbons.

'It is a poem in the Goidelic language of Ireland. I am...'

She rises quickly from her seat, announces that fatigue has overtaken her and will retire. At the door she turns and says, 'You will stay this night, Doctor Constable. A maid will show you the chamber that has been prepared.'

Perhaps I should have anticipated that the token from her eldest would affect her so. I am no further forward in my investigation into the threat of invasion. With only a few hours this next day to complete my task, I will have to be more straightforward in our exchanges if I am to extract any worthwhile intelligence.

Sixteen

It is a warm night and I throw off all the bed linens save one. I am restless, sweating freely and may have been too generous with my pouring of wine after the lady left our table. My thoughts swing in confused manner from my attack in the wooded valley, Charles and the killing, the trial, arrival of Wynter and my consultations with Hawkins and Gilbert. It is a wonder how all those events led to this place and supper with Lady Fitzmaurice. I rise to relieve myself in the piss pot, then step to an open window searching for a cooling breeze. At last, I am calmed and heavy perspiring has lessened. I lie in the bed, close my eyes and summon images of Helen. I will be with you soon, my sweet.

A dream.

A movement.

Helen is here.

She slides under the flimsy sheet… soft and slow… playful… teasing.

I shiver at her touch… a gentle press of naked flesh… she toys with my hardness…

Naked breasts brush my skin as she climbs me…

A kiss.

Her scent… is…

Ah! This is no dream…

Not Helen.

She is on me… mounted.

I am… inside her.

Cannot stop… her urging… moaning... it is… her…

Forgive me… I must…

Finally, I am spent. Her swaying subsides; she gasps and flops beside me.

Our breathing is loud in the still grey of the night. What should I do? Surely she will slip away without comment. I will be requested to leave in the morning and without further meeting. I have failed my mission here. This interval is too long

– too quiet.

'My Lady, that was - unexpected.'

'You must call me Katherine, William. We have enjoyed each other and should be familiar in these private moments.'

Our voices are cushioned in the heavy air between us – so different from our clacking in the dining chamber. I can find no words and stare into the canopy above. There is movement. I sense she levers on an elbow and cups her chin. I dare not return her gaze.

'What is the true reason for your visit here, William?'

'It is… the token from your son, Maurice.'

'You are not sly enough to lie with conviction, even when darkness hides the twitching on your face.'

There is only a small hesitation before I say, 'I am here to enquire into the intentions of Thomas Stukley and Nicholas Sanders, who I understand have dealings with your husband.'

'Hah, so Walsingham is behind this. Now that I could believe if you were here some months ago, but you must know Stukley is now dead.'

'There is an opinion that news of his death was a lie to cover up his present activities.'

She lays her head on my chest. My arm has a mind of its own and folds around her naked back.

'Stukley is indeed dead. It is certain.'

'What is the basis for your certainty - Katherine?'

'Mmm, your discomfort eases, William. There can be no shame in our coupling. No one will know of our small delight unless you choose to tell Helen.'

My belly lurches at mention of her name. I slowly untangle my limbs and rise from the bed, saying I must piss. Decency and thoughts of Helen mean I should dress and end this intimacy. But is there more to learn? I return to the bed and lie on my side facing her shape.

'My husband and Sanders were here at the turn of the year. They had spoken to men who witnessed the scene of his death from a large gun.'

'Thank you for your openness, Katherine.'

'Why is there an urgency to know of Stukley and Sanders in

England? Stukley was a vain and stupid man, while Sanders is full of hot air and boasting of his high friendships with papal legates. Neither my Lord nor I would have chosen them as confederates, but…' Her voice trails away, she breathes deeply and then turns to lie on her back. 'And Sanders is an unnatural man?'

'Unnatural?'

'He professes to be a holy man, devoted to Rome, but with a fondness for young boys.'

'You are uncommonly direct and honest in your assessments.'

'Why should I not be? England has naught to fear from my husband. His quarrel is with Earl Desmond in Munster; it was Stukley who bragged about designs on the English state and flung insults at your queen. My Lord has pledged fealty to Queen Elizabeth and England was never in our planning. Stukley was a fool we led by the nose because his swaggering and loud noise was listened to by some in Castile and Lisbon.' She turns and kisses me lightly on the lips. 'You believe me, William?'

'I do, Katherine.' My response is near the truth. I cannot detect any pretence or evasion in her words. 'Tell me, do you have a close concern with your husband's affairs?'

'Ha, you mean do I stand in dark corners to scheme with him and his associates. I share his yearning to return to Ireland, but I have long since given up any attempt to influence the thinking of such men. I despair at their dithering and inaction.' She twirls a finger around the hairs on my chest. 'You will understand from my presence in your bed, that I am no longer enamoured by my husband.'

Her fingers move from my chest down to my belly. I grab her hand before it reaches its intention. She is still for a moment, then leaves the bed and moves towards the window. Her figure is outlined against the pale light as she twists and wriggles into a nightshift.

'It seems that the wisdom of Walsingham's intelligencers is not to be feared as the common supposition holds. There was another in his employ who came to consult with my Lord about Stukley in the month of February.'

'Do you know the name of that man, Katherine?'

'He was a common, fierce and ugly man. I did not wish to be close to him. He was called Black… or Hack.'

'Was it Stack?'

'Yes, that was the name – Stack.'

*

I am at breakfast, my head in a whirl and thoughts running too fast to catch and hold for examination of logic and veracity. A maid comes and goes, but I am alone in the dining chamber. I have heard voices of children and others, but none have entered and joined me. There is no sign of Katherine. Any sense of shame from the night's pleasure is outweighed by the significance of Katherine's disclosure about Stukley – and Stack. If she is to be relied on, then there is no imminent threat of invasion to our West Country ports. Stack will have known this unless Fitzmaurice fed him with false intelligence. But there would be no reason to lie if there was never any design on an incursion to England by Fitzmaurice and Sanders. Indeed, England appears too grand an objective set against a small difficulty in an Irish earldom. And what of Charles? There is no doubt he acts for Walsingham, but is his story an elaborate fabrication? And to what end? Was it a ploy to try and secure a reprieve from hanging, or some other purpose? Can I have read that man, my friend, so wrong?

And Helen. My love for her is undimmed by the romp with Katherine. I am no saint and have lain with many women, but never one so high-born. There is an untidy scratch on the promise I set myself that Helen will be my one and only love from the date of our betrothal. This will fade in time and she will not know. Would she forgive me if she was to learn by some devious means? Perhaps I am more troubled by this than I care to admit. My musings are interrupted as the door opens. It is Vaisy, the steward.

'Good day to you, Doctor Constable. I am to inform you that my lady is away from the house this morning and requests that you meet with her in the parlour in the third hour after noon.'

'Good day Master Vaisy and thank you for the message. Does Lady Katherine travel far?'

He ignores my question and says, 'My lady has suggested that you may wish to examine the collection of books in the library during this interval.'

'Yes, that will be agreeable.' He bows his head stiffly and turns. 'Master Vaisy, may I pose a question?'

'What is it, Doctor?'

'In the month of February do you recall a visitor to this house from England?'

'We have many visitors. Was this a particular person?'

'The man I have in mind is of middling rank; a ship's master and grim-faced fighting man; of my height, but broader. He may have consulted with your lord and a holy man.'

He hesitates; shuffles his feet. 'I... I cannot say. Your description is imprecise.'

'Does the name Stack help?'

'No – there was no man with that name.'

His answer is quick – too quick. He leaves without further word. I may have been intemperate with my direct asking, but it served its purpose. I do not believe him. There was recognition in his face when I spoke that name.

*

I found only one book of interest in the library. I have read the *Grete Herbal* before, but it made the adjournment a little more bearable. I am impatient for my return to the town of St Malo and our journey back to Plymouth. The intelligence I have gathered must be relayed to Wynter promptly. The third hour is almost over and still there is no sign of Katherine.

At last, she has returned. I hear her voice in the corridor.

'Ah, Doctor Constable, I am sorry for my absence.'

''Tis no matter, Lady Katherine, I am grateful for access given to your library.'

We are returned to more formal relations and I note her manner is a little strained.

'I had hoped for another conversation about your practice of physic and herbal medication, but find I am weary and must rest.'

'In that case, I regret I must make immediate arrangements to return to Plymouth. I thank you for warm hospitality in your house, Lady.'

'My thanks in return for the token from Maurice. It has been interesting, Doctor, and as you say... unexpected.'

There is no further acknowledgement or backward glance as she exits the chamber. Was something amiss? Or was it simply awkwardness and guilt following our intimate night entertainment? Whatever the cause, this has been an unwelcome delay and I should make haste for the harbour and our short sea passage.

*

I dismount in front of the bar to the town, walk to the guards and hand over my letter of passage. He examines it and shows it to another guard who nods in recognition.

He says, 'You will surrender your horse and sword here, then I will escort you to your place in the town.'

'Why is that necessary? The letter is from the Commander's office.'

'It is the Commander who has given our orders. If you do not comply easily, we will be more direct with force of arms.'

What has led to this change in our circumstances? Has the crew been unruly; with fighting; a killing? Whatever the cause, it is bothersome and must hope that any postponement in our sailing is a short one. The guard escorts me to the inn where I took my leave of Pennes. The door is open; he shoves me roughly on the shoulder and I am inside. I turn to protest, but he has already marched away. There are many in here and it takes some time before I spy Pennes seated on a stool, hunched over a cup at a corner table. He raises his eyes in recognition as I approach and he pulls out a stool for me to join him.

'What has transpired in this place? My sword and horse have been taken.'

He shrugs. 'It is not clear. We are confined here. The ship is close-guarded and our men held below deck. All arms have been confiscated, save small daggers.'

'Confined; held; to what end?'

'A body of men came around midday. They had orders from the Commander for our detention under suspicion of fermenting religious discontent.'

'Discontent – why that is absurd. It must be a pretext for some other intention. I had thought that this place enjoyed independence from holy laws and politicking in France.'

'Even so, they will not wish to cross the zealots who hunt for those seeking to overturn the old faith. A papal emissary comes from the church at Dol to question us on the morrow.'

I had expected some danger on this mission but thought this may have come from hard men with daggers and swords, not a dispute over religion. Wait – my thinking is jolted in another direction. Does the source of our predicament lie at the Fitzmaurice house? Katherine was absent this morning. Or was it Vaisy? But Katherine's information was given freely. Was the naming of Stack behind this?

I say, 'Do you have a chamber here?'

'No longer,' he hesitates and adds, 'though we could hire a nook for a private supper.'

It is early to eat, but we should have a retreat where we can talk openly. We are taken to a small, panelled recess at the back that will serve. I order wine and request the maid brings us a steamed fish.

When she is gone, I say, 'Is there a way we can take back the ship and sail under cover of night?'

'No, it is well-guarded and the men are locked away.' He shakes his head. 'And with that small chance, we would be noticed before we made open sea and we cannot outrun their bigger ships.'

'We are not guarded here.'

'Because there is nowhere we can go.'

'So, you consider we must wait for questioning? We may be taken from here and detained elsewhere.'

'They will find no extreme religion in our number – unless you...'

'No, it is a ruse. There is some other influence at work here.'

He narrows his eyes. 'What have you uncovered at the Fitzmaurice house?'

'I believe there is no danger to our ports from Stukley.'

'Walsingham's intelligence was mistaken?'

'Yes, it is near certain.'

'Then why…'

'I judge that we are to be put out of the way so that our news will not reach Devonshire.'

'Who directs this scheming?'

'I have no ready answer for that.' I do not voice my opinion that we are in mortal danger, but he may surmise this from my urgent tone.

We are served the wine and a heavy quiet settles as we sup.

He places both hands on the table and says, 'So, we must be gone this night.'

I bow my head and can think of no other response. We cannot take our ship. We have no arms to fight. We cannot flee inland. 'Could we take a small boat; the two of us; under cover of dark?'

'Our ship is guarded. We could not…'

'Another boat; not from our ship; a small fishing boat perhaps.'

I see an idea take hold in him. 'An oared boat would be difficult to detect, but… two men…'

'There is a large number of small boats on the little quays, away from the ships.'

'There may be a way.'

Our fish is served with a long bread that has a scent of nutmeg. What have I said? Only now does imagining bring substance to my words. Two men taking an oared boat across the Narrow Sea would be foolhardy in the extreme. We would be easy prey to chasing ships, or we would drown. Do I have a preference for drowning against other means of death? No, my words were spoken too hastily. We must find another way.

After a long silence, he says, 'It may be done. It is a heavy risk that must be taken.'

'But, how many days to row? It would not be safe. There will be guards.'

'Small boats will not be well-tended and guards may be persuaded by gold or my dagger. You have it, Doctor. We must set our minds to it in the hour up to midnight. That will offer enough hours of darkness to row into open sea.'

Seventeen

The hour has arrived and a steady, light rain has set, which Pennes welcomes as a help to our discretion. We are unhindered in our departure from the inn and make our way to the quays, both of us carrying a skin of wine on a shoulder. The gate is manned by two guards and I hold back as Pennes confers with them. Our tale is that we carry wine for the crew detained on our ship. If we are allowed passage it will require coin, maybe gold. He turns and beckons me to follow. We stroll, as if untroubled, past the ships and towards the place where small boats are berthed. A drunken fellow, propped against a wall mutters a strew of meaningless curses as we make our way to the far end of the quay where it is darkest. We are not alone – a lantern sways thirty paces on as a man clambers from his boat. As we near, Pennes calls a greeting, as might a friend, and holds his arms ready to embrace. It is quick and quietly done - a dagger under the man's ribs. After a brief trembling, he flops and Pennes lifts him on his shoulder. He hands me his wineskin, takes a rope and scrambles down the wall into the boat. He hisses a command for me to follow and bring the lantern. We are in. It is small – shorter than the length of three men with places for four sets of oars.

'Untie the rope. I will row quietly 'til we are away from the harbour.'

The rain is heavier now. It may aid our escape but makes the rope like iron and it takes many moments before my frantic fingers work it loose. He takes the lantern and dips it in the water to douse the flame. All is black – a stinging, wet black. I am at the stern facing Pennes with the body between us and there is a gentle rocking. I close my eyes to picture Helen and pray to God for our deliverance from this peril and my welcome into her embrace. We are moving – slowly.

Pennes has warned that there will be a chain across the boom towers at the harbour entrance. A small boat could pass through the centre, but we must take care not to become entangled. I see small, twinkling lights by the town walls to my left side, but there are no guiding lanterns on the quays. I blink and wipe my eyes against a sleeve; catch a faint grey edge of cloud in the darkness. A dark shape looms. I lean forward and touch Penne's arm so that he should steer away. 'More', I say; my voice strident; seemingly disembodied and distant. Will I be heard? There. I spy a gap ahead. We are too close to one side. I reach to tap his other arm; my knees pressed on to the soft, dampness of the unfortunate fisherman.

My teeth are clenched tight; my legs and shoulders braced for scraping against the barrier; or a shout from the harbour walls. Our motion has changed. We are through.

'Take the oars, now.' His voice is hoarse; urgent.

'The body?'

'Later - when we are away.'

I scramble over the body, shift it to the stern, take my place on the bench next to Pennes and set the oars. I try to match his calls of, 'Dip,' and 'Pull,' but am clumsy and it takes some time before I find a rhythm to the strokes. We are together now. I have a sense that our progress is good, but the lights of the town appear no further distant.

What will become of the crew we have left behind?

Dare I begin to believe we could make good this escape?

Dip and pull.

...

The body is tipped over the side. We are lighter; the swell higher. My shoulders burn.

...

'Rest.' His voice cuts sharp through a mist; a dream. 'A wineskin.' I remove the stopper, drink a little and reach behind for Pennes.

The rain has eased and growing wisps of moonlit sky testify to clouds dispersing.

'How far?'

'Huh,' he grunts, 'not far enough.'

We take up oars again.

...

'Stop... must stop.'

132

I am gasping. My body is on fire; shoulders; back; thighs. There is a pale blush in the sky to my left side. We are in open sea with no sight of land.

'Here.' He hands me the wineskin. My arm trembles; hands blistered.

'Your hurt will fade,' he says. 'Fill your thoughts with pleasant things – a woman; roasted pig; a past triumph.'

...

Daylight. How long?

I am in my bed at West Cheap. Helen sleeps by my side. If only...

Wet. How am I wet?

I hear a curious rumbling, deep within my chest. I am talking. Another man is near. He tells me to tear my shirt and wrap my hands.

...

I have been asleep; my neck angled against something hard. I wince and pant air, struggling to rise. The boat... and Pennes is here. I have been lying with my head pressed against the back of the boat. Pennes has his bald scalp facing me, drooped over folded arms. He dozes. I straighten and gaze around. The sea has calmed and the sun is setting in a coloured sky. I look down and see two hands in bloody, tattered rags. Mine? My feet are numb. It is as if body parts are not joined to my senses. I feel pain and cold.

My head has cleared. It is a mixed blessing, for although I recall our actions and purpose in taking this boat, the agonies in my body are heightened. I drink from the wineskin, then take my place at the oars and start to row. We still head north and put distance from St Malo as the sun sets to my right side. Our toil thus far has not been wasted.

The sun is almost gone. Pennes stirs behind me and begins to row.

I say, 'We have near twenty-four hours behind us. Can you hazard the distance we have travelled?'

'Less than fifty and more than twenty.'

'How is our heading?'

He grunts a word lost in the effort of pulling. Our route to

Devonshire will waver markedly from a direct line in this boat. If he is right and his numbers are sea miles, then we face between four and eleven more days at sea. Will we survive?

...

A new day is on us and the sky promises fair weather. We have alternated short rests in our pulling during the night and agonies have subsided to a dull ache. The swell is light and our progress steady. Pennes stops for another mouthful of wine. He stands, unsteadily at first, shades his eyes and gazes around. He adjusts his stance and mutters some words.

'Do you see anything? A ship?'

'Land.'

It will not be England. Have we drifted back to France? I rise from the bench, waiting until we crest the swell before straightening to my full height. There is a grey smudge on the horizon, dead ahead. It is small – an island or headland, perhaps. He signals that we should resume our rowing and I hold further questions until we are nearer.

We are close enough to see jagged grey cliffs edged with uneven lines of green and flecks of white. It has the look of an island, although there is more land to the east – another island, or mainland France?

'Do you know this place?'

'I cannot be certain. We must row to the east and be wary of rocks.'

Another hour or more passes; we have rowed to the eastern tip of the south coast and turn north. We have seen two fishing boats heading south and a larger ship heading north-west, but we are too small to be seen.

He rests his oars and says, 'It will be the Isle of St Peter Port, that is called Guernsey.' He taps me on the shoulder. 'There is a strand in that cove.' He points to a thin line of pale yellow at the foot of a break in the cliffs.

'Who rules here and will we be welcome?'

'It is Her Majesty's, but with free license.'

What does that signify, I wonder? I have heard the name but know naught of its character. Well, we have little choice. We must set down here, trust that we are well-received and offered assistance for our onward travel to Plymouth.

We beach the boat and clamber over the side. My legs fail me and I crawl on hands and knees away from the tide to lay flat on the wet sand. I close my eyes and offer silent thanksgiving for our return to solid earth. Pennes is sat by my side with knees raised and head bowed. It is peaceful, with a warming sun and the lulling of breaking waves, but… I should not sleep.

How long have we been here? We have moved past a ribbon of shingle on to dry sand and continued with our rest. Pennes is asleep. I lean over – he wakes with a start and grabs my outstretched hand - 'Ahh!' It is tender. He loosens his grip but makes no apology. I stare at my hands and slowly unwrap the blackened and bloody rags that were once my shirt. I rise on unsteady legs and survey the scene around us. We are alone, but there is a small barn or house at the top of the cliff. I stagger to a small pool of seawater in the shingle and rinse my hands. It is time to plan the next step in our escape.

'You mentioned St Peter Port, Master Pennes. Will there be ships at this port bound for Plymouth or Dartmouth? We should try to negotiate our passage.'

He grunts and considers for some moments before replying. 'There will be a handful of trading ships, but whether we can persuade one to sail to our ports is uncertain.'

'Do you have gold remaining?'

'A little; most was given in St Malo.' There is a hesitancy in his manner as though troubled by the thought of coming difficulties.

'Come then, we will make for the port and trust we find a sympathetic hearing.'

'I am known here.'

'Known, how?'

'I was there in 'seventy-two and crossed a man named Leighton. He was the Governor then and may be still. My ship was falsely accused of piracy. Men were sent to take me and three were slain. I will not have been easily forgotten.'

This presents an unwelcome obstacle. It will be impossible to conceal the presence of a man like Pennes. I have encountered a few sailors from Maroc, but none with his size and fearsome appearance.

'What manner of man is Leighton? Can his past hostility be converted by arguments of loyalty, influence or coin?'

'I think not. He has a haughty air with fixed views. He was not liked by the Bailiff, Guillaume Beauvoir, who has a more balanced humour. But... he was an older man and may not be here.'

'Well, we must take care in our approach and hope that we can secure a passage without troubling either of those gentlemen.'

'The quays are likely well-guarded and we will be fortunate in the extreme to avoid their attention. It is a small isle where confidences are not easily kept close.'

My spirits are dampened by his words. Our time in the boat has given us a bedraggled and unkempt appearance. Will our story be believed, or will we be assessed as a pair of cutthroats, vagrants or brigands from a sunken pirate ship? Whatever we encounter, we must be bold. We will try the Bailiff.

It takes no more than a half-hour before we sight the port. It is a substantial harbour for a small isle, with a large fortress guarding the entrance on a long, thin spit of land. There are five ships among a number of small boats sheltered there. The few people we have encountered on our brief walk here have eyed us with suspicion, stood back and stared at our progress. It seems we are already tainted with the mark of unsightly strangers.

We are into the town making for the Bailiff's house, which Pennes informs is near to the church. We march with purpose up to the front door and I tap the heel of my dagger on the nameplate. A maid answers. I announce my name and state that we wish to attend the Bailiff on urgent business. She peers at us closely as though her eyesight is poor, then opens the door and bids we remain in the hallway. She has been some time when the door opens and a bent old man enters, shuffling along with the aid of a stick. I must assume he is the Bailiff.

'Good day to you, Bailiff Beauvior, I am Doctor William Constable and this is my companion Master Pennes.'

He studies us in silence for a few moments. 'Hmm, Doctor,

you say. You have the look of a sailor – and one that has fallen on hard times.' He turns his gaze to Pennes. 'You are from Maroc?'

Pennes grunts confirmation.

'Bailiff, I beg that you excuse our uninvited call and the roughness in our appearance. We are on the Queen's business and have lately escaped the attentions of Her Majesty's enemies in France. We took an oared boat into the Narrow Sea and landed here by a stroke of good fortune. We are here to request your assistance.'

'Ha, you spin a tale fit to warm a midwinter hearth.' He hesitates then ushers us through the open door. We are offered stools at a small table and then he departs, murmuring that he will seek refreshment. He returns and joins us at the table.

He says, 'Now, you must fill some of the holes in your story. What is the nature of your business and under whose orders were you in France?'

'We are gathered in Plymouth and Dartmouth making ready for a great venture to the New Lands, with a fleet led by Captain General Hawkins and Sir Humphrey Gilbert.'

'Naturally, we have heard tell of this scheme by two renowned sailors and adventurers. And you, a doctor, intend to sail with this fleet?'

I see this will not be easy. He is distrustful and cannot be blamed for suspecting a wild tale from dishevelled strangers. Despite his age, he has a bright eye and keen mind. I must elaborate and convince with a full account, omitting only the finer details of the conspiracy. I beg his indulgence, then begin my narration from the time of my betrothal to Helen and acceptance of an invitation from her father, Sir George Morton, to sail with the fleet. I request that he holds all I will tell him in strict confidence. Beauvoir raises his eyes and considers a moment before giving his word. He crosses himself in the way of the old religion and quickly excuses this display through force of habit. He shows a particular interest at my invention of a navigation instrument and the sending of a message to Walsingham about the conspiracy. I do not mention Charles as the source of this intelligence.

The door opens. In place of the expected maid with refreshment, four soldierly men enter with swords unsheathed.

'Your story is interesting, Doctor, but we will continue without your companion, Master Pennes. There is an outstanding warrant for the arraignment of Jacques Pennes from Maroc on the killing of three men in this town. There cannot be many who will match the description and name of that brutal man. He will be detained under force of arms and his identity verified.'

I turn to Pennes, who has a moment of indecision before he submits with a shrug. Even he cannot overcome the odds set against him here.

'Bailiff Beauvoir, I beg you do not take him away from your house, yet. Please settle Master Pennes under guard in some other chamber while I finish my recounting.'

He looks to me and Pennes, consider for a moment and answers, 'Very well, chain and confine him to a stable in the yard. I trust that we will not be overlong in our conversation here.'

His last words are not encouraging. When we are alone I say, 'Might I beg the promised refreshment before continuing – a cup of ale or wine to ease a dry throat.'

My request is unexpected and I see I have pricked his sense of guilt at weak hospitality. He rises stiffly, shuffles to the door and calls for a maid. He returns and sits on his stool with a deep exhalation.

'Forgive my poor manners, Doctor. Pray, proceed with your account.'

'Sir William Wynter was despatched to Plymouth by Secretary Walsingham to investigate intelligence about a gathering of ships and men in Biscay. There is a concern that this may signal an imminent threat to our West Country ports.'

A maid enters with two cups and a jug of ale. Beauvoir pours into my cup and leaves his untouched. I drink quickly, refill, and drain to the last, savouring a freshness on my palate and renewed vigour seeping through mind and body.

'I was sent to a place in northern France in a ship with Master Pennes and his crew.'

'Why would a man from Maroc with the appearance of a savage fighting man be given charge of this ship?'

'He is the trusted Muster Master for Captain General Hawkins.'

He arches his eyebrows at my reply, then shakes his head while clicking his tongue. 'You say that your intelligence concerned Biscay, yet you sailed to northern France. You will understand my puzzlement at this contrary logic.'

'There was reason to believe that a source there could provide speedier confirmation or denial. If our mission failed, then Biscay would be the next objective.'

He places his stick between his legs, rests both his hands, then his chin on top and studies me closely. 'You have the manner of a scholar beneath a bare chest, crumpled doublet and soiled hose. Your wounded hands would also indicate soft living. But why would a scholar be entrusted with the dangerous work of an intelligencer? You must tell me more of your colourful background to convince you do not spew a fantasy as thick as cold pudding to hide some devious end. I must warn you that, even in this small island outpost, to profess a false connection to Her Majesty's security is treason and will be punished according to law.'

He means we will both likely suffer a hideous traitor's death if the circumstances of our predicament here are not accepted. I begin to think my direct appeal for his assistance was unwise. We should have been more circumspect and approached ships' masters with quiet promises of reward for a clandestine sailing. Well, it is too late now for regrets. I must sway his thinking.

'I have a fascination for the stars – both for physic and an understanding of our place on this earth in relation to their movement. Astrological divination will inform on the nature of human temperament and the application of physic to aid wellbeing. An accurate reading of heavenly bodies with a measuring instrument will aid navigation of ships that are distant from sighting land. My capability in these matters led to my involvement in the uncovering of a plot tied to an astrological natal chart for our queen and the great adventure to the New Lands. I was fortunate to receive commendation for assistance in this affair from Sir Francis Walsingham and Lord Burghley.'

'You know these great men?'

'It would be audacious to claim I am on intimate terms. Lord Burghley, I met only briefly, but I have worked closely with Sir Francis. It was Secretary Walsingham who offered my name to Sir William Wynter as one who could be trusted to assist with his intelligencing.'

'Ah, I have also had the good fortune to meet with Sir Francis; once in Paris when he was the Queen's Ambassador there; and a second time three years past at his house in Barn Elms. Perhaps you have visited Barn Elms?'

'Indeed, I have. Allow me to offer a brief description in confirmation.'

I describe the main features of the house at Barn Elms and for good measure Walsingham's town house on Seething Lane. Still, he holds an expression of doubt.

'You are familiar with some of Walsingham's associates?'

'Francis Mylles for one, and his captain named Askham, who I count as a friend.'

'Are there others of a lower standing?'

What can this signify? Does he require a listing of household servants from steward to kitchen maid? Wait – there is a name that may satisfy. 'His housekeeper, Mistress Goodrich, was someone I came to admire and understand that she is not merely a house servant, but also a trusted advisor to Sir Francis.'

His expression softens and there is a light of recognition in his eyes. He purses his lips and nods his head slowly. 'I think I must accept your assertion of a connection with Sir Francis. I have met with Mylles and my late wife formed a high opinion of Mistress Goodrich, who is more than housekeeper to the great man.' He pauses and eyes me directly. 'You will forgive my caution, but your appearance alongside Pennes the Maroc and your wild tale was problematic. What would you have me do?'

'We must hasten to Plymouth town. Do you have a ship that will provide us with passage or can you instruct one of the traders in the harbour to divert there? There would be a reward in gold.'

'I am the law keeper on this isle and do not have influence with trade or ships in our harbour. The Governor would not take kindly to interference in his domain.'

'Then, can the Governor be appraised of our situation?'

'That would not be advisable. He is quick with his judgements and you would likely be damned by your association with Pennes.'

'Is there another way?'

He considers for a few moments. 'I own a small two-masted caravel. I had a fondness for the open sea in my younger days, but now I am too old and need a degree of comfort in larger ships.'

'Could we…'

'It can be sailed by four men and is quick through the water. If you have coin, then I can find three men to take you to Plymouth.'

'Three? We will need only two men.'

'My offer is for you alone. Pennes must remain here for investigation.'

'No, that cannot be. Master Pennes will accompany me.' I am forceful, perhaps too strong in my assertion, and must hope this does not lead to a withdrawal of his offer.

'You are direct, Doctor. I am charged with the rule of law here and will not countenance your meddling.'

'If you have accepted my story, then you will know that I have influence with the highest in the land. They would not look favourably on any obstacle placed in the way of Her Majesty's business.'

'Do you threaten me, Doctor Constable?'

'Yes, you leave me with no other option. I know the value Captain General Hawkins places on Pennes and it would be no surprise if he decides to sail here with hard men to recover his trusted aide. It would go badly for this quiet and pleasant island should that circumstance be deemed necessary.'

'Your situation here is precarious. I could have you arrested now and save a deal of trouble.'

'Yes, you could, but I am confident that honesty and diligence in your service to Her Majesty will lead you to choose the honourable path.' I trust I have not misjudged this man. He does not answer. His mind will sift through choices and their consequences.

I say, 'Tell me about the warrant held against Master Pennes. When was the action and who named him?'

'It was some years past, but his violent actions are well-remembered here. He was accused of piracy by the master of a ship named *Falkin*. The Governor sent three armed men to arrest him, but he killed them all with sword and dagger.'

The *Falkin*; I have heard that ship's name before but cannot recall the reason.

'Bailiff Beauvoir, you have said yourself that the Governor is quick to judge and I have heard he is an intemperate man. It is unlikely in the extreme that Pennes was involved in piracy. Captain General Hawkins would not consider employing a man with a tainted background.' This is not true. I hold no faith in Hawkins' character, but I have changed my opinion of Pennes. He is proven to be reliable and trustworthy in our mission thus far and I cannot desert him. 'I will offer you an undertaking, which I trust will satisfy. I swear in the presence of God that I will return here to face the force of your law if you send later word to Plymouth of your confidence that Pennes committed an act of piracy. I cannot speak for Pennes, but I give holy word on my part to obey your instructions.'

He puffs air in surprise at my declaration. 'Ha, I understand now why Secretary Walsingham places his trust in you. You have a clever way with words and the mind of an intelligencer. But... I will accept your assurance, Doctor.'

He rises from his stool with difficulty and advises that he will make arrangements for our sailing. I thank him and offer gold. He demurs but says that he will be pleased to receive favourable mention in the ear of Sir Francis, should our mission end in success. Finally, he states we should act quickly as sighting of Pennes will reach the Governor's ear before long. We must be gone within the hour.

*

Under sail with fair wind and St Peter Port is lost from rear view as we pass the northern headland of the island. Beauvoir was true to his word, with his caravel and two men readied and waiting for us within a half hour. It is a small ship, but its lateen sail helps cut through the water with good speed. I have little to do now we are underway and stand amidships waiting for any call to pull or loosen a rope. I am thankful that Beauvoir gifted me a pair of gloves for sore hands and a linen blouse to cover my bare chest. It was a stroke of good fortune to find a thoughtful man of balanced humour who was willing to hear me out. Many would have dispatched us to the cells with determination to see our twitching at the end of ropes.

I have time to consider all that we have found on this eventful mission. The interlude with Lady Fitzmaurice has the feeling of a different age, although it was less than three days past. Now there is distance between us and no distraction of her beauty, I am convinced that there was no dissembling about the fate of Stukley and the limited designs of her husband and Sanders on a province of Ireland. Why was she absent that morning? Was it Vaisy who sent word for our detention in St Malo? And why? What would he or the Lady have to gain from stopping our news reaching Plymouth? Then there is Charles. Could he have relayed false intelligence about Stukley in all innocence? If it was indeed Stack who consulted at the Fitzmaurice house in the month of February, Charles will have known of Stukley's fate. In that case, why would he spread false information about the threat of invasion? My musings are interrupted by Pennes, who joins me.

'How was it done, Doctor? You will have sprinkled magic dust on that old man, Beauvoir, to arrange this passage.'

'Ha, it was more an appeal to his loyalty and the threat of anger from men of influence that decided in our favour.' Our escape is not complete, but my spirits are lifted and I am thankful for the companionship of this brave fighting man. 'We have shared an adventure and should be more familiar in our conversation. You must call me William if I can use your given name of Jacques.'

'By all means... William.' He bows his head. 'I was wrong to regard you as a foppish man of letters with no manly substance. Many gentlemen look on those from Maroc as inferior and undeserving of such openness.'

'We are both guilty of early misjudgement in character, then. I was too persuaded by your fierce look and my mistrust of your master.'

'The Captain General is a fine man but will admit he takes some knowing.' He turns to face me. 'I can understand how you, a scholar, could use fine words for your own passage, but it will have required particular inducement to secure my freedom.'

'I could not leave you there, Jacques. I did no more than you. There was no insistence we row on. Instead, you set us down in a place you knew would likely see your arrest and hanging.'

Have I erred in my assessment of his character only, or are there others I must appraise with a fresh eye?

Eighteen

We arrive in Plymouth with no fanfare or cheering crowds. The quays are quiet as men have finished their day's work and head to inns and lodgings for supper. Any watchers will have a keen eye for *The Griffin,* in which we departed; a small caravel such as ours will be regarded as of little consequence. Another sleepless night at sea has left me with aching body and grainy eyes - a poor state to face Wynter and Hawkins. And Helen will be here. I ask Jacques to report to our principals and beg their forgiveness for a short delay while I bathe and dress at my lodgings.

There was much fussing and clucking as busy hens by Mistress Gredley and her maid at my appearance and request for a tub of warm water. I would happily dawdle in the soothing calm of the bath and retire to my bed, but this interval must be short. I am rinsed, dried and somewhat restored in fresh hose and shirt when I hear a commotion in the house and my door opens without warning. Helen.

She rushes to me. I open my arms to receive her, but she stops short, places her hands on her hips and stares at me with – what: defiance; anger; concern?

'William – why…'

I take her and gently fold her in my arms, murmuring her name. She is stiff at first, then slowly surrenders to my urging. Our bodies press together with a growing impatience and I thrill at her scent; the curve of her back; a shiver as I kiss her soft neck. Her body heaves. She is… crying.

'My love, what is it?'

She breaks away and dabs at her eyes with a silk cloth. 'Why were you not here? They would tell me naught, save that you were at sea to trial your instrument.' She breathes deeply to compose herself. 'I did not believe them. There was more to it. I could see the concern in their eyes when your return was delayed.'

I should be better prepared for this. I cannot lie as she will find out soon enough that *The Griffin* and her crew are detained in St Malo. I will offer at least an outline of our enterprise across the Narrow Sea.

'What has happened to your hands?'

We both stare at them; strange, ugly, swollen things blistered and scabbed black.

'I – we – spent some time in an oared boat. They are more accustomed to handling quills and tumblers of wine than heavy, wooden oars, but they will heal.'

She ignores my poor attempt to lighten the conversation. 'You say "we". Were you with that dark, severe man who called at the Hawkins' household?'

'Yes, that man is Jacques Pennes who was my partner these past days. His frightening appearance hides a steadfast and thoughtful mind.'

'What were you about... and... why did you have to sail away at the time of our arrival?'

'There was a rumour that foreign ships may threaten this harbour and halt our venture to the New Lands. I sailed with others to the French coast and made enquiries about the veracity of those rumours – 'tis all.'

'Ha, 'tis all. I have heard no talk of a danger to the great adventure. Why would you, a physician and man of letters, be chosen for that task? There are fighting men aplenty here – rough men who can row oars without injury.'

'All in good time, my sweet. It was considered prudent to guard the reason for our sailing from all but a few, so please do not reveal to others until there is a general understanding. Come with me to Hawkins' house where I must report my findings.' I place my hands on her waist. 'But this is a cold welcome; I would have a kiss from my dearest love, who I have missed sorely these past months.'

She slaps playfully at my chest, then submits. Her lips are honeyed-soft and eager fingers explore my back as our embrace lingers. A noise at the door. Her maid, Lucy, stands there with head bowed in awkwardness at our display of affection. We break gently and Helen leaves with Lucy while I pull on my boots and finish dressing.

Two of Hawkins' men accompany us as we walk through the lanes with a bright, low sun casting shadows at our feet. Helen and her father are lodged in chambers at the Captain General's house. She tells me her father is somewhat recovered, but his dizzy spells remain and she worries about his health. He is in a high mood at the prospect of the fleet's sailing and has been given to excessive eating and drinking these last few days. It would seem that Sir George has not been informed of the peril that may threaten his venture. The meeting to receive my report will have to be handled with delicacy.

We are expected at Hawkins' door and ushered directly into his dining chamber where three are sat at a table scattered with the remains of a supper. My belly growls its displeasure at missing a fine spread.

Sir George rises from his seat and comes to welcome me with open arms. 'Ah, William, my dear. How good it is to meet with my future son again. The sea air agrees with you; there is a vital glow on your complexion.'

He was always a large man, but a puffiness has been added since our last meeting and he walks stiffly as though his legs are troubled to bear extra weight. He mocks Helen for her haste in prising me from my lodgings and shoos her gently from the room so that we can discuss our business. I exchange greetings with Hawkins and Wynter and take a seat at the table.

Wynter says, 'We have spoken briefly with Master Pennes and only now informed Sir George of the true nature of your undertaking at sea.'

'I should be ruffled at your secrecy, gentlemen,' Sir George waves a hand airily, 'but I am relieved that your news brings no obstacle to the sailing of our venture.'

The door opens and a maid appears to clear the table. Hawkins rises, dismisses her and instructs that we are to be left alone.

'We are eager for your full report, Doctor Constable. Pennes has given only a short outline of your actions and findings.' Hawkins bows his head as a signal that I should begin my report.

I have resolved to tell all, save the intimate nature of my conversations with Lady Fitzmaurice and any mention of Stack.

I will set about my own examination of Charles and Stack, trusting there will be an innocent explanation. If not... then I must decide what is to be done. I can see no purpose in his spreading of a false alarm, unless it was a desperate attempt to be freed of the noose. All three men listen in silence as I narrate the events since our departure from this place over five days past.

I have finished. Sir George sits back in his seat and thumps the table.

'A brave tale, William. It was well done. I had not understood the mortal hazards you faced and have overcome with daring and subtlety.'

'Indeed,' adds Wynter, 'it was a fascinating oration. How can you be certain that the disclosure from the lady was not an attempt to confound and mislead?'

'The information was given freely and her manner strongly suggested there was no attempt to dissemble. Her household had received direct intelligence from those present at Maroc and she was adamant that Stukley was killed there. I believe the ambitions of the lady and her husband lie in a longing to return to Munster, either to be reconciled with Earl Desmond or to challenge the earldom.' I pause before adding, 'Lady Fitzmaurice holds no great attachment to her husband and his associates.'

'Then it is a puzzle to comprehend why you were detained in St Malo.'

'I agree. I have considered this carefully and do not believe it was Lady Fitzmaurice who sent word for our detention. I suspect it was her steward, named Vaisy, who perhaps has a strong devotion to the old religion and is hostile to all from Her Majesty's state.'

'Your escape from St Malo in an oared boat was a triumph, William. I shall take great pleasure in recounting this escapade to my grandsons.' Sir George spreads his arms and smiles broadly at this imagining.

'Master Pennes should take the credit for our successful flight from that place. I should not be here were it not for his actions and determination to complete our objective.' I turn to Hawkins.

'I trust that efforts will be made to recover our crew and ship?'

'You can rest assured on that count, Doctor. I am acquainted with the Commander in St Malo and a small ship is readied to sail with my message on the morrow. He would not wish to stir my anger in this matter.' He pauses and folds his arms across his chest. 'Sir Humphrey and I both have interests on the island of Guernsey. The Bailiff there is a sly and calculating man. I wonder how you managed to negotiate your freedom, knowing that Pennes has a history there.'

'I gave my word I would return there if there were matters there requiring resolution.'

Hawkins tilts his head with a questioning look. 'May we know the nature of these matters?'

'It is in regard to Master Pennes' naming for piracy some years' past.'

'Then why would the promise be on your part and not Pennes?'

'It was the way my conference with Bailiff Beauvoir unfolded. Pennes was held in chains and in no position to offer his own undertaking. I confess that I was forceful in my warnings that our detention there would incur displeasure from men of high influence. I saw my oath as the final piece in an argument to sway his decision in our favour.'

'Do you intend to stand by your word?'

'I do.'

Sir George puffs air in disapproval and exclaims, 'Do not be rash, my dear. You will be tangled in trouble, not of your making.'

'Sir George has it right, Doctor,' joins Hawkins. 'The Bailiff may be relied on to act with honour, but the Governor is an intemperate fellow who holds a grudge against my Muster Master. It was the Governor, Sir John Leighton, who named Pennes on false testimony by another ship's master. Pennes was attacked by his men and killed them in self-defence. Leighton would be likely to have you hung or throttled for the affront to his authority.'

'I do not see...'

'Do not fret, Doctor, you will be gone from here soon with

our fleet and if by small chance word comes from Guernsey then we will send you with a force of armed men to calm their temper.'

'I am grateful for your concern, Captain General.' I am also greatly relieved in light of his cautioning. 'Do you have the name of the ship's master who gave false testimony?'

'It was Wicken – Charles Wicken.'

I cannot stop a small mewing noise in my throat at the mention of his name. Yet again Charles' name appears in circumstances which throw doubt on my regard for him as a friend. That will be the reason why Hawkins holds him in low standing. Charles will have known that, but why did he not disclose this information when explaining the hostility of Hawkins? There may be a blameless explanation behind the naming of Pennes, but it is troubling.

'Ah yes, Captain Wicken,' says Wynter. 'It was his intelligence that brought us here. I am inclined to accept your account, William, and surmise that Wicken's intelligence was mistaken. Of course, that is the nature of intelligence gathering; much of the gossip and tittle-tattle is unreliable or given in mischief.'

Sir George thumps the table again. 'Ha, at last, the way is clear. Well said, Sir William. Do we understand from your words, that our fleet may sail without further delay? How long will it take to gather the ships from Dartmouth and ready for our grand departure from here, Captain General?'

'Three days, no more.'

'Gentlemen, I must stretch your patience a little longer. I will prepare an urgent message bound for Secretary Walsingham in London this night. Caution demands I establish if there is any further intelligence from London or this place before your fleet sails. However, I have a strong notion that William has it right and that the threat to these shores is mistaken – or a malicious fabrication. Let us say eight days; there will be no dallying beyond that.'

Sir George mutters some words to himself and turns to Hawkins who bows his head in assent and it is settled. We sail in eight days. I feel no sense of satisfaction. My brief re-joining with Helen has confirmed my misgivings. I will seek a way to excuse myself from the great adventure, but it must be done in a way that will not incur the displeasure of Sir George.

Our conference is over. Hawkins and Wynter rise from the table while Sir George reaches for a gammon and proceeds to cut a generous slice for his plate. I am hungry and my belly tells me to sit with him a while, but I have a more urgent call on my senses. I ask Sir George's permission to call briefly on Helen before I retire. Further, say I have in mind a diversion for her while we wait to sail. I would ride with her to Dartmouth and introduce Helen to the Gilbert household. My suggestion meets with approval from her father and gratified expression from Hawkins who begs me to carry a message detailing our present deliberations to Sir Humphrey.

Helen is alone in the parlour, having sent Lucy to ready her bedchamber. We embrace in silence for a while, savouring our closeness. I wonder if she shares my reluctance to be parted for two years or more on my voyage to the New Lands. She has not voiced a concern, but perhaps that is because she understands the great weight her father places upon the venture. It has been some years in the planning and Sir George's fortunes are tightly bound to its success.

'What is it, William? Your mind is on other affairs outside his chamber.'

'Forgive me, my love, I had not understood you could read my thoughts so early in our togetherness.'

'Dear William, you were open to me from the first. I trust that we will hold no secrets from each other now, or in our married years.'

I shake my head to be free of an image of Lady Fitzmaurice. 'No, you are right. I was planning how we might be together while we are delayed in our sailing, which is to be in eight days and...'

She looks into my eyes. 'Then we must make the most of this time... if you are still intent on being part of the adventure.'

'This next day, I thought we could ride to Dartmouth and meet with Sir Humphrey and his wife, the Lady Anne. It will allow us an interval of freedom from the interests and anxieties of ships, trade and intrigue.'

She lays her head on my chest and murmurs her pleasure at the imagining of our attachment in the next few days.

Nineteen

I am here before nine bells to collect Helen. The weather is set fair; there are high spirits and chattering as Helen is gathered in the courtyard with her father, Lucy, Hawkins and two of his children, together with an escort of six soldiers from the fleet. I dismount and go first to Hawkins who hands me a message for Gilbert and wishes me a pleasant journey.

'Will you travel via Loddiswell?'

'No, we will take the Ivybridge road.'

'Ah, that is a wise choice.'

Sir George claps me on both shoulders, leans towards me and whispers in my ear, 'Have a care, William. Let there be no excitement and daring on this excursion. When you return I should be grateful for your consultation as a physician.'

I bow my head in acknowledgement, grateful that I am not the one to broach this subject. He is not a man to fuss over his ailments or welcome the attentions of a physician. I take Helen's hand as she steps on the mounting block and settles on her grey palfrey, then do the same for her maid on her bay cob. With a few clicks and gentle urging, we are away.

We ride in a comfortable quiet to the bridge where the estuary narrows before I turn to Helen and tell of her father's wish to consult on his health.

She says, 'He is reluctant to discuss his ailment. He has finally accepted my daily soother of comfrey and elfwort, but I fear a cure is beyond my reasoning.'

'His flesh is bloated with an unhappy colouring. It may be the result of an imbalance between blood and phlegm.'

'Will you draw his star chart?'

'Yes, it may help with an understanding of his bodily inclinations.'

'You must be delicate in your conference with him. He will likely bristle and snap if you offer a remedy to shrink his belly.'

Our first stop is on the brow of a hill past Ivybridge. I sit with Helen under the shade of a tree while we slake our thirst with small beer and the horses take a pick of grass.

'Were you welcomed on your arrival in Plymouth by Oliver and Charles?'

'Oliver was there, but no Charles.'

'Did he offer my excuses?'

'Yes, he said your absence could not be helped; you were at sea trialling an adjustment to your instrument of navigation.'

'Yes, that was our cover. We did not wish to spread alarm at the thought there may be a threat to the ports. There is no harm in knowing now, as we have found the rumours were false.'

'Was it Walsingham's doing – that you sailed to France?'

'Yes, he sent Sir William Wynter here to examine our situation.'

'I wonder that you, a scholar, were chosen for this undertaking. Are you able to confide the events of your enterprise to me, or is it a tale not fit for the ear of a dainty woman?'

She mocks the way men hide matters of business and state from female sensibilities. It is an attractive trait and one that I find it difficult to resist, but I must be circumspect – at least for the present. I take her hand and kiss a cheek softly.

'It will all be out in good time and ask that you bear my discretion for now.' She wrinkles her nose as a sign of her displeasure but does not press her case. 'How do you find Oliver?'

'He is a pleasant man. He was invited to a supper along with others at the Hawkins' house on our second night in the town. He converses well and has good learning. I can see that he is a good companion to you.'

'And Charles – have you met with him, yet?'

'Yes, on one occasion only. We were introduced on the quays by Oliver.'

I wait for more, but naught comes. 'Do you have an opinion of Charles?'

She brushes her skirts and gazes at the sky before answering. 'It was too short an encounter for any understanding of the man, but…'

'But?'

'Lucy confided later that she heard the housemaids gossip about him. He appeared at the quarter session here accused of a killing and you, my dearest, were named as the one who spoke strongly in his favour and gained his freedom.'

'Yes, that is…'

'There was naught in your letters about this matter. I heard only of his friendly manner and good conversation on politicking.'

'It is no easy thing to write of a comrade blamed for such a foul act. I believed he was innocent. I felt compelled to uncover the truth and question the testimonies.'

'Well, that is a mark of a true friend. If you were certain…'

'Yes… yes, I was.'

There is an awkwardness about the ending to our conversation as if both have left thoughts unsaid. We mount our horses and resume our journey.

The air is thick with heat from the afternoon sun as we leave Townstal behind and make our way up the Dart estuary to the ferry. The harbour presents a fine view. Helen and Lucy point and chatter about the handsome scene and how it differs from the busy, narrow streets of their house in the Leadenhall district. We leave the horses and soldiers at the ferry crossing and climb up the hill to Gilbert's country house. It is young Humphrey Or who greets us and guides to a receiving chamber. He is eager to inform me about his work on ship navigation following our previous meeting. He has begun to make his own observations of the stars and I promise to confer with him and inspect his findings later this day. Lady Anne enters and exclaims in delight when I introduce Helen.

'My, what a handsome pairing you make. It will be a joy to entertain you to a supper here.'

'Thank you Lady Anne, I have told Helen of the fine welcome and pleasure from my last visit here. Is Sir Humphrey at home?'

'He is on the quays but will return in good time for our table.'

Helen is clearly taken aback by the fussing and flattering over her beauty and fine clothes. Her expression is a mix of bafflement and gratification at the Lady's attention. We are offered both refreshment and the opportunity to rest from our journey and she dithers over which should take precedence. Eventually, it is decided that she will instruct Helen's room to be readied while we take a glass of sweet wine in the parlour. I beg to be excused, saying that I will take a boat into the harbour and meet with Sir Humphrey.

A stable man is sent with me to the boathouse and rows me down the estuary to the quays. We moor by the small building pointed out as the harbour mater's place of business. The quayside is busy, but I see only one man inside through an open door. I knock as I enter and introduce myself.

'Good day to you, Doctor, I am Edwin Grant, the harbour master in this town. I have heard your name from Sir Humphrey. Is it he that you seek?'

'Yes, Master Grant, but I would have a short word with you before that. Do you have a journal of trading ships that berth here?'

'Indeed, I am meticulous in the entries recorded here.' He points to a square piece of leather sitting atop a pile of papers, bound tightly with two strings. I ask if I may examine it and he slides it across the table.

'I have an interest in a ship that arrived here some three weeks past.'

He folds back the cover with care and turns over three or four sheets of paper. I run my finger down the dated entries. There – I see the entry for the ship *Falkin*. The fifth day of June corresponds. There is more… sailed from Antwerp… cargo of fire powder, matchlocks, muskets, ironmongery… depart the seventh day of June… destined for Sandwich. I check the entry again.

'Could there be an error or hiding of the true ports of origin and destination recorded here?'

He is swift in his indignation. 'Indeed, no, all ships must carry license to and from their ports. Any ships found to be meddling with their papers would be held and their cargo forfeit to Her Majesty.'

'I am sorry if I gave offence, Master Grant. I know little of the handling of trading ships in ports and did not refer to the particulars of your duty.' My thoughts run fast. If the record is right… 'Do you know the name of the master of this ship – *Falkin*?'

'The master of the *Falkin* is James Blount.'

'Blount – not another?'

'Her master was named Wicken, but it changed hands some four or five year's past.'

'Is it recorded how the cargo was discharged?'

He reaches for another journal and sifts through its pages. 'It was moved to another ship, the *Brave Edmund*, in the ownership of merchant Jeremy Sindell.' He leans over the table and points to the quay outside. 'That ship remains moored over there; one of Sir Humphrey's fleet for the New Lands venture.'

'My thanks to you, Master Grant for your openness and I congratulate you on your diligence as harbour master.' I place a silver coin on his table and take my leave.

I make only a cursory and failed attempt to find Gilbert, then take the boat back up the estuary. How should I interpret these findings? Does my memory fail me or did Charles tell me that the final piece of his intelligence was received from one on board the *Falkin*? Yes, I am sure that was the ship name he gave as the reason for his visit to Dartmouth. That was not the only falsehood; the ship sailed from Antwerp, not Corunna; and did he state the cargo as sweet wine? I cannot be sure of the latter, but I am convinced on the other points. Was my mind so scrambled with relief at his saving my life that I viewed him cloaked in a heroic halo?

I am about to enter Gilbert's house when Helen calls me from the side. She slips her hand through my arm and says she will show me Lady Anne's garden, which has a good stock of herbs, aromatics and other florae. It is easy to leave my troubled thoughts in her company. She has a lightness in her mood as she takes my hand and leads me around the side of the house. She stops under the shade of a tree, pulls me close, cups her hands around my face and kisses my lips. We are both quick, fervent and excited with hands exploring and bodies urgently seeking a greater closeness. I slide a hand up the curve of her hip to her breast.

'Not here, not now.'

Her hands push me away and she withdraws, panting and flushed with a glint of mischief in her eyes.

'If this is to be the object of a stroll in a garden, we must set to it each day, my love.'

She smiles, links her arm again and we step through the bricked paths, stopping now and then to take in a scent or examine a particular flora.

She says, 'You were quick to leave me with the Lady Anne and seek out Sir Humphrey.'

'She is a lively woman with a cheery manner. Did you enjoy her company?'

'I like her, she is an easy companion, even on first meeting, but I confess I could not keep pace with her flattery and compliments.' I agree with her, remembering my first encounter with the lady. 'You missed Sir Humphrey, who returned here by ferry a short time after your leaving.'

'Yes, I will hand him the message at our gathering for the table.'

A maid appears around the corner of the house, bobs a curtsey and says the Lady Anne begs our presence inside for supper.

Our hosts are waiting for us in the dining room. Sir Humphrey takes me aside and enquires if there is any news from Plymouth. He takes the note with an expression that is a mix of eagerness and trepidation. He scans it quickly and claps me on the shoulder.

'Ha, we are near there – a sailing in eight days. It was well done, Doctor. The Captain General writes of your bravery and cunning in uncovering the true nature of the intelligence.'

We take our seats at the table. Only four are here, but the supper is generously spread already and would feed twice our number with oysters, thickened soup and a large halibut. Helen pleases the lady with her compliments on the table and admiration for the garden. This sparks a conversation about the use of herbs and aromatics in food and potions for small illnesses in her children.

Lady Anne says, 'Doctor, I wonder at your good fortune in capturing the heart of your lady. Not only is she uncommonly fair of face, but her wisdom and learning belies her eighteen years.'

'Indeed, I am the most fortunate of men. I am a slave to her beauty and must be alert with my intellect if I am not to be outdone in our discussions.'

Helen colours a little, thanks Lady Anne for her kind words and lowers her head to hide a smile that plays on her lips. We exchange a furtive and knowing glance before I turn to Sir Humphrey and enquire about the readiness of the fleet moored in Dartmouth.

'All is set. We have encountered fewer troubles here than in Plymouth.'

'I wonder why it was decided to split the fleet between the two ports. When I departed from London, I understood that all would be harboured in Dartmouth.'

'It is a matter of prudence, Doctor. The size of our fleet grew as more joined in the New Year. We have forty-three ships now, and although both ports can accommodate our number there is more safety in their separation.'

'Safety – how?'

'A gathering of many sailing and fighting men in one place for too long is apt to bring difficulties and nuisance to the towns.' He pauses and waves his knife. 'Then there is a danger of accidents in a large fleet, close-moored.'

'What nature of accident do you guard against?'

'There may be fire or an explosion. There are other reasons and although the dangers are small we considered a separation would be safer and calm the fears of our backers.'

'You will join the ships in Plymouth soon.'

'Yes, but that will be only a short time before our grand departure. It will be a triumph, imprinted on the minds of all who are there to witness the magnificence of the event and hear the orations. We will sail from here in four or five days to assemble in Plymouth as one united force, the like of which has not been seen before.'

He lifts his head and his eyes mist with imagining the scene. I understand, but cannot share, his excitement and impatience for the fulfilment of a scheme, so long in the making. As our supper progresses, Sir Humphrey becomes carefree with his wine and is merry and loud with his talk. Lady Anne is discomfited and tries to soothe him, but there is no stopping. He congratulates me again on my bravery in the expedition to St Malo and then, to my dismay, mentions my attack at Loddiswell as another sign of my courage. Helen glances at me with a questioning expression. I must prepare for her probing.

Gilbert's head soon droops and he is asleep in his seat with much snorting and bubbling of lips. Lady Anne takes Helen to her bedchamber while I go fetch a servant to help me heave our drunken host to his rest. It will not be long before I am in the quiet of my chamber longing for Helen to be by my side. And then there is Charles. I must consider how to take forward the disturbing and contrary facts I have discovered about my friend over the past few days.

Twenty

Helen joins me as we ride away from the ferry and up the path to Townstal. She holds out her arm and bids me hang back so that we may ride together at the rear.

'Tell me about Loddiswell.'

'My love, you will forgive me...'

'I am no fool, William. I understand why you may wish to keep mention of killing and peril from my ears, but it is out now and I would know more.'

There is no profit in hiding that episode from her any more, and so I relate my story, holding back only the most gruesome details. Her mouth gapes and she shakes her head in wonder at my good fortune.

'So, that was the time you wrote a letter about your visit to a church remembered fondly by John Foxe. I remember his telling of the place around a cosy winter hearth in your parlour?'

'Yes, the prayers I said in the church of St Loda for our future together were answered.'

She is thoughtful for a few moments, then says, 'Is that why you hold Charles Wicken in such high regard? He saved your life and 'tis no wonder you view him so well.'

It is a question I have not resolved in my own mind. I shrug and answer, 'We were on good terms before that incident, but I do not deny that his action there may have raised his standing in my eyes.'

'Let us take the path back to Plymouth via Loddiswell. I would see the place of your deliverance and give thanks to God.'

We are well-guarded and I can see no reason to object. I urge my mount forward and instruct our guards to change our course.

The sun is high when we arrive at the scene of the assault in the wooded valley. It is another warm day, the trees offer welcome shade and the place has the aspect of a pleasant summer idyll. Whispers of the terror and murder here intrude on my thoughts, but for others this will appear as a benign place, encouraging innocent and gentle remembrances. Helen dismounts, takes my hand and I lead her down the slope to the edge of the stream.

'This was the position I saw my assailants and believed my time was done. My first thinking was of you, my love, and the injustice of our final separation in this world. Fright and alarm came later.'

She lowers herself to her knees and clasps her hands in prayer. I stand by her side, try to free my head of the ugly memories and give thanks to God for rekindling the promise of our future together. I help her rise, she rests her head on my chest, folds her arms around me and murmurs words of devotion and affection.

We ride on and I have a sense that my mind has been cleansed of the dread that lurked in the shadows from that encounter. I turn our conversation to lighter subjects, but there is little response and she returns to a topic that seems to nag and itch in her mind – Charles.

'I am ever grateful for Charles Wicken's actions in saving you, but could this service have clouded your judgement on his involvement in the killing?'

'Why do you ask? Have you heard gossip about the trial?'

'Yes, some of it indirectly, but there seems to be a general opinion in the town that your intervention secured his release, perhaps unjustly.'

I react with a sigh of impatience, which is heavier than intended. I recount my examination of the testimonies, the findings that swayed my opinion and the arguments presented at the quarter session. It was less than three weeks past, but it feels like an age ago and I struggle to recall some of the finer detail. Then, I remember the immediate aftermath of the trial when Charles, Oliver and I adjourned to celebrate his freedom. It was an oddly subdued gathering and I am reminded of my surprise at the verdict.

'William.'

I am brought back to the present by her sharp reminder and apologise for my inattention.

'I had said that, from your telling, it was problematic to decide on guilt or innocence. So, I suppose it was right that he was freed.' She pauses, then adds, 'I wonder you were not questioned on the purpose of your counting men with height and yellow hair. The numbers do not appear to hold any significance.'

'It was simply to illustrate that Charles Wicken was not the only large man in town with fair hair.' I hope there are no more questions on those numbers as I am pricked with guilt at trickery in the way they were used.

'And why do you think the maid from the inn changed her testimony?'

'Now on that, I cannot be sure. I was taken aback at the switch in her story and I can only guess that she misremembered or could not countenance telling a lie in such a formal gathering.'

'Or, that she was persuaded by some other, devious means.'

'What - what can you...'

She clicks her mount and rides ahead, ending our conversation with troubling abruptness.

*

I took my leave of Helen at Hawkins' house. I had intended to consult with Sir George, but he was engaged at a meeting with fellow merchants arrived for the grand departure. I called on Justice Shanning and met with a gruff reception. I inquired if there was progress in finding the culprit responsible for Tremayne's killing and received short affirmation of none. I was left in no doubt he believed my intervention had led to the unwarranted release of a man who deserved hanging. Investigations had uncovered naught and his words about my 'conscience' and 'meddling in local affairs' raised my unease a further notch. It is time I talked with Charles.

I meet with Oliver on the quays. He is in high spirits at the news of our sailing and congratulates me warmly on the news brought back from St Malo.

'I have heard only snatched gossip of your brave enterprise across the Narrow Sea, William. You must relate the fine detail of your clandestine mission over a cup of ale or wine.'

'That would be welcome, my friend. It is some time since we have supped and conversed together. Have you spoken with Charles these past days?'

'No, I understand he has been busy with his preparations, here and in Dartmouth.'

'Then, I will seek him out and bid him join us. Let us meet in the *Seven Bells* in one half hour.'

Stack is on the deck of Hawkwind. I hail him and ask if Charles is aboard. He doesn't reply but moves to the captain's cabin on the stern. A few moments later he appears with Charles who waves a greeting. I invite him to join me and Oliver at the inn. He hesitates, appears undecided, mutters some words to Stack, and then says he will convene after a tiresome interval with his journals and letters.

Oliver is already seated at a table with a jug and three cups. I sit heavily on a bench and remove my cap, feeling weary, thirsty and hungry.

'Your brow is creased and your shoulders droop as if under a great weight, William. Are you troubled?'

'Ah, 'tis naught but tiredness and a missed dinner. This will soon put me right.' I take the cup, swallow the ale and lick my lips. 'Charles promises to be here when his business is done.'

He bows his head, refills our cups and we are quiet for a few moments.

'It was a delight to meet with Helen, your betrothed. She has a rare beauty and I wonder you can bear to be parted.'

Does he read my thoughts about the venture? There is naught to be read from his expression. 'I thank you for your compliment, dear Oliver. She is all to me and it is a joy to be with her again. I am grateful to you for attending her arrival and explaining my absence.'

'I was happy to meet with her but wanting in a complete understanding of the reason for your departure. She questioned me closely and cast me a look of daggers as the bearer of words she did not wish to hear.' He pauses and sups. 'Still, it was soon forgotten and we had a pleasant conversation.'

'I am sorry for the secrecy surrounding our small mission, but Wynter was cautious and insisted only our small group should know until we returned.'

'I heard only that you returned with news that there was no imminent threat to these ports and that you met with an element of peril.'

'Our enquiries in St Malo revealed that any gathering of ships in Biscay is more likely to be directed at a small dispute in Ireland. All seemed well until we were detained through an absurd accusation of religious mischief. Pennes and I escaped in an oared boat to the island of Guernsey, but the ship and crew remain in St Malo.'

He whistles his astonishment at news of our flight. 'But why… Pennes I can see is a man equipped for danger. Did you not question your inclusion in this hazardous task?'

'Ha, you do me a disservice, Oliver. You think I am a soft scholar and… well, you have it right. It is not my preferred way of entertainment.' How much should I tell? I must keep Lady Fitzmaurice close, but the rest… 'I have not told you before, but I have worked for Secretary Walsingham lately. It was he that put my name to Wynter as one who could be trusted to wheedle and prise intelligence.'

He sits back in his seat and stares with open mouth.

I say, 'I will add that I have misjudged Jacques Pennes. He is a fine, brave man and I would not be here, but for his efforts.'

He shakes his head, then glances over my shoulder. I turn and see Charles approaches.

'Welcome Charles, you have become a stranger to our assembly of friends these past days.'

'Yes, good day to you both, I have been taxed with onerous duties in our readying to sail.'

Oliver grunts sympathy for his industry and states he is likewise occupied. Our cups are filled and the jug empty. I signal to a maid for more ale and see it is Amy Wearing. She sees my hand, but turns on her heel and disappears towards the kitchens. I can understand that she may be even now discomfited at the reminder of her testimony, but it was an extreme reaction. Another serving maid acknowledges my hand and takes our jug for refilling.

Oliver says, 'We are all relieved that your intelligence was mistaken, Charles. I would have my backers baying for blood if our venture was postponed, or worse.'

'Yes, it is a curious sensation to be so glad I am proved wrong. Still, it is the nature of whispers and chatter about secrets to wander from the truth. I was never certain of the veracity of the threat, but prudence demanded its disclosure.'

'Nevertheless, you must scold the master of that ship from Dartmouth when you next meet.' I pause and feign a lapse of memory. 'What was its name? Ah, the *Falkin*, I remember.'

His head turns quickly and he gapes at me. 'Yes... yes, you have it right there, William. I hear it was you who brought the news back over the channel.'

I relate the same story told to Oliver, then add, 'It would seem that Stukley was killed in Maroc, after all.'

'Yes, it is a blessing the rumour was false and Her Majesty need fear his insults and scheming no more.'

Stack has appeared. He sidles up to Charles and whispers in his ear. He drains his cup and begs forgiveness, but he must attend to urgent business on his ship.

When they are gone, Oliver folds his arms, puffs air and declares in mocking voice, 'Stukley – I couldn't swallow that tale about faking his death.'

I drink the last of my ale and say, 'Come, Oliver, our thirst is slaked with ale now; I will stand a bottle of this inn's finest claret if you have a mind before I adjourn to Mistress Gredley's for my supper.'

I order the wine, a tub of oysters and settle to conversation about Helen, Sir George and the other merchants and backers who will be there to watch the fleet sail. Oliver admits his circumstances will benefit greatly from successful trading and a share of Spanish treasure. Unlike others, he is not encumbered with large debts and, while failure would hurt, his family has land and assets that would see him through.

'Do you have a mind to marry, Oliver? Maids are rapt by your splendid figure and few would find a finer match.'

'Huh, that is a kind thought, but I am wed to the sea now.' He sips the wine, then circles his cup between his hands. 'I was married some nine years past when I was barely twenty. Kate...

fair Kate... I loved her deeply but lost her and a babe in the birthing.'

I did not know and am stunned into silence. He leans over and claps me on the shoulder. 'Do not let thoughts of my misfortune spoil your eagerness for Helen in the marriage bed. She has a strong and healthy glow to match her beauty and, after all, you are a physician.'

The serving maid, Amy, passes close by and I note that Oliver catches her movement.

I say, 'That maid reminds me of your supper here with your man, Charles and Tremayne on the night of the killing. Do you remember the topic of disagreement between Charles and Tremayne?'

He is surprised at my question and considers for a few moments before confessing that his memory fails. 'I wonder that you return to this subject, William. Ah, now... there is some fragment I remember. Tremayne was rambling about the great adventure, but he often talked of it. He was enamoured at the thought and he... yes, he accused Charles of obstructing its progress. But he was in his cups, as you know, and I regarded his chatter as meandering nonsense.'

I let the quiet between us linger a while before I continue.

'Do you consider Charles could have invented the threat and sent word to Walsingham so he could be spared the rope?'

'Ah, that is a towering and worrying matter, William. It would be an act of treason to falsely manufacture a tale about such a scheme. But you must hold a suspicion to pose the question.'

'There are some small markers in that direction; his denial of a strong belief in Stukley's death; his general manner after the trial; and one circumstance in particular. He related to me the particulars surrounding his final piece of intelligence from a ship's master in Dartmouth.' Oliver tilts his head, inviting me to disclose more. 'I visited the harbour master in Dartmouth and discovered that the ship, *Falkin*, had not sailed from Corunna, as Charles claimed. Further, he stated the cargo was sweet wine, but it was fire powder and ironmongery destined for his own ships there.'

'So, that is why you named that ship to Charles. It was an

awkward query that appeared to discomfit him.'

'Yes, and I had hoped he would stay with us, so I could have probed more.' Should I tell him of Stack's visit to the Fitzmaurice house? That is my strongest logic against Charles. No, I must set that aside and keep it close until this puzzle unravels more.

Oliver says, 'Perhaps there is also a doubt of Charles' innocence in the killing. I know you are convinced and spoke well in his favour, but I have grown to mistrust the man. I have seen his temper and quick violence on the quays.'

I find I am nodding my head in agreement, thinking of his treatment of young Huckle. But what is to be done? There is no certainty on either his killing or creating false intelligence. Oliver pours more wine and picks at the oysters. I have not eaten any. I try to clear my head, sip the wine and gaze around the inn. There is Amy Wearing again. She keeps her distance. Should I attempt another conversation with her?

'William.' Oliver leans forward on his seat and places his hand on mine. 'There is no profit in pursuing these matters. You must forget these doubts about Charles Wicken, look to your preparations for our sailing and care of Helen in your absence. Charles' trial is over and there can be no going back now. He will be in the open seas with our fleet soon enough and we have need of his fighting ships. We cannot always choose the character of those we will stand alongside in times of adventure and endangerment. If he is at fault then God will surely bring his mischief into the open and see to his just and timely punishment on this earth.'

Twenty One

I have resolved to accept Oliver's advice. I deny my suitability as an intelligencer and aver my dislike of intrigue to all who will listen. I am a scholar with a devotion to mathematics and physic, so why would I wish for involvement in matters of law, politicking and statecraft? Yet, an itch nags away at my thinking. Is it my pride that will be hurt if I have misjudged Charles' character? Am I shamed to have defended a man who may be guilty of a terrible crime? If Walsingham will accept Charles' intelligence as a mere error, then why should I delve deeper into his motives. I must forget this. I will be away from this place soon and these vexed thoughts will fade.

My early morning has been fretful and unsatisfactory. I confess I was inattentive to Mistress Gredley's chatter during my breakfast and she left my chamber with much 'tutting' and shaking of her head. My time as a lodger in her house is near an end; I will seek out a small gift for her as a token of thanks for her care, admirable table and my occasional rudeness.

I called on Helen at Hawkins' house hoping we might ride out of town together on another fine day. She begged to postpone this invitation until after dinner. Her father had retired to his bed after breakfast complaining of stomach cramps, she was preparing a soother for him and would stay to tend him. It was plain that she had great concern for Sir George's wellbeing and I offered to consult with him, but she was forceful in her opinion that it was not a good time. He is prickly and ill-disposed to communicate in a calm manner when poorly. She anticipated his belly would ease in a few hours and promised to arrange a firm time for my consultation with him.

So, I have naught to do and find myself horsed and plodding through the streets and lanes of Plymouth with no clear purpose. I am on the lane through the marshes by Rope Walk. I pull the reins, stiffen my legs and turn towards the cabin where I met with Stack. Contrary voices in my head tell me to stop...

continue... no purpose... there can be no harm... Curiosity wins out and I head to Hagger's tannery.

I thought I would be prepared for the stench, but it is overpowering and I am forced to cover my mouth and nose with a linen cloth as I draw near. There are men working in the pits and further on two figures in front of his house. It is Hagger and the other... must be his wife.

'God's blessing to you both on this fine day. I beg forgiveness for my unplanned intrusion Goodwife Hagger, but I would have a brief exchange with your husband.'

She smiles at my greeting, bobs a curtsey and makes to retire to her house, but Hagger grabs her arm.

'We do not offer refreshment here to unwelcome visitors, my love. This is Doctor Constable who is no friend to me.'

I dismount, remove my cap and approach gently.

'I am here to offer my apologies for belligerence on my previous visit here. I confess that my manner was abrupt and ill-judged to one so well-regarded in this town.' He is not one to give way to flattery, but his wife may be receptive. 'The industrious work here, your healthy complexions and sturdy figures speak strongly in support of the kind words spoken about you in my neighbourhood.'

She reddens, bows her head and I see that his expression softens a little.

'What is it you want here, Doctor?'

I gesture with my hands. 'No more than a few moments' conversation to ease my conscience over our last meeting.'

He shrugs, mutters to his wife and invites me to join him in his house. I am taken to the parlour, which is a small, dark room, barely furnished with only a chair, two stools and a candlestick atop a little table. Goodwife Hagger brings in two cups of ale and closes the door as she leaves. He lifts his ale and waits for me to begin our exchange. I may as well be direct.

'Is it still your firm belief that Charles Wicken killed Walter Tremayne?'

'It is.'

'Then, why did you not attend the quarter session to deliver testimony? It was said that you had an illness. I have no doubt that your word in person would have carried force in those proceedings.'

He mutters words I cannot hear and beg him to repeat.

'My family was threatened with sly words that did not state mortal danger directly, but in a way that left no space for misunderstanding.'

'Who gave you this intimidation?'

He describes a grim, hard man that leads me to believe it was Stack.

He says, 'I was offered coin at first in a soft, coaxing way, but would not have it. I cannot be bought for a handful of silver.'

'That does you great credit. Were you asked to alter your testimony?'

'I was but would not. I steered a middle path trusting I could defend my family around my house and business. I sent a message to Justice Shanning, feigning illness, and stating I stood by my original testimony.' He sups his ale and considers for a moment. 'It was my intention to keep my family close-guarded here 'til your fleet had left, but Wicken was freed, so there will be no benefit in his threats now.'

'Was his freedom a great surprise to you?'

'Well, you must know, Doctor.' He waves his arms as if to dismiss unseen pests. 'There were jurors who received handsome reward for their compliance, or so it is said.'

I shake my head and mutter denial at any knowledge of this corruption. Yet, I am not startled by this assertion. Perhaps I half suspected but did not wish to allow this tainted thinking creep into my conscious mind. Hagger is a gruff man, but his actions are to be commended. Is this another character I have read badly? Was I too easy in taking Mistress Gredley's disdainful reaction to his name as damning? Perhaps it was simply the stink associated with his trade and which sneaks faintly into this parlour.

I break an interlude of quiet and say, 'May I know the cause of your disagreement with Captain Wicken? I was informed that you insulted his person.'

'Huh, I remember it clearly, although it was some months past. It was not a direct hostility between us. I was on the quays and saw him beating a young lad, no more than ten years; a cabin boy from his ship, I surmised. The lad was screaming and the punishment severe; he was marked and bloody. I intervened and begged that he spare the lad more blows. He rounded on me and struck me fiercely on the shoulders with the flat of his sword.'

'Did it end there?'

'He kicked the lad in the arse and sent him away, sobbing. I was not carrying a sword and would not face a man like that, even armoured and bristling with weapons. I left for an inn and set about a long swigging of ale.'

I depart Hagger's place and return to the town strangely comforted by my time there. My confusion has cleared and I am set on unravelling this puzzle despite Oliver's practical advice. Helen will have to know. I would not be able to hide my concerns from her; she will understand; there must be no danger to her in my enquiries; and I will cease at any sign that Charles has scent of my investigation.

*

Sir George is somewhat recovered and rests in his chambers. Helen is pleased to tell me that he ate only a modest portion of mutton pie and small beer for dinner. She has arranged my consultation with her father for the next day after breakfast. There is an eager glint in her eyes as she willingly agrees to postpone our diversion on horse for a stroll around the town shops to choose a gift.

'It will be a small present for Mistress Gredley, my hostess here these past months.'

'Ah, well, we must not disappoint the Mistress and I am sure she is deserving.'

Her tone has set me on a path to greater expense. I am reminded of my inexperience in matters of the heart and tokens of love. We are followed by Lucy and two guards as we wander the crowded streets arm-in-arm. Helen guides me to the shop of a silversmith and we browse a display of trinkets, bowls, candlesticks and other shiny wares. I follow her as she picks up a chain, a little casket, then shows me a small bowl for sugared dainties. I nod my head, she offers a price and after a short exchange on numbers, it is done. But not quite.

'What now, my love?'

It is decided even before I note the sign of a goldsmith a few paces distant. We are there in short time and the process is much the same. I stand back while Helen picks, examines and discusses matters of quality and value with the craftsman. A fine, jewelled brooch is chosen; glittering and pretty, but more modest than many on display. It is handed to me and I take care in pinning it to Helen's bodice. Relieved that the final price does not require me to fumble for a scrivener's note of credit, I am taken aside and my purse near emptied. My reward is a kiss and whispered promises of ardent love.

On our return journey, we are approaching the Guildhall when we pass a building that I remember Oliver pointed as Tremayne's town house. I wonder if I should offer my sympathy and respect to the mother and father of the young victim. Their grief will still be raw and my support for Charles will cast me in a poor light. I know little of the character of young Walter Tremayne and there may be some benefit of understanding more why he had an attachment to Charles and others linked to our venture. Would such an enquiry be too sly and unworthy? Well, it cannot be done now. I will ponder this question further before making a decision.

Our mounts are readied when we arrive back at Hawkin's courtyard and we are soon on our way after a short refreshment. We head east and follow a coastal path around a headland under a warm sun tempered with a sea breeze. When we cannot be heard by others I turn to Helen and tell her of my misgivings about Charles, doubts of his innocence in the killing and a wish to re-examine earlier suppositions.

'I had thought you were quite firm in your friendship. Why has there been such a change?'

'I have come to learn more of his character in recent days. You may have scratched a scab to reveal the truth, when you suggested my opinion was skewed by his action in saving my life.'

'Was there also a finding in St Malo that altered your thinking? You have not shared the complete nature of your business and actions at that place with me. All I know is that Walsingham was behind your inclusion in the enterprise. In that case, I cannot imagine your mission was carefree jaunt for bracing sea air and a cup of French wine.'

'That concerned a different, but related matter. It... it is complex.'

'Then you must explain to me in simple words I will understand, William.'

Her mischievous charm is hard to resist, but I had not wished to delve so deep into the affair for this conversation. Sir George will not thank me for my openness with her on matters which he considers unsuited to the female disposition. But if she is to help and advise, there can be no harm in her knowing more if she keeps it close.

'I will oblige, my dear, but first you must promise to hold this as our secret and will not mention this conversation to your father.'

'Very well, William, I know my father believes I will faint at the mention of men's rough schemes and I will hold it in our confidence.'

'Charles claimed he had intelligence that there was a threat of an invasion on our West Country ports backed by Spain and Rome. We were despatched to St Malo to establish the veracity of his information. If the intelligence was confirmed then our fleet of ships would be diverted to defence of the ports under royal warrant. Your father's great venture would be abandoned. Fortunately, the intelligence proved to be false.'

She gapes at me and halts her mount.

'Does my father know this?'

'Yes, but he was informed only when we returned with good news, so did not have time to fret and stew while we were gone.'

She shakes her head, then urges her palfrey into a walk.

'Why St Malo? Do they hold secrets from Spain and Rome there, which are easily given over a cup of ale?'

I explain the connection of Stukley with Fitzmaurice and the pretext of our visit with a token from his son held hostage. She listens to my words and when I am finished we ride in silence as she considers all I have said. It is some minutes before she speaks.

'It is indeed a dense and confusing intrigue. Did the man Fitzmaurice give his information freely?'

'Lord Fitzmaurice was away from his house. It was Lady Fitzmaurice that confirmed there was no design on English ports.'

'You discussed these matters with a lady? What manner of lady: old; young; welcoming; sour-faced; fair?'

'She is young, fair and has three children.'

'So, you were sent there as a handsome young emissary to charm her.'

'No, my love, she was suspicious of my motives and connections, but there was no benefit to her cause from hiding the truth. Lord and Lady Fitzmaurice disliked Stukley and their quarrel is with an Irish earl, not our queen.'

She nods her head, but I see from her furrowed brow there are more questions to be asked. Could it be simply mistaken intelligence and not malicious? Why was there concern at the delay in our return? What role did Pennes play? Did I encounter danger? I tell her all about Stack's visit, our escape from St Malo and bargaining for our assistance in Guernsey. Finally, I am done and there is another long interlude of quiet while Helen mulls over my long and intricate tale.

She says, 'I am happy that you have told me all this, William. After all, I begged that there should be no secrets between us.' She hesitates and has trouble forming her next words. 'But what is to be done? Charles Wicken will be gone from here in a few days and surely it is for others to decide if he has acted in a way that obstructs the security of our state.'

'Yes, you are right and Oliver has urged me to abandon thoughts of further investigation. But... my conscience will not let it lie. I must know if my trust in Charles was misplaced and I was too easily led.'

'And if you find strong evidence of his guilt; what then?'

'I do not know whether our laws will allow a re-trial, but Walsingham and Wynter will wish to know if he has spread false intelligence.'

We reach a point on the headland named Prince Rock. I signal it is time we made our return. I have a sense of release from my telling to Helen. Of course, it is not complete. I have not scrubbed away a nagging at the edge of my thoughts from the intimacy with Lady Fitzmaurice. I will reveal that to her, but at a later time.

We have reached the edge of the town streets when Helen touches my arm and bids me move aside and let the others pass.

She says, 'Am I to be your helper in this affair, William? I understand the reasons for pursuing your investigations but would be more content if I could assist in some way.'

I had intended to let our conversation settle on her consideration more before broaching this subject, but I am thankful she has spared my asking.

'Yes, my love, there is a delicate enquiry I cannot undertake, but to which you may be well-suited. Will you accompany me back to my lodgings on the way to Hawkins' place so I can explain?'

We divert to the Gredley house in Lockyer Lane where our guards lead the horses through to a water trough in the yard while Helen and Lucy follow me into the house. The maid fetches her Mistress and I am pleased to introduce Helen. I hand her my gift. She is full of flutter and gratitude, twirling, brushing her skirts and wanting to set about preparing refreshment. I beg we are excused under pressure of time but will take up her offer in the next days.

'Well then, I must thank you in a proper manner.' She kisses me warmly on a cheek, then follows with Helen. 'You will keep your promise, Doctor. It will be a delight to converse with you and your fair lady.'

'Of course, Mistress Gredley, now I would show Helen writings in my chamber if you will allow? It will be only a brief interval.'

She casts me a knowing look and bows her head in assent. She will be imagining our wish to share an intimate exchange. She is right, but there is also more to be done. I make to leave, then stop as if remembering another matter.

'You may be able to assist with a small enquiry, Mistress Gredley. Do you know the maid, Amy Wearing? She serves the gentlemen in the *Seven Bells*.'

'Why yes, I know her family.'

'Helen and her maid, Lucy, are new to this town and would know more about the notable gentlemen they will encounter in the days leading to the celebration of the grand sailing. Do you know the house where she resides? She will be well-placed to offer advice on the character and inclinations of those gentlemen.'

I have a sense that it is a weak and unusual request, but there is no hint of wonder as she informs the location of her modest family dwelling close by the inn.

I close the door and take Helen in my arms, but she pushes at my chest and I am left to kiss the air.

'First, you will tell me the reason for that exchange with Mistress Gredley. "Notable gentlemen", indeed; "advice on their inclinations" – you have much to learn in subtlety, William. Do I understand that Amy Wearing is the maid who changed testimony in Charles Wicken's trial?'

'You have it, my dearest, and as for subtlety – my enquiry served its purpose well enough.'

'The mistress was dazzled, and her senses overwhelmed, by your gift. If you had asked her directions to the gates of hell she would not have blinked.'

At another time there would be entertainment in the thrust and parry of our conversation. But I must explain before a tap on the door comes.

'Amy Wearing will not talk freely with me. She has me closely connected with Charles and she is wary, perhaps frightened, of my intentions. You and Lucy, on the other hand, are not known to her and would put her at ease with innocent enquiries about the gentlemen she serves. Her service could be rewarded with silver.'

'Lucy will have to know the true motive behind our discussion.'

'Can she be trusted to hold a secret?'

'Yes, she has already heard the gossip about Wicken's trial.

She is apt to chatter but would not cross me if I give a stern warning.'

'I do not have to warn that you must tread softly in your questioning?'

'No, William, you do not. I take it that the nub of our enquiries will be to uncover the reason behind her change in testimony. Is there aught else?

'I leave that to your discretion, my love.'

There is a knock at the door and we must leave. Time only for a hurried kiss and a suggestion that she visits Amy the next morning when I will be in consultation with Sir George.

Twenty Two

Helen and Lucy have already departed when I arrive for my consultation with Sir George. I do not relish the prospect of our meeting; it will be a prickly affair and I am certain he will not find my counsel agreeable. But it must be done. I am shown to the chambers set aside for him on the first storey. A maid opens a door and I find him spread across a seat with his feet on a stool. He holds a leg of cooked fowl in one hand and is dabbing his lips with a linen cloth in the other.

'God's blessing to you on another fine morning, Sir George.'

'And to you, my dear. Pour us some wine and draw your seat close.'

A bottle of claret and two glasses wait on a table. He is dressed for comfort in loose blouse and hose. He appears in good humour, but his face is blotched with an unhealthy pallor and the mound of his belly is unnaturally large. It is early in the day for wine, but it may serve to settle the air between us. I pour two small measures and hand him his glass. I must tread gently and dance around other subjects before touching his health, so we begin with talk of arrangements for the grand departure of the fleet and his oration. His eyes light with eager anticipation as he describes the scene he imagines in a few days. He says that four other merchants will be here and have been invited to offer orations.

'Will Master Sindell be among those present? I hear he has cargo in three, well-armed ships commanded by Captain Wicken.'

'Jeremy Sindell – I know him only by repute. He has an estate near York and we have exchanged letters.'

'Do you consider it strange that his considerable interest in this great venture is done at arm's length?'

He shrugs. 'It matters little to me. He has good wealth and brings assets to our undertaking. I understand he trades in wool and ironmongery.'

'He also has a captain with experience in raiding Spanish

179

treasure in Biscay.'

'Indeed he has.' He pauses, then adds, 'It is rumoured that Sindell adheres to the old religion and stays North to avoid examination. Still, that is no concern for our commerce and this adventure will enhance the glory of Her Majesty and her dominions.'

Then, abruptly his mood changes, he drops the chewed meat on the floor and picks up his glass.

'But we are here to discuss my wellbeing, are we not? I must warn you, William, that I do not hold physicians in high regard. I have had more relief from Rosamund and Helen's herbal soothers than the ministrations of learned men.'

'You are right to be wary, Sir George. We physicians have much to learn from the herbal preparations from goodwives and healing women. Our profession is too quick to ignore their knowledge and intuition.'

He grunts then sips his wine.

'Will you prepare my astrological chart? It has been done before with no benefit.'

'That may not be necessary. Perhaps you can explain your bodily sensations when you are overcome by dizziness and nausea.'

He considers for a moment and then describes head pains and a tightness in the chest as though a great weight is placed on it. There has been no vomiting accompanying the nausea, but his dizziness persists after the head and chest pains have eased. I question his eyesight, which he avers is clear, but admits that his extremities have a tingling and numbness with the pains. It is not a physician's normal practice to examine the body of a patient, but in this case, it may be revealing. He is hesitant before allowing my gentle probing. I put my ear to his chest and belly, then feel the heat in his head, neck, hands and toes. He has an amused look when I am finished.

'You have an unusual way of examination, my dear.'

'I find the heat and sounds of a body can be informative. In this case, they confirm my opinion.'

'You have reached an opinion already?'

'There can be no doubt there is an imbalance in humours. The blood is weak and the phlegm strong.'

'Do you have remedies?'

'There is but one. Each body has an ideal construction and the vital organs do their work in maintaining a healthy balance within the limits of that framework. When the extent of the construction becomes too large or too small, the organs strive to keep this balance. Your body has grown too great for the vital organs to work effectively. The flesh on your bones must be reduced.'

'Ha, you and Helen are of the same mind. But is it also not true that good food and drink sustain bodily functions?'

'Yes, but there should be moderation. Your organs cannot keep pace with your nourishment.'

'It is as I thought. You have naught to offer me.' He drains his glass and throws it on the floor in a show of petulance.

It is a reaction I half-expected, but perhaps not so extreme.

'If you search your mind, Sir George, you will find that you agree with my words. You deny them because they are unwelcome and the remedy will be troublesome to see through.'

His jaw is set firm and I see he will not be moved.

'You will die before your time if you continue unabated.'

'That is impudent beyond...' His temper explodes but does not finish. His body sags and a tear slides down his cheek. 'I know, I know... you have it right, my dear. I feel... my end is near and... there is so much to be done.'

He is soon blubbing like a babe and I hand him a cloth. His body heaves and words like 'Helen', 'treasure', and 'finance' lurch through his breath. It is some minutes before his distress subsides.

'What should I do?'

'You must confine your food and drink to no more than one-half of your present servings.'

He gasps in dismay, then collects himself and announces that he will abide by my recommendation.

'I have a sense in my being that... that a darkness is near and I will soon be called to His mercy. I have a longing to be present for the fulfilment of a dream and the success of the adventure fleet. It is also my dearest wish to see my precious daughter wed to a man I know loves her well and will care for her. But… it will be two years or more before my ships are returned here and you… you must survive.'

I share his dread but cannot voice it. It is plain that he struggles with his thoughts and takes some time to form his next words.

'I understand the hardships and dangers that will be faced on the adventure. I had a desire to keep Helen close to me and find a man who endured the adventure and would be worthy of her hand. But now… now I would happily see her wed, and quickly, before I am gone from this earth.'

Does he mean… 'You wish me to forgo my place on the voyage?'

'Aye, would that be so terrible; an end to your dreams of discovery and a voyage of adventure?'

'No, Sir George, I would willingly forsake all for Helen's hand in marriage. It is the prize I treasure above all. I have come to regard my sailing with the adventure as an unwelcome hazard that confronts our happiness together.'

I see that my words are a surprise. He eyes me directly to ensure I speak true.

'Well then, it is settled. Come kiss me, my dear, as a token of our agreement. You will hold our understanding close 'til I speak to the Captain General and Sir Humphrey. Your expertise in the mathematics of navigation will be a loss, but they must bear it. In particular, please do not mention this to my daughter for the present.'

I rise from my seat and embrace him fiercely with a kiss on both cheeks. I am flooded with relief and joy, but guard against an outpouring of these emotions until I leave the chamber. I close the door, shut my eyes and offer thanks to God for this unexpected and joyous end to our encounter.

*

I indulge in a quiet celebration of my release from the New Lands venture with a cup of claret in my lodgings. My mind is filled with visions of our marriage day. Will it be at St Giles in

Cripplegate or one close by the Morton house at Leadenhall? There is much to be done in short time if it is to be quick, but my mother will delight in its arranging. It is vexing that I cannot share my news with others but must be patient and wait for Sir George's signal. I hear voices in the corridor; a knock at the door; Mistress Gredley enters. She tells me that Helen and her maid wait for me in the parlour. Helen. She will have visited the maid from the inn. I had forgotten.

I am quick and flustered in my greeting, but it appears to pass unnoticed. Mistress Gredley bids Lucy help her with a small task in the kitchens and I am alone with Helen.

'Well my love, did you speak with Amy Wearing?'

'Yes, she has a pleasing manner and likeable family. Her mother welcomed us warmly and provided refreshment.'

'Was she open in her conversation?'

'I will get there in good time, William. She was suspicious of our motives at first, but Lucy put her at ease with tales of her service in London and our travel to Plymouth town.'

'Did you offer silver?'

'It was not offered or sought at the outset, but we left some on the table at the end. Now, may I continue?'

I murmur my apologies. I would take her in my arms and whisper my secret but must be patient.

Helen says, 'We had a long conversation about her gentlemen at the inn. She has her favourites and there are a few we were told to watch carefully in our encounters. It was Lucy who mentioned your name and described your appearance. Amy had spoken well of Oliver and it seemed a good opportunity to refer to you as his friend.'

'I'll wager she had no sweet words for me.'

'In fact, dear William, Amy said you are a handsome fellow with a pleasant air, but you are condemned by your association with Charles Wicken. She despises that man and his close associate who she portrayed as a terrifying monster.'

'That associate will be Stack.'

'Well then, it was the man named Stack who came to her and offered coin for a changed testimony. After a refusal, there was bullying with talk of violence against her and her family. She talked of being cloaked in shame by her dishonesty at the quarter session, but felt she had no other course.'

'So, it is the same as with Master Hagger; bribes and threats. I am sorry for her distress and glad that you left her with coin.'

'There was grief and sobbing at her memories of Walter Tremayne. Despite a diversity in their stations, they were of an age and she clearly had a fondness for him. She cautioned against following Wicken but was ignored. Apparently, Tremayne was entranced by him and his reputation as a man of action.'

'You have surpassed expectations, my love. It would seem you have a talent for gentle interrogation.'

Damn that man. He has soiled and demeaned my efforts on his behalf for his trial. I cannot be certain that he was guilty of the killing, but his actions weigh heavy in that direction.

'There is more.'

'More?'

'Amy overheard snatches of the argument between Wicken and Tremayne as they left the inn. Tremayne was saying that Wicken must deny some matter, or he would reveal all. She could not be certain of the issue but was adamant that Wicken was hot and aggressive in his conduct. There was little doubt in her mind that Wicken was the killer.'

Twenty Three

Two days have passed since my consultation with Sir George and Helen's with the Wearing maid. Still, there is no indication that I may share news about my liberation from the venture and I cannot settle my mind on a course of action that should be taken on the question of Charles. Helen is all for informing Justice Shanning, but do I have enough to challenge the original verdict and would that be allowed in law? It is a general presumption that there is a corruption in our system of justice, jurors would deny their pockets were stuffed and Amy Wearing would not thank me for bringing her shame into the open. Perhaps, only Hagger would be happy to share his experience of intimidation and half-measure of defiance. It is much the same with his intelligence on the threat of invasion; I am sure in my own mind that it was a contrivance; doubtless as a tactic to avoid the hangman, although another, unknown, motive cannot be discounted. However, all I have to offer as evidence is a possible sighting of Stack in St Malo and Charles' dissembling over a ship's journey to Dartmouth. This could easily be refuted as my misunderstanding or his misspeaking.

All these untidy notions, circle and swoop, vying for consideration and control as I sit in Wynter's receiving room, waiting for dinner. Wynter has taken a house for the short time he has left here. A strong disagreement with Hawkins is much discussed in the town and is the cause of his move from chambers in the Captain General's house. Helen reported that angry words on the subject of the defence of the seas around our land were heard by many outside the confines of their chamber. He is here at last.

'Ah, William, good day to you and apologies for my delay on the quays.'

He leads me through to the dining chamber with an admission that our dinner may be found wanting due to hurried arrangements in this house. It is a small house, certainly smaller than those Sir William will be accustomed to occupy, but it is neat enough.

'I have employed a housekeeper at short notice, she has a nervous disposition and is apt to misunderstand or forget my instructions for the kitchens.'

'It is no matter, Sir William, our talk will be more important than our nourishment.' I do not know why I have been invited here. I can only assume it will be concerned with the intelligence from St Malo. Perhaps he has received fresh instructions from Walsingham.

A jug of wine waits on a small table. He pours two cups and sits in his seat with a contented sigh.

He says, 'I will be pleased to be away from this place. God willing, all will be clear in a few days,' He pauses and twirls his cup. 'How do you view the prospect of sailing with the venture fleet, William?'

Has Sir George mentioned my release? I must be circumspect until I am sure. 'I have a mixed opinion. I am stirred by the splendour of the undertaking, but also anxious for my part.'

'Your honesty is appealing. Many will not admit a sense of fear, but it will be a hazardous adventure and you are wise to weigh grave dangers against profit.'

'Should I assume you have no new intelligence that will obstruct our sailing?'

'There is naught from London, but it will be too early for a reply to my letter. The *Griffin,* in which you sailed to St Malo, has been released and her crew is back in Plymouth. The men have been questioned closely on their stay in that French town and a few scraps of information have drawn my attention.'

I had heard of this homecoming but did not expect the crew would bring any news of value. 'Can these snippets be relied on?'

'On their own, no, but they confirm a piece you gathered from the Lady Fitzmaurice and are at odds with Captain Wicken's assertion. It is concerned with Ireland. The name of Nicholas Sanders and a possible incursion to an Irish port from Biscay were joined in gossip overheard by two men.'

'Is this a vital matter? I had thought the notion of a quarrel between Irish lords was regarded as trivial.'

'Its importance would depend on the intentions of a landing in Ireland. If it is simply one or two ships conveying Fitzmaurice so that he can make his peace with the Earl Desmond, there would be no concern for our security. But mention of Sanders is troubling. He is an ardent proclaimer of the old religion and severe enemy to Her Majesty.'

'Lord Fitzmaurice has sworn fealty to the crown and has a son held as hostage.'

'The Irish lords make an unpredictable and untrustworthy alliance. They could be sparked into rebellion if the incursion is significant and carries promises from Spain and Rome. Also, Fitzmaurice will know there is no mortal danger to his son; only continued containment with Sir John Bond.'

'I confess I know little of Irish politicking. Do you have an opinion on the likely danger posed to our security from these morsels of intelligence?'

'It is in the balance, although my mind sways towards a harmless rather than perilous meaning.' He pauses to sip his wine. 'There is another service you could render, William. I am not convinced of the character of Captain Wicken. I know his stories can be excused through over-eagerness or error but would know if there is more behind his actions and messages of intelligence.'

'What would you have me do?'

'I suppose there is little to be accomplished in the few days before his sailing, but it would put my mind at ease if you could prise a little more from him through innocent conversation.'

'He knows of my visit to St Malo and would guard against offering any information that may question his reliability.'

'Indeed, but your recent history, indicates that you have a rare talent for extracting valuable intelligence from unlikely circumstances.'

This is another request I cannot refuse. But he ascribes too much to my efforts in St Malo and Walsingham's praise for my earlier work in London. It was fortune, not guile, which produced those favourable outcomes. I have steered away from Charles these past days through... what: fear; awkwardness; or reluctance to confront my error in judgement? Whatever the reason, I should do it. It may settle my thoughts one way or another, as well as guiding Wynter's. What pretext should I use for approaching him? I cannot be direct, so must manufacture a topic that concerns us both and worm my way gently into his confidence.

'Very well, I will seek an early opportunity to converse in private with him.'

'And it must be quick. There is little time remaining.'

The door is opened by a small woman of middle years who I take to be the housekeeper. She lingers by the door with hands clasped tight, while a young maid carries a tray to our table. The smell and appearance of roast meats offer some promise, despite Wynter's cautioning.

*

Diffidence and delay will not do; I will seek out Charles before my mind can conjure up reasons not to meet with him alone. His ship is at the end of the main quay. An imposing galleon, *Hawkwind* makes a pretty sight in the afternoon sun with a light wind humming through taught ropes. Charles is not in evidence on deck and I ask a fellow who loiters on the forecastle to request his captain join me on the quayside. It is some minutes before he appears from his cabin and leans over the rails.

'William, I had not expected to see you on the quays. You should be with your lady or dawdling over a feast with Hawkins and Wynter.'

I ignore the barb in his comment. 'I would speak with you, Charles. Can you spare me a few moments for advice on a private matter? I will stand your choice of wine in an inn close by.'

He hesitates and runs a hand through his long, uncovered hair to consider my request. 'I have too much business about the ship to leave it now, but you are welcome to join me in my cabin.'

I had hoped to have an open location for our conversation. The closed, familiar surroundings of his cabin may give him an advantage. Nevertheless, I cannot dither, so step across a creaking board and on to the deck. He opens the door to his cabin and waves me through with a flourish. It is an impressive space; larger than I have seen on other ships and well-furnished. Glazed windows to the rear throw light on a sizeable cot bed, a small working table scattered with papers and a more extensive, carpeted table with two chairs and four stools set around it. He points me to a chair and unlocks a cupboard.

'Will you take a glass of this wine from Madeira Island? I was gifted with a crate by the master of a Portuguese trader the last year.'

He places unusual emphasis on the word, 'gifted' and I must suppose that it was given under duress. The glasses are small, but finely-crafted and add to the air of wealth shown by a number of gold and silver objects arranged in the cabin. They will also be pickings from his raids in Biscay. I compliment him on the wine, which is sweet and flavoursome.

'You said you seek advice, William.'

'Yes, it is a delicate affair and you are well-placed to guide a decision which has nagged and pricked at my conscience for some time.'

'Oh, and what is this affair?'

'I believe my temperament and inclinations may be unsuited to our great adventure and would value your opinion.'

'Why, William, this is a surprise, and so close to our departure.'

'I know that I will be regarded as cowardly and weak if I withdraw at this late stage. I see hard, fighting men such as you, Hawkins and Stack in our number and feel exposed as soft and unprepared.'

He raises his eyes at my admission and considers before giving a response. 'You are indeed unsuited, William. I wonder you have tarried here so long.'

'Yet, it is a magnificent adventure that captures the imagination and admiration of many. There would be great credit in my taking part. Why, I understand that poor unfortunate Tremayne was besotted with imaginings of glory and pestered you to take him on your ship.'

He is stilled at that name and his face distorts to a scowl. 'Why would you mention that name and where did you learn that story? It is not true.'

'I thought that was the reason for your disagreement in the *Seven Bells*. I forget who informed me, but it was doubtless learned during my investigations for your trial at the quarter session.'

'I would mark it as a favour if you do not speak that name.'

'I did not think you so squeamish, Charles. He is dead and you are cleared of blame.'

'Yes, and you were a finely-played instrument in my freedom.'

'Instrument? Played?'

'Ha, I picked those words in error. I did not mean…'

'Do you have an opinion that I was fully convinced of your innocence?'

He stares at me with an expression I have not seen on him before; doubt crossed with puzzlement. 'Indeed, that was my understanding – and so I am - innocent.'

'Come now, Charles, let us not play games. The killing of Tremayne meant naught to me. I was fixed on clearing the name of a friend who had done me a great favour in the rescue by Loddiswell. Your trial was well-managed. I sowed unease about your identity, used a little trickery and I had no doubt that you would spread your influence among the jurors.'

He sits back in his seat, folds his arms and gazes at me. Have I played my hand too quickly? The silence between us sparks and froths with heavy consequence. I have an urge to speak but will hold for his comment.

'Well, William, it seems I may have misjudged your character. It appears you are not the trusting, guileless soul I took you for. But let us talk no more of this. You will not wrench an admission of guilt from me, even though the trial is done and I will be gone from here in short time.'

'That was never my intention, Charles. As you say, a confession would serve no purpose. But there is an aspect that perplexes. Why was it necessary to manufacture an elaborate tale of threat to these ports that included the name of Stukley? You must have known his death in Maroc would be confirmed.

After all, Stack knew some months before following his visit to St Malo.'

His eyes narrow and there is a growling sound rising from his throat.

'You will leave my ship now, Doctor, before my patience and good manners are exhausted. You are indeed the fuckwit I took you for if you believe you can muddle my thoughts with a clever tongue.'

I do not need a second warning. I can do no more here. I rise from my seat, thank him for his advice on my participation in the venture and exit his cabin with as much grace as I can muster. My legs are unsteady as I stride across the deck, around a pile of small rafts and across the plank to the quayside. I keep my eyes ahead, stop after twenty paces or so and breathe deeply to settle my senses.

*

I hurried back to Wynter's from the quays, but he had quit his house on urgent business. I passed a note to his housekeeper requesting that he call at my lodgings at his earliest convenience. I learned her name as Mistress Sibson. True to Wynter's words, she was tremulous and wary of my presence at the door. I stood back so as not to intimidate and she was pleased to tell me that she knew of my good nature from Mistress Gredley, her long-time friend. She confided that she would be pleased when the venture fleet sailed and her town returns to its normal state.

I have stayed in my lodgings, waiting for Wynter, but his delay has stretched past nine bells. I have had supper, turned a few pages of my books and written a letter to my mother. I have confided in her about my withdrawal from the New Lands adventure. I believe she will be thankful for my release and certain she will be overjoyed that preparations for our wedding day can commence on our return to London.

I have been confined in the close heat of my chambers too long, so go to the front of the house for cooling night air. It is unusually busy for the late hour in this neighbourhood. A group of drunks stagger and gabble down the lane. They are stopped by three men. Loud words are exchanged and there is a scuffle. One man is down and is being beaten; others run away. I will not intervene. It is a too common occurrence here these past weeks and no doubt the primary reason for Mistress Sibson's timidity. I turn and open the door when a voice calls me.

'Doctor Constable, I apologise for the late hour.'

It is Wynter with two guards. They were the three men who scattered the drunks. His guards hold the one who was beaten. He can barely stand and his face is bloodied.

'Were you attacked, Sir William?'

'No, those men were unruly and in need of correction. This one here will be taken to the cells.'

He orders his men to take him and return here. Wynter appears to be in a high temper. I invite him inside and then to my chambers. I take his cap and offer him a seat. He declines refreshment.

He declares, 'Discipline of the men in Hawkins' fleet is wanting and it will worsen in this town once Gilbert's ships are here.' His teeth are bared and it is more snarl than statement.

I can only mutter my agreement and wait for a calming in his humour. I wonder if he has recently parted from another strong disagreement with Hawkins.

'Your note indicated that you have some news, Doctor.'

'I met with Captain Wicken earlier this day and had an interesting conversation.'

'I am glad you acted with speed in this matter. Did you uncover any vital information?'

'It was plain to me from his answers and demeanour that he was the killer of Walter Tremayne. He would not give an open admission of guilt but did not deny bribery of jurors and influencing testimony of witnesses. His manner was sly and complacent, believing that he has cheated the hangman and will soon be away from this town.'

'Is there more? What of his message to Walsingham? Did you press him on the question of Ireland?'

'I questioned his intelligence on the threat of invasion and whether it was an invention. During my conversation with Lady

Fitzmaurice there was mention of a man fitting the description of Wicken's secondary, named Stack, who visited her house and was informed of the certainty of Stukley's death in Maroc. His attitude changed abruptly when I related my knowledge of this, becoming hostile and abusive. Although I have no firm evidence, it is my belief that he manufactured the threat outlined in his note to Walsingham.'

'There was naught on Ireland?'

'I was dismissed from his cabin before I came to that subject.'

He considers all I have said in silence, eyeing me with an expression I cannot read.

Finally, he steeples his fingers and says, 'I confess I am disappointed, Doctor. Perhaps I overestimated your capabilities. I care little about the killing and whether you consider Wicken to be a murderer. All that is over and cannot be revisited.' He pauses and shakes his head before continuing. 'I had hoped for information on Ireland. Your supposition on the false intelligence is of mild interest, but I cannot act upon the sighting of a secondary in St Malo. Wicken and his crew are privateers and that French town is well-known for hosting their kind. This meeting leaves me no further forward in my deliberations.'

He rises and exits my chamber without further words. I am left feeling like a boy who has been scolded by his tutor for a dismal failing in Latin grammar. This is a side to Wynter I have not seen before. It is a small blow to my pride that I have not met his expectations, but my main concern is that my conviction on Charles' guilt on two counts has nowhere to go. It seems he will escape justice for murder and there are insufficient grounds to condemn his act of treason.

Twenty Four

If there is no more to be done with an investigation of Charles Wicken I am determined to pass much of my time remaining here in the company of Helen. I will banish thoughts of murder and intrigue and dwell on gentler aspects of life. It is wet and blustery outside, so there will be no ride out of town this day for intimate exchanges under the shade of a tree. I am cloaked and hooded as I step around mud and ordure in the streets on my way to Hawkins' place.

A maid takes my damp outerwear and boots for drying then goes to fetch Helen while I wait in a receiving chamber. I am called through to the parlour where Helen sits with Lucy and a child, which must be Hawkins' youngest daughter. The chamber is cosy with a warming fire in the hearth. Helen is reading a book and Lucy appears to be instructing the child in needlework. Our greetings are over and Helen bids Lucy take the child to her chamber under the pretence of obtaining more threads for their task. We kiss sweetly on the lips and I take a seat by the fire to cure my wet toes.

I say, 'How is your father this day?'

'He declares he is well, but I detect from his manner that he ails. He puffs and blows when taking stairs and there is a general listlessness about him.'

'Has he mentioned our consultation?'

'Yes, but in brief outline only. You had an effect on him and time will tell if he takes your advice to any benefit.'

'You will know that I recommended a reduction in his intake of nourishment. Does he follow this instruction from your observation?'

'He does not starve, but there is a little more restraint. He had only eggs and small beer when breaking his fast, but last supper he could not resist sizeable servings of a gammon.'

It is plain that she worries about Sir George, and with good reason. It is too early for another consultation, but I should request one before we depart this place for London. She has made no comment on my place in the venture fleet, so it would seem Sir George has not informed Hawkins or Gilbert.

'Has Sir George discussed arrangements with you for celebrations to mark the grand sailing?'

'I know only that there will be decorations on the quays and a platform will be built for the notables to give their orations. Father is distracted in his discussions with the Captain General and Sir William. There was a fearful dispute the last night with much commotion, stamping and strong words.'

So that was the reason for Wynter's foul humour at my lodgings. It is to be hoped relations will mellow in short time or there will be others in this town discomfited by harsh words and actions.

'Is Sir George here, in this house?'

'He is on the quays. The Captain General was thoughtful in arranging a litter for his transport. He will be occupied there much of this day as Sir Humphrey brings his first ships from Dartmouth.'

I take her hand and we sit in quiet for a few moments. If only I could tell I will be accompanying her back to London.

'What is it, William? You have a dreamy look to your eyes.'

I murmur words about my contentment to be alone in her company.

'You have not mentioned Captain Wicken.'

'No, my love. I would be happy to forget I ever met with him.'

She looks into my eyes as though she would share her thoughts but does not speak. I kiss her lips and whisper in her ear that there should be no confidences between us.

'Ha, I hold no secrets, William. I was choosing the right words for the telling about my visit this last day.'

'A visit. Who did you visit?'

'I went to the house of Robert Tremayne to pay my respects for the loss of a son.'

'That was a bold move.'

'It may be considered polite and usual practice for the family of a noted merchant of London to visit one of similar standing in this town. I was received with courtesy by Mistress Tremayne. Her husband was away with business in Crediton.'

My wonder and admiration at her resourcefulness and daring grows. How many maids would have taken this task upon themselves? She will know that I wish to question the Tremaynes but would doubtless be turned away because of my actions at the quarter session. I hold no great hope for her findings but will hear her out.

'What manner of woman is Mistress Tremayne and is there any relief to grieving from her loss?'

'She is an upright, somewhat stern woman of middle years. It is a large house and neatly kept with many servants. She did not hide objects of devotion to the Catholic faith around her chambers, but I have learned that many in the West Country cling to the old faith. She was composed when talking of young Walter, but there was also sadness and regret in her bearing.'

'Did she talk freely about her son and the manner of his death?'

'First, we discussed the great adventure to the New Lands. I enquired why her family, as one of the wealthiest merchants in this trading town, chose not to join with the fleet.'

It is not a question I would have thought to put, and I wonder at its significance.

'How did she answer?'

'It was a great surprise to me that she was dismissive and unflattering about the possibility of its success, even suggesting the ships would be fortunate to quit this harbour. All that was out before she had considered my connection to the venture. She begged forgiveness for her quick words and tried to soothe my alarm by marvelling at the scale of the operation and offering sympathy for those who manage its diverse interests.'

It is an extreme view but perhaps formed by jealousy. As I know, there are also many in this town who have come to hold a poor opinion of the venture fleet because of prolonged delays and the nuisance created by ships' crews. Helen continues to relate her conversation with the Mistress, which ranges from her husband's recently acquired land and the tutoring of her children.

'We came gently to the subject of her son, Walter, who she portrayed as a headstrong youth, but with a good heart. He was the third son and she admitted her grief at his passing was lessened by the comfort of his elders. I also gained the impression it was shame at the manner of his killing that was her primary concern.' Helen wrinkles her nose in dislike at her recall of these sentiments.

'Was Wicken's name mentioned?'

'Indeed it was, and that was another amazement. His name was spoken fondly. He has visited their home many times and it seems he is still held in high regard by the Tremayne family. She did not believe that Wicken could have killed her son. She blames an unknown vagrant or band of thieves. She would gladly see a handful of beggars and vagabonds plucked off the streets and hanged as an example and warning for her loss.'

I am stunned; speechless. I clamp my mouth when I realise I am gaping like an imbecile at Helen. Why was that not mentioned by Charles? And why did the Tremayne family not come forward to speak on his behalf at the quarter session? But this does not alter my position. I remain convinced of his guilt and I have heard naught that could influence his supposed intelligence on the threat of invasion.

'Was there more telling of significance?'

'I think not. Our conversation was overlong and my attention strayed. I remember asking if Walter had a longing for a life at sea and if he had an admiration for adventures to faraway lands. She denied this and said only that he had expressed a fondness for Ireland.'

'Ireland?'

'Why, is that noteworthy?'

'I am unsure. Were there any other particulars stated about his interest in Ireland?'

'No, it was a small remark and easily forgotten. I remembered thinking only it was curious for a young man to fancy the familiarity of a neighbouring island above the mysteries of undiscovered, alien lands.'

Twenty Five

There are but three days before the grand departure. Wynter has received a message from Walsingham affirming he has no intelligence that will hinder the sailing. Sir George, Hawkins, Gilbert and other masters are in high spirits at the lifting of this final barrier. Wynter also presents as a man who has had a burden lifted from his shoulders and the rift with Hawkins appears to be mended. They talk together in a civil manner and he has been affable enough in my company. Ships from Dartmouth are gathering in the harbour; a platform has been built on the main quay, decked with heraldic banners, standards and decorative tokens from backers and well-wishers. Sir George has employed the services of a Dutch artist, Cornelius Ketel, for sketching the occasion to incorporate into his portrait, which will be completed back in London. The town is teeming and unruly as numbers grow. Our principals have paid for extra watchmen and guards to patrol the streets. Their aim is to keep the crews confined to the inns and whorehouses around their ships after five bells, but there have already been disturbances in the finer quarters. I fear the townspeople will have to bear more mischief before our ships are gone.

At last, my withdrawal from the great adventure has been announced by Sir George. He begged forgiveness from Hawkins and Gilbert, claiming he required a physician he could trust to attend him in London; also, that his daughter would not forgive him if I failed to return. The great men were easy in their acceptance and declared all their ships' masters were now confident in the handling of my shadow-staff for navigation. Hawkins' half-smile hinted at a welcome freedom from responsibility for my care, rather than regret for my loss – a small hurt to my pride I bear gladly. I was allowed to break the news to Helen in private and I will always treasure her joyful expression and our too-brief moment of passion that marked the occasion.

I had a mind to throw a supper at an inn for friends and

acquaintances in the fleet to mark this change in my situation. All the inns are harried and overflowing with eager patrons, so I have resorted to a more intimate gathering at the Gredley household. Sir George begged to be excused and I am left with three guests: Helen; Oliver; and Jacques Pennes. Those first two are here, but it seems our number has dwindled more as a note from Jacques advises of his delay.

Helen says, 'I have not met with Master Pennes. Do you know him well, Oliver?'

'Naturally, we are acquainted. He is a trusted secondary to The Captain General and has been his principal aide in the management of ships and men in our fleet.' He pauses and studies his cup of wine. 'You know he is a dark man from Maroc?'

'Ha, you must not worry at my delicate sensibilities, Oliver. William has already told of his fearsome aspect and that I must not expect to be dazzled with his pretty words.'

I confer with Mistress Gredley and decide that we will begin our supper without Jacques. She has taken particular delight in preparing our food and the first serving is roast lobsters with white bread and a mess of eggs, cream and fruit, which we are told is named a *fricasie*. We set to our table in lively fashion and Helen is eager to inform Oliver of plans for our wedding celebration. Oliver is polite in his exchanges, but it is clear his mind is on the voyage ahead and we soon turn to that subject. We are presented next with boiled mutton and a capon stuffed with oysters when a maid enters and announces my final guest. I welcome him warmly and offer him a seat at the table. He exchanges a brief word with Oliver, bows deeply to Helen and offers compliments on her appearance, which have an air of being well-rehearsed. She offers her thanks and brings Jacques directly into the conversation.

'We were discussing the thrill of discovery in the new and faraway lands across the great sea. I hear that you have journeyed to these places before, Master Pennes.'

'Yes lady, to Hispaniola and the territory named Venezuela.'

'What is the character of those places? Do they have large settlements and a pleasant climate?'

'They are unlike Plymouth and London town. It is hot as Maroc, but the air is heavy and may bring a lethargy on those from Northern countries.'

Talk of the New Lands continues, but Jacques is not given to lengthy narrations and the topic is soon exhausted. He breaks a period of quiet by addressing Helen. 'I am sorry that Doctor Constable – William, will not be numbered in our fleet. He is a fine man and I owe him my freedom. I understand you will be married and I trust you are blessed with a happy and fruitful union.'

I thank him for his kind word and, seeing that he is a little discomfited in giving his compliment, turn to practical matters.

I say, 'You were delayed in your arrival here, Jacques. Was there urgent business with the ships or men?'

'There was a minor confusion over the placement of ships to be moored for the orations. It was Captain Wicken who insisted on a particular spacing of his three ships.'

'Why is that significant?'

He shrugs. 'To my mind, it was a petty squabble and Wicken had his way in the end.' He pauses and glances at an empty chair. 'I had expected him to be present at this table as your friend.'

'He is no friend to me.'

It is out before I have considered how this hot denial will surprise Jacques. I see he is intrigued and lifts his eyes inviting me to explain. Oliver intervenes and says this is no place to discuss the character of a fighting man; meaning it would not be fit for Helen's ears. There is a strained silence around our table. We gaze at each other wondering who will speak next; to switch our conversation, or delve deeper into the sense behind my pronouncement. It is Helen.

'William and I have spoken about Captain Wicken and his actions. His dislike of the man is no secret to me and I have learned something of the nature of his corruption from my own enquiries.'

Oliver and Jacques are both stunned by Helen's assertion and I am sure they will consider her involvement unwise. She catches my eye and tilts her head as though seeking approval to continue. There is no reason to prevent her telling more, so I bow my head to signify she should proceed. She begins to recount the evidence we have gathered about threats, bribery and other reasons to believe that he was the killer of Tremayne. I will add to this with details of my conversation in his cabin when she is done, but there is an itch at the back of my thoughts. I am missing something of significance. But what? Does it concern the murder, or the false intelligence; or both? There is a piece in this puzzle that floats a hair's breadth beyond my reach.

I rise from my chair and walk to a window. I must clear my mind and consider all that I have learned these past weeks. Was anything said here this evening to prick my hidden senses? The hum of conversation has died. My name is called. I turn back to the table.

'What is it, William?' Helen joins me and slips her arm through mine.

I say, 'Jacques, please tell me again about the placement of Wicken's ships in our fleet.'

'All ships are gathered close together on the main quay, or will be once the remaining two arrive from Dartmouth on the morrow.'

'And what was the disagreement about the positioning of Wicken's ships?'

'It was a trivial matter. He would not have his ships between others. He insisted that his ships should be roped at the ends for safety of his cargoes and to protect against scuffing and scraping of the fine varnish he had applied. It could only be a matter of his pride as there was no substance to his anxiety. In the end, Hawkins relented under persuasion of Sir George as there was no profit in continuing the argument.'

I think I have it. If I am right then we must act quickly. But… I cannot be certain; loose threads in the pattern I have imagined are still to be tied.

'I have a theory I would put to you for your opinions.'

*

Our supper is left unfinished and four of us make our way through the streets to Hawkins' house. We are received with some surprise. Hawkins, his wife, Gilbert, Wynter and Sir George are at the dining table, sipping sweet wine and picking at sugared fancies. It is Jacques who begs forgiveness for our intrusion on an urgent matter. There is a bemused expression on Hawkins' face, but he signals to his wife, who hurries to arrange our places at the table. She is about to retire from the chamber and would take Helen with her. My request that she be allowed to remain until our submission is finished is granted, but with some grumbling from Sir George.

When we are all seated, Hawkins says, 'What is the affair that must be revealed at this hour. I am intrigued at the air of mystery you bring to this chamber.'

'I believe that there may be an imminent danger to the ships in your fleet.' I turn to Jacques on my left and rest my hand on his shoulder. 'It was a mention by Master Pennes at our supper that pricked my thoughts. We four have discussed my supposition and concluded it should be brought here directly.'

Gilbert mutters to Hawkins, while Sir George simply gapes at Helen and me.

Wynter says, 'Pray continue, Doctor.'

'It concerns Captain Wicken. Sir William knows of my suspicions about his intelligence on the threat of invasion that concerned Stukley and others. When we last talked, I had thought it was manufactured as a ruse to stay a sentence of hanging at the quarter session.'

'What... I know naught of this,' Gilbert looks in turn at Hawkins and Sir George for enlightenment but finds none. 'Please explain, Doctor Constable.'

'On my visit to St Malo, I learned that Wicken's secondary, Master Stack, had consulted with Lord Fitzmaurice and Nicholas Sanders some months earlier when Stukley's death in Maroc was confirmed to him. On my return, I called at the harbour master in Dartmouth to verify a statement made by Wicken. He had told me that his final piece of intelligence on the invasion was obtained from a vessel named *Falkin*, which had sailed from Corunna. In fact, that ship had sailed from

Antwerp and the cargo was not wine, as he claimed. It is my assertion that Wicken knew there was no threat to the West Country ports. His supposed intelligence was a fabrication.'

'Yes, yes, all this I know,' says Wynter, 'but it is not conclusive. The man, Stack, may have been misidentified and the cargo…'

'I agree, Sir William. This is not enough, on its own. But there is more. It is my strong opinion that Wicken was the killer of Walter Tremayne, but the false intelligence was not connected to his trial. There was no need to seek this way to obtain relief from a death sentence. He had witnesses and jurors threatened and bribed to ensure his freedom. To my shame, I also contributed to the corruption of justice by speaking on his behalf.'

There is a lively conversation between Hawkins, Gilbert and Sir George about Wicken and the killing. It is Helen who outlines the findings from Hagger and Amy Wearing. Oliver voices his suspicions and comments on his observations of Wicken's violent nature and I conclude with an account of my consultation in his cabin.

The chatter subsides and Hawkins says, 'All this points to his guilt and I do not wish to belittle the misfortune to the Tremayne family, but a verdict cannot be undone, save by Her Majesty. He will be away from here before two days are gone and it will be forgotten.'

'There may also be disruption to our plans for the departure,' adds Sir George.

Wynter has listened to the to-and-fro of our voices in quiet and is ready to speak. 'Gentlemen… and lady, I have already given my opinion to William over the murder. I am in accord with the Captain General and Sir George that the time has passed for any action on Wicken's culpability. I understand he has reason to believe the false intelligence was not connected to the killing but has some other, malign intent related to your fleet.'

'Yes, Sir William, and I will come to that in good time. First, you should know that the lady Helen had an interesting conference with Mistress Tremayne, Walter's mother. It would appear that Wicken is well-acquainted with the Tremayne family and has been a frequent visitor to their house. Unlike many others in this town, she believes that Wicken was not guilty of her son's murder. However, the family made no representation at his trial.'

Sir George stares at his daughter, glances at me, then returns to Helen. He disapproves. I continue before he has time to scold her for involvement.

'There is a connection to the old religion in this matter. Jeremy Sindell, who is Wicken's sponsor is reputed to hold to Catholic devotions. The Tremayne household displays Catholic icons and trinkets and it was clear to see those in the Fitzmaurice house in St Malo adhere to the teachings of Rome. This network on its own is not damning, but it is strange that Wicken, who professes to worship only as a matter of convenience, has associations of this kind.'

Gilbert puffs air in dismissive fashion. 'There are many in these parts who hold to the old ways.'

'You are right, Sir Humphrey, and it is only a small piece in this puzzle. It was a statement you made some days past that goes to the heart of the affair.' I pause to determine if there are other comments before continuing. 'I enquired why the fleet was spread over two ports before a short assembly in Plymouth. You answered that it was to ensure the nuisance of the crews are not clustered in one place, but also to guard against an accident of fire and other hazards that increase through enlarged numbers.'

I note that Wynter nods his head slowly as if an understanding creeps at the edge of his thoughts.

'I mentioned earlier that Wicken spoke an untruth about the cargo of the *Falkin*. It was not wine, but fire powder and ironmongery, which was transferred to one of his ships. At our supper, Master Pennes confirmed that Wicken's other ships also contain quantities of fire powder in their cargo.'

Sir George whistles at his imagining and I see that all now comprehend how my narration will end.

'The moment that marshalled my thinking was Master Pennes' mention of Wicken's insistence in the positioning of his ships. I have little familiarity with the handling of ships or explosives, but he would seem to have placed his vessels in a way that may aid mischief and escape. I had also noted a collection of small rafts on *Hawkwind's* deck when I conferred with Wicken in his cabin. I thought little at the time, but now I can envisage them strapped with kegs of fire powder and scattered at night among the close-gathered ships on the main quay. It is my conclusion that Wicken's false intelligence was created so that the fleet would be held here in order to allow preparation for their destruction by fire and explosion.'

I have finished and a heavy quiet settles as the significance of my last words take hold.

Sir George thumps the table. 'He must be taken and held for strong questioning.'

Hawkins and Gilbert murmur their agreement, but I see that Wynter has a question.

'Is there more, William? I see now that your deductions are robust and should be investigated, yet there is no absolute condemnation. Do you infer that Tremayne may be party to this plot and in that case, how do you explain the killing of his son?'

'I do not know if Tremayne is connected in any way that is harmful and I cannot be sure of the motive for the killing. It may be that Walter Tremayne knew of the conspiracy and was silenced before drunken blabbing made it common knowledge. But that is fanciful on my part. I may be wrong.' I pause, then add, 'There may also be a connection to Ireland, which I have not unravelled.'

Oliver says, 'It is a convincing case, William. Yet, I am perplexed at why Wicken mentioned a threat to these ports in his message to Walsingham if he himself has an intention to cause harm here.'

In truth, this is a puzzle that I have difficulty in understanding. 'There may be a number of reasons, deep in the chaos of intelligence gathering and counter activities. The further delay to the sailing of the fleet will give more time for preparing an attack. Belief in a danger as Wicken describes will turn our attention outward and perhaps bring a complacency within the fleet. No suspicion would fall in him who shouts the alarm.'

'And how will Wicken benefit from this conspiracy.'

'That can only come to light from questioning. I have considered whether it is devotion to Rome, loyalty to some other cause or simply financial gain. I do not have a ready answer.'

Wynter places his hands on the table and gazes at each of us before saying, 'Well then, we are all agreed Wicken must be taken now for interrogation.'

I say, 'I beg your patience a little longer, but Master Pennes has identified danger in a hasty intervention.'

Jacques clears his throat and after a small hesitation says, 'We must suppose that Wicken's masters and secondaries on all his three ships have a hand in this plot. They are large, well-armed ships with near three hundred men in their crews. If we board his ship, it is likely we will meet resistance and may initiate a small war, resulting in death and wounding to many men as well as damage to our fleet.'

His warning strikes home and their enthusiasm is dampened. Sir George asks Pennes if he has a solution.

'The lady Helen had a suggestion at our supper.' He peers around me at Helen and gestures with his hand that she should put forward her scheme.

She says, 'You will excuse my small contribution, which may be worthless as I am pleased to know naught of fighting and fierce questioning. I wonder if the grand departure should be marked by a gathering of masters and secondaries in this house on the morrow. The occasion can be framed as a celebration with food and drink to thank the principals on each ship for their steadfastness and courage in advance of the sailing.'

'Yes, yes, I see it now. It is a splendid scheme,' exclaims Sir George.

'Indeed,' says Hawkins, 'then Wicken and his associates can be taken quietly at this place while we board their ships. Lacking in leaders, ships and crews can be secured and searched with little or no blood and no harm to the fleet.'

There is much thumping of the table and agreement that the plan is a good one. I take hold of Helen's hand and brush her fingers against my lips. We exchange a silent contentment at the acceptance of our opinions and proposed method of resolution.

Twenty Six

Noon is the appointed time for the gathering of ships' masters and secondaries. Notes have been delivered to all ships. The notes were worded and delivered in a manner that would discourage any excuse for non-attendance. Over one hundred and fifty men are expected. All arms will be collected before entry to Hawkins' long chamber, which has been arrayed with carpeted tables down one side with the remaining area cleared for our assembly. Restless and fretful, I have arrived early with Oliver. We loiter in the chamber exchanging few words and watching as the servants scurry from the kitchens to lay the tables with various wines, sweetmeats and sugared fruits. It is an unusual and hurried arrangement that has taxed the patience of Hawkins' housekeeper. She is hot and ill-tempered as she barks and spits orders to ensure all is ready.

Wynter, Hawkins and Gilbert have together devised our strategy for this day. The procedures have been set and instructions given. Now, we trust the plan proceeds without disruption. Wynter will position twenty armed men in the adjoining chamber when all have collected here. They will enter when the speeches and prayers for a glorious and successful expedition are made. It is to be hoped that care has been taken in the identification of Wicken's men and there is no fault in the selection of those who will be held. Hawkins and Gilbert have selected two hundred men to board Wicken's three ships under signal from Oliver who will depart the chamber before the prayers begin. Helen has been barred from the gathering and must bide in her bedchamber. She urged her father to do likewise for fear of over-excitement, but he would not heed her words. Presently, he prowls the chamber with an anxious air, picking and sniffing from the bowls and plates. I am thankful when he is distracted by the arrival of two fellow merchants who have significant interests in the enterprise.

The pace of those entering grows and I overhear enquiries on the nature of this congregation given with short notice. The grand departure is scheduled for the next but one morning and I see Sir George huddled with a group of men. He is loud in his assertion that this meeting is a celebration of farewell and not an announcement of a further delay. Pastor Gadge approaches. He has heard of my release from the adventure and offers his commiserations. I thank him and express my regret that I must tend to mundane duties elsewhere. There is no sign of Charles. Will he suspect the motive for this gathering?

The space fills with prattling and chatter, but still Charles is absent. Someone places a hand on my shoulder. It is Wynter who whispers confirmation they are near. I join Oliver and we adjust our position to view those entering. At last, he is here. He enters with assured air and teeth bared in a bright smile as he greets fellow captains. Stack is at his shoulder with narrowed eyes scanning the chamber, followed by other principals from his ships. There is naught in their manner to distinguish them from others here. Are my suspicions misguided; my deductions clouded?

Hawkins and Gilbert are the last to enter and the door is closed behind them. Jacques comes towards me and guides me to a corner. He confides in a low voice that Wicken's men have been counted in and all is set fair on the quay.

He says, 'Your talk the last night was well done, but I wonder you did not refer to our detention in St Malo. Surely, it is connected in some way.'

'I have considered that action but can bring no light to bear on the circumstances here. I had thought it may have been designed as a signal that English ships are not welcome in France where the Catholic Church is eager to quell any whispers of Protestantism.' An imagining of Lady Fitzmaurice brings a small hesitation. 'But I cannot discount the hand of Vaisy, steward at the Fitzmaurice household. He may have been the cause through an association to Wicken.'

'We may find the answer in his questioning.'

I murmur my agreement, but the appearance of Wicken and Stack has brought a sense of unease about their interrogation. Do we place too great a reliance on what may be uncovered? They are not men who will surrender their secrets easily. This brief exchange with Jacques has also nudged the memory of my promise given at Guernsey to the fore. I fill my cup with brandywine and say a silent prayer there will be no call for its redemption.

Hawkins bangs the table and begs for quiet. Gilbert is the first to speak. He praises the steadfast nature of our crews and challenges their leaders to be firm in their resolve. Sir George is next and says much the same, but with emphasis on the wealth and fame that will surely result from a successful venture. The words from both men are well-chosen, but their manner of delivery fails to stir emotions. Hawkins has a more profound presence as a speaker and conjures pictures of glory for men and our queen in heroic battles for Spanish treasure. At the edge of my sight, Oliver leaves the chamber, quietly. Finally, it is pastor Gadge who bestows God's blessing on our righteous enterprise and promises heavenly reward to supplement earthly wealth.

I see Wynter open the door as Gadge comes to a close. His men enter with swords drawn and resting on their shoulders. Those nearest react with cries of surprise and indignation. Hawkins shouts a command for all to be still.

'My apologies, gentlemen, but we must act with caution to preserve the safety of our fleet. Most of you will be untouched. We seek only to question a few of your number.'

I glance across the chamber and see Charles surrounded by four men. He meets my gaze briefly and is led away. His men follow, each held by the arms with four or five guarding. I see they are being roped in the next chamber before being taken to the Guildhall, which will be the place for their questioning. Many gape open-mouthed at these proceedings and it is only when the door is closed that urgent voices swell to express amazement and speculate on the cause of this unexpected happening.

*

I have no part in the searching or questioning, so adjourn to find Helen. She is in the kitchens preparing a soother for her father.

'Shall we take our horses out of the town until supper?'

'It is a tempting notion, dearest, but I must tend to Father. The excitement of your meeting has made him puff and blow. He is quite drained.' Her anxiety is plain to see as she dithers and fumbles with boiling and straining her mixture.

'Then, I will sit with you both for a while, if I may.'

He is in his bedchamber, sprawled on top of the linens. His face is grey; the rasping and wheezing in his chest painful to the ear. I sit on a stool while she bends to spoon the warm potion into his mouth and murmur reassurances. She is uncomplaining and persistent, for he fidgets and wafts his hand to dismiss her care. It is some time before she is finished and his breathing is more regular. We must both know, but dare not speak of the gravity of his illness. He is surely not long for this world unless an extended rest brings marked improvement. That will not be easy to arrange. He waves a weak hand to bid me draw near.

'Well my dears, what a worthless, tiresome object I have become.' His voice is little more than a high-pitched whisper. 'This chest pains me and I cannot shake a damnable weariness. I fear your labours on my behalf will come to naught.'

Helen reaches to clasp his hand and says all will be well if he will take respite from his business.

'It is too late. If I could witness the despatch of the fleet and see you both joined together in God's union, I will be content.'

His eyes close. After only a few moments, they are opened quickly and he stares wide-eyed, first at Helen, then at me.

'I... I have made provision. You must consult with Lawyer Daunt on Canwicke Street. Your fortune is bound close to this venture. My finances are... stretched. Do not blame me... I have loved you... most precious daughter. Lawyer... Daunt has it...'

The effort is too much. His eyes are closed and he is soon asleep with regular snorts and bubbling on his lips. I take her hand and we sit in quiet contemplation at his bedside. He struggled to inform Helen of intentions laid down in his will. There was an admission her inheritance may be diminished if... But now is not the time to discuss such matters. We must pray for a successful outcome to his great adventure. We have been sat for over one hour when there is a tap at the door. A maid opens, pokes her head around and says that Master Tewkes waits for me in the receiving chamber by the hallway.

'Oliver, how was the searching done?'

'It is near finished. There was no resistance to the boarding on two ships and only minor disturbance in the *Hawkwind*. A handful of Wicken's soldiers barred the way to his cabin and threatened violence, but they were subdued after a wounding.'

'Have you heard of the questioning?'

'I know they are close-guarded in the Guildhall and Hawkins has taken the lead in interrogation, but that is all. The results of our searches will be taken there and we are to convene there at midnight for an assessment.'

'Midnight? Will it take so long?'

'We must be diligent in our examinations.' He pauses and inclines his head. 'You were with Sir George when I called. I was to invite both you and him to our night meeting, but I noted he appeared unwell at the gathering in the long chamber.'

'He has taken to his bed and I regret he will not be able to attend.'

'Until midnight then, William. I must be away to ensure all is quiet on Wicken's ships and transport our findings to the Guildhall.'

Twenty Seven

'What has been learned from our prisoners?'

It is Wynter who addresses Hawkins and Gilbert. They have managed the questioning, which has been done in two of the antechambers. Eight of us are sat around a table in the main chamber of the Guildhall where the quarter session was held. Oliver and Jaques are here with Wynter's secondary, Captain Trigg, and Master Lipton, who is attached to Gilbert.

'Naught of value,' says Hawkins. 'Wicken and Stack are hot and brazen in their denials, while the others are steadfast in claiming no knowledge of any conspiracy.'

'One of their number shows more timidity. His eyes dart and there is more behind them than he dares to speak. He is named Tuite and is the navigator on Forrest's ship. I will focus strong questioning on this man in our next hearing.' I cannot help feeling a sense of pity for the man Jacques mentions, but at least it offers some encouragement.

I say, 'Where are they held?'

'They are collected in a chamber at the rear. All are chained and the place is close-guarded.'

'Would there be benefit in placing each man away from his fellows. They may find comfort and courage in togetherness.'

Wynter exchanges a glance with Hawkins and Gilbert. 'Yes, you have a good notion, William, but we are limited by our accommodation. Let us separate Wicken and Stack in their own chambers. The others will have to stay as they are.'

There follows a discussion on the strength and nature of questioning. Hawkins and Gilbert advocate severe methods, while Wynter is more circumspect.

'There is no bar to beating with hand and stick, but we must not resort to torture that brings mortal danger. If it comes to that, it must be in the hands of Secretary Walsingham's men, who are practised in the art of fierce persuasion. Royal warrant must also be granted for torture.'

Others argue the point with Wynter, but he is firm in his

opinion and commands our group by virtue of his commission from Walsingham. I am more concerned with the questions set, rather than the manner of their putting. I enquire whether Stack's visit to St Malo, the rafts on *Hawkwind* and *Falkin*'s landing in Dartmouth have been investigated. Gilbert has an answer from Wicken that the rafts were made by carpenters to store unsteady cargo, but there is no certainty on the other queries. Wynter suggests I draw up a list of critical questions and their reasoning to assist our interrogators.

'What has been found in the cabins and personal compartments, Master Tewkes?' Wynter points to an array of objects laid on nearby tables.

'We scoured all cabins and private nooks of the secondaries. There was a fine assortment of daggers, swords and billhooks. Nine hand guns were claimed and among them, Wicken has four matchlocks of fine quality. He had many trinkets of gold and silver in his cabin. There is a particular piece which dazzles; a gold chain ringed with pearls and linked to a heavy, jewelled cross. It has the appearance of a prayer rope or rosary for Catholic devotion.'

There is some murmuring at this find, but to my mind, it does not have enough significance. He could assert it was kept for beauty and value.

Oliver continues, 'There are four commonplace prayer ropes, created from wool and beads collected from the other ships, together with a small carved crucifix fashioned from bone. The captain named Forrest has a collection of wooden carvings; finely-made, but none that can be linked with any certainty to the old religion. Wicken has two miniature portraits of gentlemen, oval in shape and ringed with gold decoration. One appears to be of Wicken himself and the other cannot be identified. There are no marks on these objects.'

A general sense of unease spreads around the table. It seems I am not alone in holding thwarted expectation of significant results from the search and questioning.

I say, 'What of books, manuscripts and charts? More may be discovered from written words than objects.'

'As to the books, each ship had a copy of *Arte de Navegar* by de Medina; two in the Spanish language and one in French. Wicken had a book on fencing by di Grassi, one on natural philosophy titled *Magia Naturalis* and *Songes and Sonnetts* - a book of poetry by Richard Tottle. Wicken had a few loose papers with written poems inserted in this volume. Stack also had the Tottle book, although it was torn and had many pages missing. Of course, there were many charts, which we did not bring here as our inspection revealed no uncommon markings.' Oliver pauses and glances around the table. 'There is a collection of letters, twenty-seven in all, taken from all men, excepting Wicken and Stack. They had no letters. A cursory examination shows them to be innocent writings received from loved ones, family and friends. All the letters were written in English.'

I know of all the books, save the one by di Grassi on swordsmanship. It is an unremarkable and disappointing collection, but perhaps there will be interest in a closer study of the letters. It seems we may have to rely on beating a confession and I am certain that will not come from Wicken or Stack.

Wynter sighs and sits back in his seat. 'Well, we have little to show for our efforts. Let us resume in five hours. There is but one full day before your planned sailing. We must be quick, but also diligent and careful in our work. William, you are the scholar here, so it is natural to request you take on the commission for scrutiny of books and letters.'

*

I have stayed in the Guildhall to write my notes for the interrogators. There would be no profit in trying to snatch a few hours' sleep as my thoughts run too fast. One of the guards has brought ale and cheese to sustain my awareness and I have started on an examination of the letters. Thus far, they contain commonplace scribblings about small family events: a sick child; the passing of an elderly relative; a modest bequest; the sale of a horse. Can these ordinary men be complicit in a conspiracy against our fleet and our state? It is strange that neither Wicken nor Stack have any letters. Have they been destroyed? I have had a brief inspection of the books and found naught that strikes as unusual in the annotations. I wonder if there is significance in the two books of poetry by Tottle? Stack is not a man I would take for a lover of pretty words.

The shutters are opened by the guards and a grey smudge of dawn is edged in the casements. Hawkins enters, followed by Jacques and Master Lipton. We exchange muted greetings, then they go directly to the chambers holding our prisoners. I return to the papers on my table when there is a shout of alarm and commotion through an open door. Two of the guards hurry there. I follow at a more sedate pace.

We are in the chamber that holds six of Wicken's men. Guards hold chained men in a corner while Hawkins and Lipton are bent over a prone figure in the centre.

'Who is it?' I ask Jacques.

'It is Tuite. Dead.'

'Tuite? How?'

Hawkins beckons me and requests that I should examine the body. There is graze with dried blood on his head and his mouth is swollen and bruised. I glance at the other prisoners. They also bear marks of beating and mistreatment, but none so severe as to warrant a death. I turn back to Tuite's body. The skin is cold, but with little sign of stiffening. His death will have occurred within the last two or three hours. His eyes are set oddly; one protrudes and stares, while the other is near shut from a swelling. It is as though I know his secret and he winks an understanding. There is a small rip and other streaks on his ruff. I know what I will find before I pull it back; red and purple marks of pressure and bruising are on his neck. He has been throttled, perhaps by chains. It cannot be Wicken or Stack as they were moved to their own cells more than four hours past.

'Well, Doctor?' Hawkins guides me away to talk in confidence.

'He was strangled.'

'It was not from a beating around the head?'

'No, that would be unlikely. The death would have been between the hours of two and four.'

Hawkins turns to confront the other prisoners and demands to know the circumstances of Tuite's death. He is hot with anger and lashes at them with his fists and boots. They are defiant, declaring their surprise at the discovery and blaming blows to his head during questioning. Jacques has to intervene and quieten Hawkins; holding him gently and leading him away. Wynter and Trigg have arrived and stand in the doorway, surveying the scene. We retire to the main chamber and I inform them of what has taken place.

Wynter says, 'That is both disturbing and encouraging. It was Master Pennes who mentioned Tuite as the one he expected may dance to his tune. By killing Tuite and attempting to hide their intentions, they have deepened suspicion of their guilt.'

I agree with him. It was a clumsy act, but perhaps they had no other option if he was inclined to break under Hawkins's and Jacques' pressing. No doubt, they will resort to sterner methods in their questioning now. It is a shaming thought, but I must not let it distract my attention from the papers and books.

Another two hours have passed and I have finished with the letters. I can find no suggestion of a hidden message or cipher, so will turn to Tottle's books and the poems. Stack's volume is in a poor state with near half the pages missing. Four torn pages are tucked inside the binding. Here is something... a series of numbers written in a small hand on the pages. They are difficult to distinguish... rows of common or Arabic numbers alternate with Roman numerals.

I have toiled for another two hours on the numbers and can find no pattern. The substituting of characters for numbers failed to progress my analysis. The numbers range from one to forty; some lines contain only four numerals, while others have as many as fifteen. I call Jacques over and request that he accompany me in questioning Stack.

He is sat with manacled hands resting on a rough table. His eyes meet mine as I enter and his mouth twitches – a smile; a sneer? Despite two guards at his back and Jacques by my side, he has an unsettling presence.

I say, 'You are educated in writing and mathematics, Master Stack?'

He grunts a noncommittal response.

'We have seen your scraps of paper in the book of poems. Do you tear strips of paper for some unwholesome purpose, or because you mislike the way the words are arranged?'

I pass him the book and point to a page. 'Please speak the first line in this poem.'

He is reluctant, but his pride wins out. 'O happy... dames that may... embrace,' is a halting, but accurate rendering.

'So, you can read. Do you also have an understanding of numerals and their significance?'

He sits back on his stool and does not answer. I pick a piece of torn paper and place it on the table.

'Did you write these numbers in common and Roman form?'

He is impassive; silent and staring into my eyes.

'What is this number here? If you will not speak, then show me the number on your fingers.'

He breathes deeply and says, 'Make merry at my expense while you can, Doctor. I will seek you out when this is finished.'

I would end with a clever remark but can think of none. His threat is unnerving, despite his position. I leave the chamber and return to my table with Jacques.

'Did you learn aught of value?'

'I cannot be sure. I believe he is uncertain with mathematics and numbers. Conceit would have urged an answer to my question if he knew. Perhaps someone else wrote the sequences on the scraps of paper.'

Am I any further forward with my studies on the papers? If Stack did not write the numbers, then was it Wicken? I pick up his printing of the Tottle book and take out the papers with written poems. There are three, but the writing is larger and does not suggest the same hand as the numbers. I read the first poem. It is curious; in the form of a sonnet; declaring a love; the words 'Queen' and 'King' are mentioned, but to what end? The sense is muddled and the phrasing badly constructed.

When your hand is with mine I burn with desire
Trusting and praying you will not kill the hope
Laying deep within and quench this raging fire
Then all is done and I am gone with wind and rope
Send sweet words quick to this very hour

For I am ready waiting for the gentle smile
Of my good king who is doomed to lour
At denial, I will turn from the teasing trial
And listen to witches spinning their spell
Our queen is born to follow many and none
Holy is her name her father will not tell
You are with a steady heart where I have gone
This place as unconsidered trifle not aching to love
The lord will know I am true from his place above

It seems that Wicken is no poet if, indeed, he is the author. The other two papers are much the same, containing inexpertly-written love sonnets. I read them, over and over, trying to extract meaning from a regularity of words and characters. I cannot find any substance there. I will return to the twenty-seven letters.

*

I am lost in a confusion of mathematics, codes and secret messages. My work for Walsingham the last year began with my solving of a cipher and its connection to an astrological chart. Was that mere chance or divine inspiration? The discovery of any hidden message in these books, papers and poems is beyond me. There is a tap on my shoulder. I turn to find Helen standing there, with an impish smile.

'You are so taken up in your head-scratching and puzzling that you could not hear my call.'

'No, my love, I... am distracted.'

'I have been allowed only a short time in your company to bring you this.' She hoists a wicker basket on to the table. 'It is your supper, saved from our leavings.'

'Supper; is it so late in the day?'

'It is near the seventh hour after noon. You will need to light candles if you continue to stare at those writings for another hour.'

I lift the linen cover to find a bottle, cup, legs of boiled fowl and a codling. I take her in my arms, kiss her lips and murmur thanks for her kind thought. She brings a stool and sits by me while I drink wine and pick at the meat.

'How is Sir George?'

'He is still confined to his bed, but his chest pains have eased and his breathing offers some hope of recovery.'

I hold a sense of guilt that I have not thought of his condition since our midnight conference. She leans over and sifts through the papers on the table.

'Do you have any results from examinations and searches?'

I will not tell her about the death and I am hesitant to discuss the questioning.

'I try to find a connection between these numerals and some other writing. Presently, I am defeated.'

'Why, William, surely a renowned scholar such as you can see through the mischievous design of simple ship men.'

She teases, but quickly puts on her serious face and examines the papers.

'This is a poor attempt at a poem. I trust it is not your scribbling.'

I laugh, 'Even I could make a better fist at dainty words than whoever wrote these.'

'There are more?'

I hand her the other two written poems. She reads them, wrinkles her nose, makes no comment, and then takes back the first poem. Some detail has taken hold, for she frowns and reaches for the papers with numerals.

Eventually, she says, 'They are contrived.'

'Are not all poems somewhat unnatural in their design?'

'Yes, but it is as though the arrangement of words is for some purpose other than a declaration of love.'

I take one from her and scan each word slowly and with care. If there is some hidden message in there I cannot detect it. One of the guards clears his throat, signalling that her stay here should end. She begs for a short delay.

'Look here.' She points to a page with numerals. 'The poems each have fourteen lines; the same number of rows on each torn scrap of numbers. Could that be significant?'

She is right. Is that the key? I have been too deep in the particulars of the writing to recognise this coincidence. I pick her up and twirl her around, praising her perception and beauty. She pummels my chest in a playful manner, asking to be set down before fainting. We embrace strongly and our kiss lingers with each of us pressing to be closer. Helen takes her leave with reluctance and makes me promise to send word on the outcome of my deliberations on her insight.

My eagerness makes for clumsy writing and finish my third attempt before I am happy with a fair copy of the first poem. Now to the numbers. I take the first torn sheet and count from the left for each corresponding character in the first line of the poem. It is meaningless nonsense. The second set of numbers may hold more promise.

j ij iij iiij v vj vij viij xxiiij xxv xxvj xxvij

6 7 8 9 10 11 29 30 31 32

iiij v vj xxviij xxix

10 11 12 13

j ij iij iiij x xj xij xiij xx xxj xvj xxix

1 2 3 7 8 9 10 11 16 17 18

iij iiij ix x xj xij xviij xix xxj

10 11 12 13 14 15 16 17 18 19 20 21 22 23 24

xij xiij xiiij xv xvj

4 5 6 7 8 15 16 17 18 19 20 21 22 23 26

j ij iij iiij xvij xviij xx xxj xxij

1 2 3 7 8 9 10 12 17

v vj vij viij ix x xj xiiij xv xvj xxxiij xxxiv xxxv xxxix

4 5 6 7

It begins to… Yes, it is here. This must be it. I circle each character in the poem. The full sense is not clear until I finish. Now I have it in plain sight, it takes an effort to have faith in the reasoning. I stop, blink and gaze around the chamber. This is no dream; it is real. Helen has uncovered the construction of the cipher. Soon, I am finished with all the poems and have written the translated messages.

Wynter is in an adjoining chamber with Hawkins. Both men are sat at their leisure with cups in hand and feet on stools.

'Gentlemen, I have discovered some interest in the writings.'

They straighten with keen interest and beg to be informed.

'Before I disclose the nature of my findings, I wonder whether you will allow me a short conversation with Wicken to confirm issues which still niggle?'

'Of course, William, but our patience will not stretch too far. Shall we accompany you?' Wynter starts to rise from his seat.

'If you will excuse my rudeness, I believe there will be more profit if I converse with him alone.'

'The guards must stay.'

'I had not thought otherwise.' Indeed, I would not feel safe without their presence, even chained and with help in the next chamber. It is Hawkins I would keep from Wicken as I consider their dislike for each other may hinder proceedings.

I enter a small chamber with three guards at the walls and Wicken sat with bowed head on a stool in the middle. There is no table between us, so I will stand. He lifts his head and nods slowly in recognition.

'A good day to you, William, my dear. What brings you to this merry place?'

'I see your humour is not broken, Charles.' The pride of his yellow hair is matted with dried blood and one side of his face is cut and swollen. 'You will know why I am here.'

'Indeed, you have come to seal an unpleasant death on a friend who granted life to you only a few weeks past.'

'That was another age. I doubt you ever counted me as a true friend, but I will never forget your brave rescue. I counted part of my debt repaid when you were freed at the quarter session, but it seems my efforts on your behalf were not required.'

'Nevertheless, you enjoyed the occasion to display your clever mind to so large a gathering.'

'That was…'

'Do not tinker and fiddle with words on your finer sentiments, William, you must come to the nub of this meeting.'

'Very well, Charles, it is tampering with your poetry that has confirmed my suspicions.'

'Ah, so you have done it. I feared it would be the working of a shrewd mind rather than a strong arm that would unfix me.' He stares at me with defiance. 'Do not expect me to congratulate you on a magnificent accomplishment.'

'All is known, Charles: your planned assault on this harbour;

connivance with Fitzmaurice and Sanders; your reward in Ireland. But why did you kill young Tremayne?'

He shrugs. 'I will admit it was a rash act, but I could see no other course of action. I liked him, he was an amusing companion, but in his cups, he would blab and gossip. It was a necessary killing.'

'Necessary?' The calculation and coldness in his phrasing make me shiver. I do not ask about the killing of Tuite as I am certain he will answer in the same vein. 'Do the Tremayne family hold the same opinion? Was their son sacrificed to a greater cause?' His face is fixed with no expression I can read. 'And what of Sindell? Is he a party to your plotting?'

'You have me, but do not probe into the naming of others.'

'Why – what has set you on this path? Is it money, fame, or some other determination?'

'You would not understand with a cosy and cosseted life, away from deeds of foul perversions and murder. You have a comfortable home, an easy living from physic and the promise of wedded bliss with a rare beauty. I lost my family - father mother; sisters - in the terrible reprisals around York, ordered by the false queen and exacted by Baron Clinton in 'seventy-one. My deeds are pale and faint set against the black devilment done in the name of your poxed queen.'

He must refer to the Rising of the North almost ten years past. 'So, you hold to the old faith and this was to be an act of revenge?'

'That was the start, although I will concede my motives are not entirely pure. I am cursed and hardened by witnessing too much evil to have unwavering regard for any way of worship. Many unplanned happenings in the past years helped to forge my destiny; Stukley's death; the approach from Walsingham; and my acceptance into the great adventure. Which common man could resist the lure of wealth and title of a lord?'

'Who has made you these promises? Fitzmaurice and Sanders do not hold the power to bestow such gifts.'

'It seems there are parts to the puzzle that confound you still. You will not get enlightenment from me.'

'Then our conference here is over, Charles. I know you will

not believe me, but I am sorry for your end.'

I turn quickly and depart without waiting for a response. Wynter and Hawkins are in the main chamber, standing with arms folded, waiting for my return. I guide them to my table, show the deciphered messages and describe the concepts and workings that led me there. I do not stint in my praise for Helen's contribution. Wynter's pleasure is plain to see from his beaming smile.

'It is a triumph, William, for you and your fair lady. With your permission, Captain General, let us convene in one hour at your house, when we will inform all principals of this famous unearthing.'

He claps me on the back as I gather up the papers and stuff them into my satchel. I note that Hawkins has not spoken. He is subdued with a firm set to his jaw. He will be wondering if these findings will cause any disruption to the grand ceremony planned for the next morning.

Twenty Eight

I am at Hawkins' house and have a short interval with Helen before she must rouse her father from his bed to join our assembly of principals. She states her pleasure at my animated telling of the deciphering but is also curiously muted in her humour. Perhaps, it is the thought of the fate that waits for Wicken and his men that depresses her excitement. I also confess my entreaties that she is allowed to join our meeting have been rejected. Wynter and Hawkins are both firm in their belief that a council with talk of reprisal, punishment and fighting is no place for a young maid. This news is not received well. She had hoped to stay by Sir George's side in order to maintain his calm during our discussions and I promise to call her if he should show any sign of pain or breathlessness. It is a finely balanced decision on his attendance; it may bring some agitation to his disposition, but we both know he would also be hot with anger at his exclusion.

I encounter Oliver entering the house. He is eager to learn the reason for the gathering and if I have found any significance in the objects from his searches. I do not wish to spoil Wynter's announcement, so simply say the mystery is uncovered and beg him to be patient. He puts his hand on my shoulder and tells me he has some recent information.

'One of the guards at the Guildhall mentioned that Tuite has a brother with a position on another ship that is not under Wicken's command. Could there be more than three of our fleet involved in the plotting?'

His suggestion jolts my senses. I had not considered that prospect. Surely, a close association with Wicken would have been noted and examined. 'You would be wise to mention this in our conference, Oliver, but it is fanciful to my way of thinking.'

We enter Hawkins's dining chamber to find all present, save for Sir George. Natural light has gone and extra candles have been lit at my request, so that writing may be read without difficulty. There is some conversation in low voice and muttering between Gilbert and Lipton. Wynter is quiet, gazing around and drumming his fingers on the table, suggesting an impatience to begin.

At last, Helen enters, with a strong hold of her father's arm and guides him to the seat between Hawkins and Gilbert. He is dressed simply in a loose, white, silk blouse and back hose. He has aged in the few short hours since we last met, with sunken eyes and a general sagging in his bearing.

Wynter says, 'Before you leave us, lady, we should record our thanks to you for your remarkable perception in sparking light on the malign intent of the conspirators here.'

She bows her head in answer to the compliment and murmurs of approval, then bobs a curtsey and exits the chamber with only a brief glance in my direction. When she is gone, Wynter thumps the table with both hands.

'Gentlemen, a plot, more devious and broader in scope than we suspected, has been uncovered. The throttling and killing of a prisoner by his fellows deepened our opinions that guilty secrets were hidden from our interrogators. Doctor Constable redoubled his efforts in examination of the books and writings. He has saved the nuisance and delay in arranging strong questioning and torture in London with a triumphant discovery.'

He signals I should continue with the exposition.

'There was a cipher in three poems and the design was unusual in the separation of the key to unlocking concealed messages on scraps of paper torn from a book. On these, certain numerals were arranged as a reference to the position of characters on each line of poetry. It was your daughter, Sir George, who noted this correspondence.'

He forces a smile and waves his hand weakly to acknowledge congratulations.

'One message was imprecise in its meaning, referring only to a meeting and preparation for an undisclosed objective. It was another message translated that shows the full nature of the conspiracy. The message was spread over two poems with two separate sets of numerals holding the secret to their true meaning.'

I hand out copies of the decoded message for inspection. It reads:

When your burning and killing is done
Send word to Vy for readying
My kingdom will turn from the witch queen
To follow my holy father
You with Sy place as Connacht lord
Meet with Fe by Fort of the Gold
Be strong. You are blessed.
GB

The paper is passed around the table, received by shaking heads, growls and gapes. When all have finished reading, I continue.

'There is still some work to be done on identifying the author of this message. I questioned Captain Wicken and while he did not deny the sense of the instructions, he would not disclose its source.' I pause to determine if there are any names put to the reference 'GB'. None comes. 'As for the message itself, it is my understanding that Wicken and his forces are intended to bring fire and killing to the venture fleet, and perhaps also to Sir William's ships. The "Vy" mentioned I hazard is Vaisy, the steward at the Fitzmaurice house in St Malo. He will be the coordinator of messages for the parties in the conspiracy. The sender of the message has pretensions to be the King of Ireland in place of our queen and Wicken has been offered lordship of Connacht as his reward. It seems that he has taken the place of Stukley in this conspiracy after his death in Maroc.'

Oliver says, 'What does mention of a "Fort of Gold" signify? Is this place real or some dreaming of a magical land?'

'I am at a loss to know, although I wager that "Fe" refers to Lord Fitzmaurice.'

'It is not an imagined place,' replies Gilbert. 'It is an ancient site close by the small harbour of Smerwick in South Western Ireland. I was there for a short time in 'sixty-nine when I quelled the headstrong Irish lords led by Fitzmaurice. It is a glorious name for a small piece of land with a scattering of rocks.'

Wynter leans on the table and rests his chin on a hand with a thoughtful expression. 'This location would seem to confirm an

227

intention to sail an invading force to Ireland, where Fitzmaurice has designs on the earldom of Munster. Their plan will be to settle matters there before moving North to Connacht.'

There is discussion about the nature and scale of this scheme. Hawkins is strong in his opinion that our capture of Wicken and the foiling of his plans for this harbour will lead to its abandonment. He is supported in this by Gilbert and Lipton, but I see that Wynter is not convinced. Sir George, who has been quiet until now, taps his hand on the table wishing to be heard.

'Who would have the impudence and daring to proclaim themselves King of this small country in place of Her Majesty?' His voice is weak and there is crackle in his breath, which speaks of a congestion in the lungs.

'I have considered this question,' says Wynter, 'and believe I have the candidate. Nicholas Sanders is known to be an accomplice of Fitzmaurice and also has the ear of the Pope. The message refers to "my holy father". I interpret this to have a double meaning of both spiritual leader and sire. Giacomo Boncompagni is the illegitimate son of Pope Gregory, the source of wicked and malicious insults hurled at our gracious queen. He will be the "GB" written as author and sender of the message.'

The chamber is stilled by his words. The significance of the plot is heightened by its intimate association with Rome. I see the troubled expressions around the table as they fear this may bring disorder to the plans for the grand departure of the venture fleet. Wynter knows he has our rapt attention and prolongs the silence before speaking.

'I have considered what must be done now to safeguard Her Majesty's interests. I understand there will be an eagerness to ensure there are no more delays in the departure of your great adventure on the morrow. When all is settled here, I will sail for Ireland to investigate any incursion in Munster. I would have another three ships accompany mine to guard against encountering a superior force and you, Sir Humphrey, will be my choice of companion commander. Your experience of fighting in that land would be a valuable asset.'

There are angry cries of dissent and strong disagreement

around the table. Hawkins rises from his seat and stamps back and forth, while Gilbert waves his arms and argues this is an unnecessary measure. It is some minutes before the air has calmed and Wynter can address the table.

'I do not deny the sailing of the majority of your fleet in the venture and Sir Humphrey can join when I have determined the threat to Munster is small or entirely gone. But it is a precaution that must be taken. Secretary Walsingham would expect no less.'

The grumbling continues, but it is muted and there is a sense of grudging acceptance, except for Hawkins, who continues to stand and glare with arms folded.

I say, 'What is to be done here, with the prisoners and men on Wicken's ships?'

'The leaders will be taken to London in covered wagons under strong guard. They will face unpleasant ends for their treason, especially Wicken. I do not see Sir Francis taking kindly to one of his agents playing him for a fool.'

'And the crews?'

'Most will be innocent of any deep mischief and simply acting for coin. I will speak to Justice Shanning here and suspect he will relish the management of high delinquency against Her Majesty in place of beggary and thievery. No doubt he will arrange a spectacle of some hangings as an example.'

Those harsh words are spoken with no hint of regret and I am glad that I will soon be released from this company of hard, fighting men, back to the gentler setting of my London home. The conversation moves on to the selection of ships for Gilbert and adjustments in the arrangements for next day's ceremony when there is a loud thud. The walls and floor of our chamber appear to tremble. Has something heavy fallen in the storey above? All is quiet as senses are pricked with wondering. Nothing follows and after a few moments, Wynter continues the discussion. Then… another thump hits the chamber and the table shifts. Jacques is instructed to investigate and exits with haste.

Hawkins says, 'Forgive this disturbance gentlemen, I deduce there may be a fault in the construction on the side of this house.

I trust it will not be too severe.'

There is a general relief at this understanding and conversation revives, although it is hesitant and disjointed. After some minutes, Jacques has not returned, Hawkins shows signs of restlessness and we sink into another expectant silence.

The door is flung open and Jacques appears staring and gasping for breath.

'It is the harbour... fire... explosion... fighting. We must...'

Chairs are spilt as we rise from our seats with much cursing and hurrying to the door. I am slower, following others, then remember... Sir George. I turn to see him heaving his frame upwards from the table with shaking arms. He stops, gapes at me with an expression of disbelief and shakes his head. He collapses slowly, appearing to fold in on himself and hits the floor. I stand; fixed; uncertain. No, this cannot be. Not now.

Time has slowed and my legs are leaden as I skirt the table and reach his side. His eyes stare and a milky liquid bubbles from a mouth distorted into a hideous grin. I am kneeling, praying, holding his hand, and pressing his neck for vital signs. I am helpless; a physician without remedy; impotent.

'Helen. Helen!'

I call her, but it is hopeless. He is already dead.

*

My sense of obligation is torn. Sir George has been laid in his bed, prayers for his departed soul have been said and continue in subdued mutterings under the guidance of Pastor Gadge. Helen is bewildered; passive; confused. She has shed no tears and I must suppose they will come later. Her state is somewhere between disbelief and an understanding that death was expected. My mind is drawn back to the passing of my father, for which I had many weeks to prepare, yet found its happening brought a sensation of numbness and shock. I should stay with her in the candlelit gloom and soothe the heaviness of her sorrow, but if danger threatens on the quays then I must be there to offer assistance. Also, I would know if the fighting goes against us so that I may return in good time and take Helen to safety. We are knelt together at the bedside. I murmur my intentions and kiss her head gently. She does not stir. I rise stiffly and exit the bedchamber.

Over an hour has passed since Hawkins and the others rushed to the harbour and the battle still rages. Even in the narrow streets I can see the sky lit from fires, hear the crack of guns and taste the acrid smell of charcoal and sulphur. I turn a corner and the quays come into view. All is chaos; shouting; running; burning. I pause to take in the scene. The two closest ships have men dousing flames with buckets. The fiercest blaze rages near two hundred paces away, yet still I feel a strong heat. Before then I see a group of men on the quayside surrounding two or three ships and silhouetted against the fire. The ships are massed with black figures, whirling arms and glinting steel. Who is friend or foe? There is too much confusion. I am transfixed. Someone touches my shoulder, my senses jolt and I reach for my sword.

'William.'

A puff of air escapes my lips and my senses are calmed. It is Oliver.

I say, 'What... what is our position?'

'We have them. Those that are not subdued and taken are trapped on two ships.'

'What has happened here?'

'Crews from other ships freed those on *Hawkwind*. They set fire and exploded some of ours and there was a battle on the quayside.'

'Did any ships escape?'

'Pennes was quick and ordered vessels to manoeuvre and block their flight. It was bloody. Cannon was used at close range. Many are killed and wounded.'

There are shouts and rumbling behind us. We stand back to allow the passage of big guns pulled by ropes. Oliver tells me that they are bringing demi cannons and culverins on the quayside to bear on the trapped ships.

He says, 'It is a matter of time. They will see their cause is hopeless.'

I walk with him towards the action. Two men heave a body

on to a cart. There are more – a mound of bodies piled against a wall. A figure crawls away on all fours and collapses on his front. I kneel down and turn him over. My hand is wet and warm with his blood. A yellow glow from the fire reveals a wide gash from throat to chest. He gurgles and reaches out with a trembling hand. I take it and grip it tight. His body shudders and I feel his life force ebb away. I do not know who he fought for. Does it matter? I murmur a few words of prayer and rise slowly. Oliver has gone to the crowd gathered by the ships holding the insurgents.

Our fighting men have withdrawn forming a deep half circle around the two trapped ships. Oliver is attending to the positioning of the big guns in the vacated space. Voices have quietened; the crackling and spitting of burning wood fills the ears. Motion on the ships seems to have stilled. They will see how their end is planned. The head of Jacques Pennes is a few paces to my left. I push my way through to his side and grab his arm.

'Will you fire the guns, or is it a threat?'

He faces me and lifts his eyes in mild surprise. 'William, you should be with your lady.' A man hands him a pike with a torn, white shirt roughly tied at the top. 'We will offer terms first.' He signals to another man who lifts a musket to his shoulder and fires into the air.

Jacques steps forward and lifts his pike into the air. He walks slowly towards the ships waving his flag. It is a brave or foolhardy act. If he is too close he may be short in an act of defiance. A shouted taunt from our force is met with urgent appeals for 'hush'. I strain to view action aboard the ships, but flickering shadows play games with the figures at the rails. Jacques is there. He will be heard.

He is loud and clear in his voice. He offers life and merciful punishment to all but five principals on each ship if they will surrender arms. They have a count of one hundred to accept these term or the cannons will be fired and no quarter given. A moment of silence is broken by a few bold shouts of denial amidst a general hubbub on the ships. Jacques ignores any questions or bargaining and returns with measured steps back to my side. Hawkins joins us and claps Jacques on his back, praising his bravery. I must hope the terms are accepted as I do not wish to bear witness to bloody slaughter.

I say, 'Will the terms be honoured?'

Hawkins stares at me wild-eyed as though I have said words of particular idiocy. He clamps his mouth, juts his jaw and turns his back on me without answering.

My count has passed sixty when planks are laid and the first men cross from ships to the quayside, throwing down swords, daggers, guns and other weapons then wait in line to be roped and taken away.

I do not stay to the end. I am overcome by tiredness and trudge back slowly through the streets to Hawkins' house. What news shall I bring to Helen? A victory - of sorts - for our state. A disaster – certainly – for the great adventure. She will not want to hear of either. They will have no meaning set against the loss of a loving father.

Epilogue

The few days after the small war in the harbour were full of misery and recrimination. Helen was, in turn, distant and sobbing, then ardent and hungry for greater closeness. I could not manage either state well. My thoughts were wayward, swaying from worries about our betrothal and the status of our forthcoming marriage now her father was gone, to concerns on the upheaval in Sir George's estate brought on by the severe disruption to his great adventure.

The ships presented a sorry sight on the main quay when we departed Plymouth town. Three other ships were part of the conspiracy and the crews on two of Wicken's ships were freed to fight. They were outnumbered but had the advantage of surprise and the battle waged long into the night before they were subdued. Near one half of the fleet was burned or badly damaged with cargoes lost or corrupted. Great rows of scaffolds were erected for hangings and the decaying bodies of twenty or more rebels draggle there, picked by gulls and crows as a warning to others. Wicken and his fellow prisoners from the Guildhall were taken in a covered wagon to London. Men from his ship were herded into derelict buildings serving as cells to await their fate. Shanning had a high time dispensing swift and arbitrary justice. Some were hanged. Others had a limb cut off and fired before being driven from the town to perish out of sight of townsfolk or hunt for another place to ply their beggary. The fortunate ones were branded on both cheeks and chased out of town by a baying mob wielding sticks and whips. Our terms for surrender were not honoured.

Wynter sailed with his three ships to the Dingle peninsula two days after the fighting and burning. Gilbert and Hawkins advised there would be little chance of encountering Fitzmaurice and Sanders in Ireland after Wicken's defeat, but he would not listen; Walsingham would not forgive him if he returned to London only to learn there had been an encroachment in Ireland. Gilbert is to follow him once his ships are readied, while Hawkins stomps and shouts around the quays blaming others for the calamity that has overtaken the great adventure. Oliver and I have not escaped his spite and anger; we should have foreseen and voiced our concerns about other rebel ships earlier, and I should have delved deeper and been more perceptive in my questioning of Wicken.

The fate of the damaged and shrunken venture fleet hangs in the balance. Crushed spirits and dampened fervour among masters and merchants have resulted in withdrawals to deplete numbers further. There are no more than a dozen ships remaining in a fit state to embark on the voyage across the great seas. Hawkins will not hear of total abandonment. He avers that recovery from misfortune and a triumphant success against overwhelming odds will bring even greater glory and wealth to those who are steadfast and determined. Oliver's ship is wrecked. Two of Sir George's ships were salvaged from the chaos and Helen has charged Oliver with their custody. They will sail to the New Lands as a tribute to Sir George with or without Hawkins when they are repaired.

The body of Sir George has been put in a wooden box with prayers from Pastor Gadge. He will be laid to rest in the church of St Katharine Cree in Leadenhall. We are a mournful band of travellers escorting his earthly remains on our journey to London. Devonshire is behind us now and there will be much relief when we reach our destination. Plymouth town had one final wound to inflict on the day of our leaving. A messenger from Guernsey arrived with a demand from Sir Thomas Leighton for my return on a matter of murder and offence to his office. Shanning arrived, flourishing the note and ordering my detention as we were readying for our departure. I would not comply easily; any word given on that isle should have meant naught set against the need to care for Helen and attend to vital affairs in London. But it was a holy promise given freely. A denial would spread a stain on my conscience that the passing of time would not wipe clean. I was fortunate that Jacques was present to ease my conflicting thoughts. He fetched Hawkins, who tore the paper and dismissed Shanning with indignation and heated words. Jacques promised that he would take my place and travel to Guernsey with sufficient force of arms and gold to silence their bluster and accusations. I must hope that is the last I hear of a connection with Guernsey - and the interlude in St Malo.

End Notes

This book is a work of fiction. William Constable, Helen Morton and most of the protagonists are imagined characters, but they do encounter historical figures and the story mentions 'real-life' events. Brief descriptions of some of the major figures encountered or referenced in the book are given below.

Sir Francis Walsingham (1532 – 1590) was Principal Secretary to Queen Elizabeth from 1573 until his death and is popularly referred to as her *spymaster*. A firm believer in the Protestant faith, he sanctioned the use of torture against conspirators.

Admiral Sir John Hawkins (1532 – 1595) was born in Plymouth to a prominent family. He was a naval commander, merchant, navigator and privateer. He is best known as a slave trader and a pioneer of the 'Triangle Trade'. Goods were sailed from European ports to West Africa and exchanged for slaves. Slaves were sold to settlers in the colonies across the Atlantic and the ships returned with cargo (usually sugar or molasses) to sell in Europe. Hawkins included privateering and raiding of Spanish treasure on his voyages.

Treasurer of the Royal Navy from 1577-1595, he was less well-known as an innovator in ship design and shipbuilder. He can be credited for much of the improvement in the Elizabethan navy that defeated the Spanish Armada in 1588.

He styled himself 'Captain General' as general of his own fleet as well as the English Royal Navy.

Sir Humphrey Gilbert (1539 – 1583) was an adventurer, explorer, soldier and half-brother to Walter Raleigh. The Greenway Estate in Dartmouth was the home of the Gilbert family. (The present house on the site was owned by Agatha Christie and is now run by the National Trust.)

He served in Ireland and was appointed Governor of Ulster in

1567. His battles against Irish lords spread into Munster and confrontation with the Geraldine lords, whose forces were captained by James Fitzmaurice Fitzgerald. He gained a reputation for cruelty and advocated the killing of non-combatant women and children.

In the summer of 1579, he was commissioned to sail three ships and intercept Fitzmaurice who was rumoured to be leading a force to Dingle in Ireland. It was reported that Gilbert's fleet got lost in fog and heavy rain off Lands' End.

James Fitzmaurice Fitzgerald (d 1579) was a cousin of the Earl of Desmond in the province of Munster, Ireland. He led the Desmond forces in the 'First Desmond Rebellion' (1569-1583). Defeated, he was granted a pardon, swore fealty to the crown and surrendered his eldest son as hostage.

Estranged from Earl Desmond, in 1575 he sailed to St Malo with his wife, Katherine, children and other followers. He sought backing from Rome and Spain for an invasion of Ireland and was supported by Thomas Stukley and Nicholas Sanders. Stukley withdrew from this scheme to support the King of Portugal in an invasion of Morocco, where he was killed in a battle. Fitzmaurice and Sanders set sail with a small force and landed at Smerwick harbour in Dingle in July 1579 and garrisoned at Dún an Óir (Fort of Gold), launching the 'Second Desmond Rebellion'. Fitzmaurice's part was short-lived as he was killed in a skirmish a few weeks later.

Thomas Stukley (1520 – 1578) was a mercenary and, in later life, an enemy to Protestantism in England under Elizabeth. It has been alleged that he was a bastard son of Henry VIII, but there is no reliable evidence to support this claim.

In his earlier exploits, he served Elizabeth, was a supporter of Robert Dudley, Earl of Leicester and held several positions for the Crown in Ireland. He also embarked on a career as a privateer and was implicated in the 'Ridolfi Plot'. Thereafter, he was a determined and vocal opponent of Elizabeth, rumoured to be implicated in a number of conspiracies against her.

He was killed at the Battle of Alcácer Quibir in Morocco,

having abandoned his support for an invasion of Munster with James Fitzmaurice Fitzgerald. It is reported that his legs were blown off by a cannonball.

Nicholas Sanders (1530 – 1581) was an English Catholic priest and prominent advocate for the overthrow of Elizabeth and restoration of Catholicism in England. Exiled in Europe, he wrote polemics against Elizabeth and tried to negotiate support from Rome and Spain for his cause.

He obtained support from papal nuncio, Filippo Sega, for an expedition to Ireland with Fitzmaurice and Stukley. He accompanied Fitzmaurice to Smerwick harbour in Ireland, raising the papal banner in 1579. The invasion fleet was routed by Sir William Wynter and Sanders was reported to have died as a fugitive some months later.

Admiral Sir William Wynter (1521 – 1589) held positions in the Council of Marine, including Surveyor of the Navy and Master of Ordnance. In 1577 he was expected to be appointed as treasurer of the navy but was passed over in favour of John Hawkins. A rivalry with Hawkins persisted and in 1582 he accused him of corruption. A royal commission under Lord Burghley, Sir Francis Walsingham and Sir Francis Drake found in Hawkins' favour.

In 1579 he commanded the squadron that sailed to Smerwick to defeat the uprising led by Fitzmaurice and Sanders.

Giacomo Boncompagni (1548 – 1612), the illegitimate son of Pope Gregory XIII, was an Italian lord and patron of the arts. He was proposed as King of Ireland if the Catholic faith was restored there following the invasion of Fitzmaurice and the Second Desmond Rebellion.

The art of navigation developed rapidly in the sixteenth century in response to explorers who needed to find their positions without landmarks. Instruments were used to determine latitude, but longitude required accurate timepieces and these were not yet available. Instead, navigators used educated guesswork or 'dead reckoning' by measuring the heading and speed of the ship, the speeds of the ocean currents and drift of the ship, and the time spent on each heading.

A cross-staff was in common use in the mid-sixteenth century as an instrument to calculate latitude. This device resembled a Christian cross. The vertical piece, the transom or limb, slides along the staff so that the star can be sighted over the upper edge of the transom while the horizon is aligned with the bottom edge. The major problem with the cross-staff was that the observer had to look in two directions at once – along the bottom of the transom to the horizon and along the top of the transom to the sun or the star.

A more advanced instrument was the Davis Quadrant or backstaff. The observer determined the altitude of the sun by observing its shadow while simultaneously sighting the horizon. Captain John Davis conceived this instrument during his voyage to search for the Northwest Passage and is described in his book *Seaman's Secrets*, 1594. One of the major advantages of the backstaff over the cross-staff was that the navigator had to look in only one direction to take the sight – through the slit in the horizon vane to the horizon while simultaneously aligning the shadow of the shadow vane with the slit in the horizon vane.

The shadow-staff in the book is an imagined forerunner of the backstaff.

The Cipher

For those who cannot resist the mystery behind a cryptic message, here are the poems, numerals from corresponding scraps of paper and the translation to the hidden message.

Sonnet 1

When your hand is with mine I burn with desire
Trusting and praying you will not kill the hope
Laying deep within and quench this raging fire
Then all is done and I am gone with wind and rope
Send sweet words quick to this very hour

For I am ready waiting for the gentle smile
Of my good king who is doomed to lour
At denial, I will turn from the teasing trial
And listen to witches spinning their spell
Our queen is born to follow many and none
Holy is her name her father will not tell
You are with a steady heart where I have gone
This place as unconsidered trifle not aching to love
The lord will know I am true from his place above

Numerals 1

Until the sixteenth century, numbers in England were generally written as Roman numerals. The invention of the printing press accelerated the acceptance of modern or 'Arabic' numerals in the fifteenth century Europe and they were in common use in Tudor England.

j ij iij iiij v vj vij viij xxiiij xxv xxvj xxvij
6 7 8 9 10 11 29 30 31 32
iiij v vj xxviij xxix
10 11 12 13
j ij iij iiij x xj xij xiij xx xxj xvj xxix
1 2 3 7 8 9 10 11 16 17 18
iij iiij ix x xj xij xviij xix xxj
10 11 12 13 14 15 16 17 18 19 20 21 22 23 24
xij xiij xiiij xv xvj
4 5 6 7 8 15 16 17 18 19 20 21 22 23 26
j ij iij iiij xvij xviij xx xxj xxij
1 2 3 7 8 9 10 12 17
v vj vij viij ix x xj xiiij xv xvj xxxiij xxxiv xxxv xxxix
4 5 6 7

Sonnet 2

Will you meet me with flowers in your hair?
Your beauty on display for all to see
My fortune though small, my prospects rate fair
Handsome of face and with shape to the knee
If you go to the place where we first met
Then you will be told in verse that should please

Of bells and jewels all triumphantly set
Fine words strung out and designed to tease
Look to your temper and tend to your dress
All manner of things are despatched this day
For amusement, blessing and wilful caress
Wherever your thoughts are led they must stay
With gladness of heart and steadfast mind
I believe I am yours with our love entwined

Numerals 2

viij ix x xj xiv xv xvj xvij xviij xxij
5 10
iij iiij v vj
9 10 29 30 31
vij viij
16 17
iij iiij
10 11 12 16 20 26
vij viij ix
18 19 20
xiij xiv xv xvj xvij
25 26
v
2

The translated, hidden message

When your burning and killing is done
Send word to Vy for readying
My kingdom will turn from the witch queen
To follow my holy father
You with Sy place as Connacht lord
Meet with Fe by Fort of the Gold
Be strong. You are blessed.
GB

For those of you who have enjoyed this book, further episodes in the life of William Constable will follow. Look for the next instalment in 2020.

I can be reached via authorpaulwalker@btinternet.com

*